SERIOUS INTENT

MARGARET YORKE

SERIOUS INTENT

THE MYSTERIOUS PRESS

Published by Warner Books

A Time Warner Company

First published in Great Britain in 1995 by Little, Brown & Company

 Mysterious Press books are published by Warner Books, Inc., 1271 Avenue of the Americas, New York, NY 10020.

 A Time Warner Company

The Mysterious Press name and logo are registered trademarks of Warner Books, Inc.

Printed in the United States of America

First U.S. printing: April 1996

10 9 8 7 6 5 4 3 2 1

Library of Congress Cataloging-in-Publication Data

Yorke, Margaret.
    Serious intent / Margaret Yorke.
        p.   cm.
    ISBN 0–89296–583–5
        1. Married people—England—Psychology—Fiction.   2. Country life—England—Fiction.   3. Family—England—Fiction.   I. Title.
PR6075.07S47   1996
823'.914—dc20   95–46450
                                                                                          CIP

No man is responsible for his father. That is entirely his mother's affair.
　　　　—Margaret Turnbull, *Alabaster Lamps*

The night my father got me
His mind was not on me.
　　　　　　　—A. E. Housman

Your fathers, where are they?
　　　　　　　—Zachariah 1:5

SERIOUS INTENT

1.

Steve had always stolen from old Tom, though Mark didn't realize it until he had been going to the house for several weeks.

"We give him our time, don't we?" Steve had said, when at last Mark, understanding, had protested. "That's worth money."

Steve's stepmother, Ivy, cleaned for Tom, and the boys—just Steve at first, but later Mark as well—often went round after school because she was anxious about the old man.

Steve overcharged Tom for shopping done, rendering falsified accounts scribbled on scraps of paper, never challenged, and accepted a pound, sometimes more, for his trouble.

So Steve was doing it on purpose, not making genuine mistakes. As the two boys walked back to Ivy's house together, Mark accepted some crisps, bought with Tom's money, and quite soon he got used to what was going on.

He liked visiting Tom's house, and sometimes he went there alone.

Tom couldn't walk far. His shuffling gait would carry him from room to room, and he managed the stairs very slowly, clinging to the handrail specially installed, making just one trip each way every day. Steve often helped him go upstairs to bed, patting him gently, urging him on with encouraging words. At fourteen, Steve was a big boy, bigger than Tom, who had shrunk down almost to Mark's level.

Mark didn't like watching Tom edge himself along, not when he remembered that Tom had been a pilot in the war and had won medals. Mark had seen them. It seemed all wrong that he could barely move unaided. But Steve was always gentle with him; there was no bullying, though Steve was tough when they were playing with other boys in the park, and he wasn't always kind. Mark had seen him elbow an elderly woman with a laden shopping basket off the pavement in front of oncoming traffic, and he had done other things Mark knew were bad. He'd pushed a boy who annoyed him from his bike, then ridden off, laughing, on the bike, which he'd later abandoned, leaving it with a buckled wheel and a lacerated tire. He'd smashed a car's windscreen because he said the driver had shown no respect at a crossroads; that time, he watched the driver park, lock his car and leave it, before carrying out his action.

"He's got to be punished," Steve had said.

Mark didn't like it when Steve was in one of his angry, vengeful moods, and he thought charging old Tom more for shopping than the real price was disrespectful, but he did not want to lose his role as Steve's assistant, so he kept quiet. Steve ran through people, Mark knew. Boys formerly his friends gave him up when he flew into a rage or "borrowed" their possessions once too often.

Tom said that without the two boys' help he might not be able to go on living at The Willows, and Ivy thought Tom was good for Steve. She worried about him. He wasn't doing well at school, and often she had no idea how he spent his time. At least she knew where he was when he went to Tom's.

Tom's money seemed to flow in regularly. Steve didn't know how it came. Perhaps the bank sent it by post. Steve had offered to collect Tom's pension from the post office.

"Wouldn't it help?" he'd suggested. "My mum gets loads for other people," he invented. He always called Ivy his mum; it saved explaining that after his mother died, Ivy and his dad had got married, and then they had a daughter, Kylie, who was now seven. Ivy already had a daughter of her own, called Sharon. Eighteen months ago, Steve's dad was killed in an accident. That was sad, and Steve did not like to think about it. Kylie had been in a terrible way at the time, and so had Ivy, but they were all right now, and so was he.

Tom hadn't accepted Steve's offer. He'd said it was all under control and the pension money went straight to the bank.

He'd got stocks and shares, too, Steve knew. Once, when Tom was dozing, he'd looked through some drawers in his desk, but he couldn't pry when Mark was around; the kid had too many scruples.

"Maybe he'll leave all his stuff to us, we're so good to him," Steve had said one day when the boys had collected a video to watch with the old man.

Tom's tastes and Steve's didn't coincide and much of what they watched was too tame for Steve, though it appealed to Mark. They'd had some comic films like *Crocodile Dundee* and *A Fish Called Wanda*, and they'd all laughed at those, even Steve, as they ate fish and chips bought from the van which parked in the market square three times a week.

It was nice, Mark thought, sitting in front of the television with the plates of food—Tom wouldn't let them eat it from the wrappings even though it meant they had to wash up later. Steve did well on those nights because Ivy gave him the money for his and Mark's meal when she did not feed them at home, and Steve also claimed it from Tom.

In the soft light from the gas fire—one which looked like

coal—the flickering television screen, and a standard lamp switched on in the corner, the room was peaceful, the atmosphere easy. Mark would imagine that Tom was his grandfather. He liked the old man's pink face and fine white hair, and his crooked smile. Mark would pretend that he lived here all the time, and his mother too, so that it didn't matter that she was out so much. She had to work hard to keep them both and to pay Ivy for looking after him out of school hours—it came to a lot in the holidays. If his mother had to be away all night, which happened when there were conferences and big functions at the hotel where she worked, he spent the night at Ivy's, but soon he would be old enough to stay at home by himself and save money. He planned to suggest it next time his mother seemed depressed when doing her accounts.

Ivy had looked after him for a long time, even before Steve's father died. Mark had liked Joe, who had played football with the boys and promised that they'd all go camping when Mark and Kylie were older. Mark missed Joe a lot, but he didn't like to say so in case it made Ivy sad. She'd cheered up when Sharon had her baby, Adam, who was four months old now. The baby, like Mark, had no dad, but nor had Steve now, and Mark didn't know what had happened to Sharon's. Perhaps he was dead, too. It was all right not to have a dad; lots of people hadn't, or shared someone else's, but Mark would have liked one.

His mother had told him that she had wanted him so much that although she wasn't married, she had decided to bring him up on her own. He wasn't quite sure what the alternative was, and at the time was not curious about his father, but he was now, only she wouldn't answer questions about him.

"I wanted you. You're mine and I love you," she would say, and she did, he knew. She gave him lovely hugs and she bought him toys. He had a computer and a Scalextric car layout, and at weekends, if she wasn't at work, they were happy together, but he wished he had more of a family. Steve had a gran, though she lived in Wales and he didn't see her much; Kylie and Sharon had cousins who visited and with whom they sometimes stayed; but Mark had no one except his mother.

Mark was going round to Ivy's after school, even though at ten, he was old enough, now, to go straight home. After his next birthday his mum would let him; he could cook things in the microwave and put on the telly. He could still visit Tom, too, as long as he was back before Mum. But he'd miss Ivy's meals. At weekends their food was brilliant; she made shepherd's pies and tasty stews, and sticky brown gingerbread which Mark loved. Mark didn't mind the small children she sometimes looked after, as she had him when he was young, but Steve found them a pain. Mark quite liked Sharon's baby, which did little more than sleep and cry at present, or hang like a limpet on Sharon's large, pale breast, a sight which fascinated Mark and yet embarrassed him.

"Such huge tits she's got now," Steve would say, and laugh. He liked staring at her, and Sharon would get cross and tell him to piss off, and then Ivy would ask her to watch her language.

She was really quite strict, much stricter than Mark's mother.

The boys knew they must watch what they said in front of Tom. It wasn't too hard; there was no need for strong words at The Willows. Tom always had time to hear what they had to say and he never failed to ask if they had done their homework. Sometimes they brought it with them. Mark didn't have very much at the moment, and Steve skimped his so that they could settle down to playing cards or watching telly. Tom had recorded a number of old films which they put on when there was no program that appealed. One of the old man's favorites was *The Dam Busters*, and Mark liked

The Great Escape. Tom had been a bomber pilot in the war, and he was shot down over Hamburg. He had spent the rest of the war as a prisoner, but he hadn't managed to escape, though he'd tried several times before giving up and settling down to study for some exams, which had been a wise thing to do, he told them both. It meant he had done well in later life.

He must have, to have bought a big house like The Willows. Ivy said it was worth a tidy penny, and if Tom had to go into a home, selling the house would pay for years of care.

She and Sharon thought it was ever so sad that Tom had no family, and so did Mark. But there must have been someone once, a boy. There was that room upstairs with the posters of airplanes, and all the children's books, which Tom encouraged the two boys to borrow. Steve wasn't interested, but Mark was.

Perhaps the boy was dead. Mark didn't like to ask.

Tom suspected that Steve was stealing from him, but the amounts were not large and he could stand the loss. However, he felt that Steve should not be allowed to succeed with his pilfering; getting away with small thefts might lead him on to larger ones and he could end up in serious trouble.

He ought to tackle the boy, bring the stealing to a halt. There was Mark, too; Tom hoped Mark was not a party to the deceit. He was so young, his cheeks round and smooth, his brown eyes trusting. Tom knew that Mark loved coming to the house. He had discovered the books upstairs and, if he did not like what was on the television, or if Tom and Steve were playing poker—which they sometimes did, for matches, and Tom usually won—he would sit curled up in a big armchair, rapt in the adventures of Biggles or William, or even the Famous Five. Tom played chess with Mark. Steve would leave them together while he went to fetch the fish and chips, and occasionally he would slip out without saying where he was going. Tom tried not to wonder what he was up to then; he hoped the boy wasn't turning his talents elsewhere, looking for more scams. Wordsworth Road was so quiet; there were other secluded houses, which might not be securely locked up, within a few hundred yards.

If he challenged Steve, the results might be costly. He would lose his errand boy and Mark wouldn't be allowed to come on his own to visit. Or would he? Children were independent at an early age now and he was a capable lad.

Tom compromised. He began to check the money handed out and the change received, and told Steve he'd need receipts in future.

"But why? Don't you trust me?" Steve asked, his thin, fair skin flushing over his cheekbones, the pupils enlarging in his pale blue eyes.

"I need to work out my budget," Tom replied. "My funds are limited."

It was close enough to the truth.

"I'll shop around a bit. Get marked-down stuff," Steve volunteered, and for a week or two he brought back receipts from various tills, though he still filched from Tom's purse.

Tom couldn't maintain strict vigilance. He was too frail and it was too much of a strain. He'd rather have the boys happy and dishonest than lose them altogether.

Then the man came.

He called on a Saturday afternoon. Steve and Mark had been watching *Grandstand* on television. They had given Tom his lunch, and he had dozed off, as he often did after eating, when the doorbell rang.

Steve answered it, and saw a stocky man with gray hair, dressed in jeans and a fawn anorak, carrying a holdall.

"Who are you?" the man asked him, stepping forward so

that his nose was a few inches from Steve's. He smelled of beer.

"Who's asking?" Steve responded, standing firmly in the doorway. He wished he'd put the chain up, but the only people who'd ever called were the do-gooders, like the vicar and the health visitor, and once some Jehovah's Witnesses. There'd been no one showing disrespect before.

The man pushed past Steve, one hand thrusting him against the doorpost as he strode by. Steve, who was tall for his age and well built, was not used to being defied and he was startled when the man marched on into the sitting room, where Mark had abandoned the ice hockey match on the screen and was reading.

"What's happening here?" the man demanded. "Are you running a kids' home now?" He spoke in an angry voice, and as he moved across to Tom's chair and stood over him, for a moment Mark thought he was going to hit the old man while he slept. Then Tom opened his eyes.

"Eh? Eh? What—who?" he muttered, blinking, trying to focus on the newcomer.

"Wake up," said the man. "It's me, Alan, come to see his dad."

Tom gaped at him, his head tilted back. He'd gone a funny color, sort of bluey-white and blotchy. Mark stared at them both. The man had brought fear with him into the house.

But Steve had rallied.

"What right have you to shove me around?" he demanded, squaring up to the intruder, bravely, Mark decided. "And how do I know Tom is your dad?"

Like Mark, Steve was frightened, but he had recognized a bully. If the man proved to be a villain, he and Mark could run out of the house fast, and get help, then be heroes. If, however, he was Tom's son, a whole new situation existed. Had Tom sent for him because of Steve's cheating over money? He drew breath, preparing to defend himself, getting ready to counterattack.

Tom had now turned red, an alarming purply shade.

"It's all right, Steve," he said, and to the man, "You never let me know you were coming. Should you be here at all?"

"Of course, as you're not well," the man replied. "I've only just heard about your illness."

"You should have warned me," Tom said.

"I thought you'd enjoy the surprise," said the man. His manner had grown quieter. "Who are these kids?"

"They're my friends," said Tom. "They do my shopping and keep me company. Steve and Mark."

"You can go now, kids," the man told them. "And there's no need to mention my visit." He tapped his nose with his finger. "It's no one else's business."

Steve thought that made sense. Mark never talked about Tom anyway.

2.

Richard Gardner was traveling back to Haverscot from his office, which was south of the river, a large anonymous building where corporate insurance was handled. His working hours were calmer than his time at home, and he was wondering what sort of reception he would receive that evening. Sometimes Verity was out at evening classes; she was studying a form of meditation this term, seeking tranquillity. She left the boys alone if he was not back when it was time for her to leave; she said that they were old enough. Justin was thirteen and Terry was eleven; they were her children by an earlier marriage.

If Verity were at home when he returned, she might greet him with moist, sticky kisses, twining skinny arms around his neck; or she might remain silent, dishing up a meal that was nearly inedible—burned or almost raw, or part of some new diet fad she had decided they should follow.

"For your good, Dickie," she would say when the menu was bean sprouts or tofu, or both, and she would burst into tears if he shuffled the unpalatable food round his plate, planning to abandon it and look for bread and cheese when she had gone to bed.

On other evenings, she would greet him with a tempest of tears and accuse him of having a mistress, deceiving her, and of planning to turn her and her children into the street. Until recently, this had been a baseless charge; now, though, there was Caroline, hardheaded and shrewd, a colleague with better career prospects than Richard, and not the marrying type, as she had told him when their casual friendship metamorphosed into an affair.

Once, Richard had hoped to be the conventional father in a happy family with two or three children, a comfortable house in the country, and a pretty, affectionate wife who would be content to give up whatever work she had been doing to stay at home looking after all of them—perhaps resuming a career when the children were no longer small. But it hadn't worked out that way.

Like many of his contemporaries, Richard, at university, had made the most of the new sexual freedom of the sixties until, disastrously, his girlfriend, Karen, had declared that she was pregnant.

Neither had considered an abortion, recently made legal, nor adoption. They had been a couple; they would marry. The wedding had been an affair of white satin and tulle with a marquee on Karen's parents' lawn in Hertfordshire; she had been princess for a day, while everyone decided that it was an occasion for rejoicing.

Anna was a fine, healthy baby, much loved by them both, and for several years it seemed that success would follow this shaky start, but Richard, working hard, hoping to climb his professional ladder, was, said Karen, dull, and she hated life in London. They moved out to the country; she began to ride and go to agricultural shows where she met the man whom Richard, to hide his hurt, called "The Jolly Farmer," and who had several hundred acres and a farmhouse in Somerset.

When Anna was six her parents separated, and after their

divorce Karen married her farmer and had three more children.

During the years that followed, he had tried to keep in contact with Anna, whom he maintained financially with willing generosity. At first he drove down to Somerset every other weekend; gradually, though, as the little girl's life developed with new friends and then her two half brothers and her half sister, Richard saw how his visits were beginning to affect her, to interrupt her social life and to cause her problems of loyalty. She was fond of her stepfather, who had provided her with a life which she enjoyed. Richard's visits grew less frequent and were tailored to suit her diary. For a while he took her on holiday each summer to a hotel catering for children, suggesting she should bring a friend, and this worked for several years; it was Richard who could no longer bear the strain of getting to know her again every year. The holidays had stopped when she was thirteen.

She was twenty-six now, and working as assistant purser on a cruise ship. Richard saw her when she had shore leave, but that was seldom; if she came to stay, the pleasant, confident, pretty girl was a stranger; it was easy to believe they were not related at all.

Richard had hoped that he and Verity would have children of their own but this did not happen and now, as her depressions, interspersed with elation, grew more frequent, he was thankful. He believed that heredity had more effect on character than upbringing and environment. Musicians bred musicians, and actors' children went into the theater, not simply because they were surrounded by music and drama from infancy; the talent lay in their genes. In Verity's elder son, Justin, he saw the same mood swings and sudden bursts of temper, and it alarmed him.

Verity's moods were getting worse and were less predictable. Richard had devised various ruses to avoid spending too much time with her: he had a workshop in the garden where he carved figures and animals. He'd given Verity a swan; once, he'd thought she looked like one, with her long neck and her way of pointing her head upwards. She'd knocked it off the shelf where she kept it, and its neck had broken. Richard had taken it away to mend, but had left it in two pieces in a drawer where he kept some of his tools.

Leaving the train at Haverscot, he saw a thin, pale young woman whom he had often noticed on the train. She always read intently, never looking up from her book, and Richard wondered who she was and what she did. Tonight, in driving rain, she hurried from the station while he went to fetch his car. She looked malnourished; was she a starving student? Richard reminded himself not to get interested in anyone who might be a lame duck. Verity had been one when he met her, stranded with a puncture by the roadside with her two small boys. He had changed the wheel for her, pumped up the flat spare, and followed her home to Reading to make sure she arrived safely. She had seemed so forlorn and helpless, standing there with the wheelbrace in her hands as she ineffectually sought a means to jack up the car, tears rolling down her face.

At first she had said that she was a widow, but he soon discovered that her husband had left her and the boys, and gone to work abroad. The boys had told him; they remembered their father. Richard could have been on the brink of bigamy, he thought later, but soon after he met her there was a divorce because her husband had wanted to remarry.

She had lied about that, and she had lied about her name. She had been christened Vera, after an aunt, but had elected to be known as Verity—no great sin, perhaps, but an embellishment. She was good at disguising the truth.

These days, people did not set such store by marriage. This saved trouble if things went wrong; there were fewer legal hurdles to negotiate. If he hadn't married Verity, he could have left her when her accusations and her tantrums became so extreme, but he had wanted to provide security for her and to build a family, and had bought a large, solid house in which to do so. Merrifields was a solid Edwardian structure, set in a quiet road not far from the church, its acre of garden running down to a field which bordered the river, where willows grew along the bank. Richard was still improving the garden, creating leafy corners, and bowers where climbing roses sprawled; this, like his woodwork, was a solace to his troubled soul as he pruned and sprayed, clipped and weeded, prizing out every errant interloper.

Verity had said she wished to grow salads and vegetables on which to feed them all, but two rows of lettuces which quickly ran to seed the first summer were the limit of her achievement; Richard, though, now cultivated a productive kitchen garden and had joined the local horticultural society. Verity, meanwhile, had turned an upstairs room into a studio and there she covered canvases with tortured landscapes in heavy greens and purples, always tempestuous in composition. She had told him that she had planned to be a designer before she had the boys; he never fully understood what had prevented her, for she was in her late twenties when Justin was born. For her, marrying Richard was an upward move. He soon learned that she had debts and was threatened with eviction. She had told him this when he arrived one evening to find her swallowing pills, washing them down with gin. He'd called an ambulance.

She'd been expecting him. It was not a serious attempt at suicide, but, temporarily bewitched, he had felt enormous pity for her. He had stayed overnight, looking after the boys while she was in hospital, had taken them with him to bring her home next day, and was ensnared. For a few brief months he felt all-powerful, necessary to them all.

After their wedding, Verity declared that the boys must

assume Richard's surname and think of him as their father. They all went on the honeymoon to Corsica, though her parents had suggested that the children should stay with them. At five and seven, they were too old to accept him easily and they began to idealize their real father, although they never heard from him and he made no contribution to their upkeep. The boys had managed to forget the noisy arguments they had so often heard, and their mother's tears. Now, though, when she lapsed into fits of weeping, they were convinced that she was crying for their father.

Richard took each day as it came, training himself to live within small frameworks: the office, and his colleagues there; his home with its tensions, which he shed each morning like a jacket, and resumed again at night. He began to work longer hours quite regularly, partly to delay his return and partly to make the evenings when he went to Caroline's flat less conspicuous. Then, as winter approached, he joined a choir which met on Thursdays at eight o'clock to practice for a Christmas concert. At Easter they would do *Elijah*.

Verity had no singing voice nor any sense of music. She did not encourage her sons to learn an instrument, though Richard thought they should at least have the opportunity. Neither progressed beyond the recorder at school, but when Justin sat down at Richard's piano, he was able to play by ear tunes he had heard on the radio or in television jingles. Richard was impressed by this rare gift and wanted to nourish the boy's innate ability, but Justin rejected all such help. Any idea produced by Richard was anathema to him and he became increasingly rebellious as he grew older. Maybe it was natural, Richard would think wearily. Justin resented what Richard had tried to do for him; useless to expect gratitude—that was an uncomfortable emotion.

What would have happened to them all if he had not rescued them? Would someone else have come along?

Perhaps. Verity had had an appealing bruised air about her when they met and, like Richard, she had been rejected. Coming together had seemed, at the time, healing for them both. Now, Verity simply looked angry when she was not weeping. She accused him of burying her in the country and stifling her talent, but he never saw her attempt any design work, although that could be done anywhere, as he pointed out. She spent long hours painting her somber pictures; Richard thought they represented the torment in her soul and were some sort of safety valve; at least while she was painting conflict, she wasn't setting fire to things or creating mayhem.

Once, she had set his books alight, his collection of Everyman classics and his reference works. She had done it one Sunday and he had smelled the smoke and put it out before the fire had spread to the curtains or the furniture in his study. His books were badly damaged, however, and some of them were ruined.

He'd had smoke alarms installed everywhere afterwards, and put fire extinguishers on the landings.

She hadn't repeated that, but she'd wreaked other forms of havoc—scraping marks on his desk, a valuable one inherited from his father and worth a lot of money, and she had smashed a Meissen figure he had bought at a sale when, before meeting her, he had had an affair with a woman who was a collector, but they had broken up before he could give it to her. Once, when Richard was playing the piano, Verity had come in with a kettle of boiling water and poured it over his hands. He'd reacted quickly, knocking the kettle from her grasp and moving away, so that although he had been painfully scalded, he had saved the piano keys from serious damage and himself from worse injury. While he did so, water had spilled over Verity's flowing cotton skirt and thin, bare legs, so that she was also hurt.

She'd cried then and, for once, had said that she was sorry

and she didn't know what made her do it. Richard believed her remorse was genuine as he led her upstairs, sponged her legs with cool water and made her change her skirt. She wanted to make love then; she often did, after such scenes, but this time Richard's own scalded, blistering hands demanded his attention and he would not be won round.

Bandaged awkwardly, he gave in later.

It was soon after this that his affair with Caroline began. To be with her was so restful. They had always got on well at work; she was capable and assertive but never needed to challenge Richard, whom she liked and saw as no threat of any kind. He often wondered how they had ever become so intimate. She sometimes gave him a lift to Paddington, which was near where she lived, and occasionally she asked him in for a drink. He always accepted, because to do so meant he won a domestic reprieve by catching a later train. It was pleasant in her large, ground-floor flat. Her sitting room had pale gold curtains and two huge sofas covered in cream brocade; her bedroom, he discovered later, was a peaceful place with mushroom-pink curtains and calm seascapes on the walls. Making love with her was not a fight; it was, he began to understand, a mutually rewarding encounter, unalarming and enriching rather than exciting. He did not pine for her between their interludes together, but he often thought about her.

Caroline had been hurrying off this weekend, going down to the country, she said, visiting friends, not telling him who they were. He felt mild curiosity; he would have liked to have gone with her, he thought, spent a casual weekend, free from stress. Instead, he had to face Verity and the boys.

As he drove through the town in the heavy rain, he saw the pale girl hurrying along, a small umbrella over her head. Where was she going? Where did she live? He slowed the car; if he offered her a lift, would she cry "rape" and flee? Probably, he decided, sighing; it would be folly to try.

Current fears had put an end to such kindness among strangers.

He had had such high hopes when he bought Merrifields. There was space for them all—a room each for the boys, and a playroom where they had their toys at first, and now a computer and their own television, a retrograde step, he felt, but taken in the interests of avoiding discord. Justin had a compact disc player in his room. Terry was so far content with the simple stereo system which they used in their playroom. Richard, in his workshop, could escape the noise and, because the house was old and solid, built by a prosperous Edwardian tradesman, his study was almost soundproof. It would all have been much more difficult if they were forced to live in a cramped box attached to a row of similar boxes on each side. No wonder murder was done when people were forced to live like battery hens, denied personal space.

Verity had recently given up cooking, which was an improvement on earlier days, Richard thought. She shredded vegetables and grated cheese for the boys, who were not satisfied with such fare. When Richard came home they demanded pizzas from the shop that delivered or to go down to the fish and chip van which came three times a week to the square. Richard thought growing boys needed plenty of protein and fruit, and at weekends he roasted meat or made thick, nourishing stews and steamed puddings which they loved. They were often punctual for these meals and had been known to praise them.

This evening there was peace. Verity was in her studio; she discouraged interruption. The boys were in their playroom watching television. Richard decided to assume that everyone had eaten and made himself an omelette. There was lettuce in the fridge, and he found a tomato, slightly squashed, on the floor where somebody had dropped it and left it to rest in peace. There was cheese, and he thawed some frozen bread in the microwave; Richard had invested in timesaving equipment.

Verity appeared just as he had finished eating, and made a scene because he had not gone up to her studio to say that he was back.

"You've made it clear that you don't like being disturbed when you're working," he replied.

"I could have been dead for all you cared," she raged, and he thought, Yes, you could.

Richard had never allowed himself to think like that before. He made a business of putting the plate and cutlery he had used in the dishwasher, and wiping down the sink while he fought to put himself into a more charitable frame of mind, but as he did so, Verity sprang at him and began clawing at his neck and shoulders, screaming that she hated him.

He swung round quickly, which wrong-footed her, and she stumbled against the table, catching her hip on a corner. That hurt, and she doubled over. Richard left the room, not shutting the door on her, not leaving her completely cut off from an audience.

What was the matter with her? Why could she not enjoy her life, her security, her children? She often said that all she wanted was to be happy, yet she was the one who made happiness impossible.

It couldn't go on, but if they broke up, what would happen to her and to those boys? Wouldn't all three of them be doomed?

Justin and Terry were in their playroom—or their personal room, as Verity had taken to calling it, since they were too old now to have a playroom.

"Why not the den?" Richard had suggested mildly, and she had answered that it made them sound like wild animals.

She was as defensive as a lioness in relation to her young,

he thought, but did not fault that, although in his view she was overindulgent with them, set no store by consideration for others—him, for instance—and was no stickler for truth. But, though hostile to him, the boys were not too troublesome; they were rude and noisy sometimes, but what boy wasn't? He did not think they were bad boys.

Now, he went into their room. If she followed, she might restrain her behavior in front of them. Perhaps it was a craven action but he would do a lot to cut short one of Verity's fits of histrionics.

"What are you watching?" he asked, and sat down in a spare chair beside Justin who was glued to some game show.

Verity came into the room behind him and stood in the doorway with tears rolling down her face. She sobbed audibly. Her husband and her sons kept their faces turned to the television screen until she crossed the room and switched it off. She stood glowering at them.

"None of you cares," she told them, quivering, her thin hands clasped across the black knitted tunic she wore over a purple polo sweater. "I spend all day slaving here to keep the house decent and none of you gives me a word of thanks for all I do."

At least she was not swearing at them, which often happened. But her sons ought not to see her in this state. A swift memory of Richard's controlled parents came to him: one must keep up the facade of behaving well, even if the world was crashing round one's ears.

He rose to his feet and took her by the elbow.

"Come along, Verity," he said. "You're tired. I'll take you upstairs."

He led her away, and she permitted it; she had got his attention now, and once upstairs, he helped her take off her clothes, bundling her into bed, touching her as little as he could. He felt no desire for that thin body with the prominent ribcage, the small drooping breasts, but she was vulnerable and he still pitied her. He fetched a glass of water and a Valium tablet; their own doctor rarely prescribed tranquilizers but during his absence she had persuaded a locum, an older man, to do so and she had been able to get more. Richard, unaware that this was not straightforward, blessed the pills because they brought peace—tranquillity, their very purpose, albeit intermittently.

She went to sleep. The storm was over for the evening. Tomorrow was another day.

3.

On Sunday Terry had a guest to lunch. Richard had roasted a leg of lamb—it would last, cold, for a day or two, giving him and the boys something to eat even if Verity preferred to toy with bean shoots and lettuce.

"There's enough for Mark, isn't there, Cat?" asked Terry.

They wouldn't call him Dad, or by his name, and Justin had bestowed this nickname on him after a visit years ago to a pantomime when at first he'd called him Whittington. Richard had regarded it as a sign of acceptance, but when the name was switched to Cat, uttered in a sneering tone, he realized that he was wrong. However, Justin knew his limits: He was offhand, graceless, but not overtly rude to Richard, testing him sometimes, trying to see how far he could go without incurring open wrath but not quite overstepping what Richard would tolerate.

"You're not my dad," he sometimes said, when told to tidy up his possessions, put his bike away, or finish his homework.

"I pay the bills," Richard had started saying several months ago. On the whole, both of them avoided conflict. Terry, so far, was less difficult, but he could flare up into sudden rages.

22

The brothers were very much alike, both dark, with heavy eyebrows and almost black eyes. Justin's hair was longer than Richard thought it should be, but Terry had a bristle cut, each hair standing up about an inch, like a mop.

They seldom brought friends home, so Richard was pleased when Terry said that Mark Conway was coming over with a new computer game he'd got. The two boys had spent a contented morning before coming into the kitchen. Beside Terry, Mark was short and stocky, and his brown hair fell in a true pudding bowl cut around his chubby face.

"You'd better ring your parents to ask if you may stay," said Richard.

"There's only Mum, and she's away," said Mark. "It's OK." Then, seeing Richard's expression, he added, "It's just for the day. She's on a course. She's got a mega-important job. Ivy knows I'm here."

"Who's Ivy?"

Mark explained about her.

Steve had made the plan, because he did not want to be stuck with Mark as he wanted to go off with some friends in a car. They'd run into Terry in the park the day before and Steve had proposed that Mark should take his computer game over to show Terry. The idea had caught hold, and Steve was highly delighted with himself.

Mark hadn't minded. Terry was all right, and afterwards he could go round to The Willows and see Tom. He wondered if the angry man would still be there, Tom's son.

Justin had loafed off somewhere and he was late for lunch, but he did turn up. Richard's cooking made the effort of coming home worthwhile. Verity was still in bed, and, cravenly, Richard sent Terry up with a bowl of soup, a warm roll and two bananas, some of which she might decide to consume. He returned without the tray. Even martyrs needed food.

Mark did not know when he had eaten a more delicious

meal. It knocked spots off even Ivy's stews and pies. The pudding had a kind of meringue on top and was all lemony underneath. Mark had never had it before. Richard was pleased when he accepted a second helping. It was nice to be appreciated.

"You ought to run a hotel," Mark told him. He was unsure of Richard's name; he wasn't Terry or Justin's father so it might not be the same, and he couldn't really be called Cat. As uttered by Justin, it hadn't sounded respectful. Mark was interested in respect because Steve was always on about it. "My mum works in a hotel," he added.

"Which one?" asked Richard, thinking it might be The Red Lion or one of Haverscot's several pubs.

"The Golden Accord. It's on the way to Swindon," Mark replied.

Richard knew it. He and Verity had even spent a night there once, when the boys were visiting their grandparents.

"It's a very good hotel," he said truthfully. .

The weather improved after lunch, and Richard decided that the boys should play outside, but first they must help clear away and load the dishwasher.

"Ivy could do with one of those," Mark said. "She's got a big family."

"I expect she could," said Richard. "Now, why don't you take your football out, Terry, and kick it around?"

"It's too wet in the garden," Terry said. "Can we go to the park?"

Before agreeing, Richard made sure that Mark, who was younger than Terry, was allowed there unsupervised. It was true that recent rain had flooded the river below the garden and made his lawn very soggy; they'd damage it if they played out there for long. The park was on higher ground, though much of its turf was sour and dog-fouled. Children had to be independent and streetwise these days. At Mark's age, Richard had already been a pupil for two years at a boarding school housed in a mansion amid twenty acres of grounds, some of them woodland, where there was freedom to play both organized games and the other kind. Contrary to popular belief about such places, he had not been abused, nor bullied, but during his first weeks he had felt utterly forsaken, unable to understand why he had been sent away from home. He had concluded that this withdrawal of love, as it had seemed to him, had made him the more anxious to seek it in his adult life. He had certainly been eager to give affection, liable to fall seriously in love rather than indulge in passing fancies.

You had your whole childhood in which to grow used to your family; even so, there were quarrels and misunderstandings. Yet people frequently chose a partner with whom they intended to share the greater part of their life on a very brief acquaintance. It worked sometimes; there were couples who fell in love and married within weeks, and remained content after forty or more years together.

It was pointless to think like this; it made him feel too sad. He blamed himself for being bad husband material, although he had tried, both times, to be reliable and kind. He was dull, he supposed; that was the main problem. He wanted a quiet life, absence of strife even if romance had withered away. He still didn't know where he had failed Karen; her farmer, also, seemed rather dull, but perhaps she liked the country existence he provided. Verity, he now understood, could not deal with life except through confrontation; she was like a panther, poised ready to pounce, except when she had swallowed a pill and lapsed into an exhausted torpor.

"Is your mother coming home tonight, Mark?" he asked.

"Oh yes," said Mark airily. "She won't be late."

"You must go back before it gets dark," Richard said. "I don't want either of you out there then. Understood, Terry?"

Terry nodded. He had suggested the park because he had wanted to demonstrate to Mark how he could manipulate his stepfather; in fact, there was plenty to do in the garden here; Cat had built a tree house, quite a high one up a large beech tree, and he would have liked to show that to Mark, but it would do for another time.

The two boys set off together. Mark skipped along. It had been a good day so far, and it would end with a visit to Tom.

He said nothing to Terry about the old man, and the visitor who had turned out to be Tom's son. His visits to The Willows were a secret. Terry's stepfather was nice, but so inquisitive. Mum had said it was rude to ask questions, yet adults always did it—wanting to know what you'd done at school, where you were going, who with and such, and had you done your homework. Even Mum did that. In the park, they'd be on their own.

Rare calm settled on Merrifields when the boys had gone out. Verity was still in her room, but might not remain there if she had revived and felt like creating fresh drama. Richard snatched some time with the Sunday paper; then he went out to his workshop, where he was carving a figure from a piece of old yew he had found in the churchyard. It had seemed to him that there was a gnarled old man with grizzled hair and a beard trapped inside the timber, waiting for release. He always worked like this with his wood sculptures, seeking form within the branch or log he had picked up either in the garden or when walking in the countryside. He worked slowly, enjoying the sensation of the wood beneath his fingers, watching the gradual realization of his original idea.

He had given Caroline a pale, galloping horse he had made from a length of ash; she had exclaimed with pleasure, surprised that such power of observation, even artistry, could exist within what seemed to be a gray, conventional exterior. She didn't ask him what his wife thought about his skill; she was not interested in his family life.

Failing light reminded him of the time. He glanced towards

the house and saw that it was in darkness, apart from Verity's studio window. So she was up and slopping paint about; that was something. Perhaps it would relieve her anger. But it looked as though the boys had not returned. The playroom showed no light.

Of course, when you were out of doors at dusk, you did not realize how dark it was until you went inside. They'd be home soon. He locked his shed and walked slowly up the garden towards the house.

Half an hour later, when there was still no sign of the boys, Richard, with a feeling of responsibility for Mark, if not his stepsons, set off towards the park to look for them. He'd probably meet Terry; Mark, who had disclosed at lunch that he lived in Grasmere Street, would be on his way home. He'd no idea where Justin was.

He reached the park without encountering the two younger boys or Justin. There were various figures running about in the gloaming. A few children were still on the swings with two young fathers watching them. A tall woman walked a dog around the perimeter, a Dalmatian which gleamed in the dusk. He could not see Terry or Mark among the boys scuffling together in mock combat; no one was kicking a football.

Perhaps Terry had gone home with Mark. Richard thought of going to see, but he did not know which was his house in Grasmere Street. Conway—that was the boy's surname; during lunch they'd joked about the castle because Mark had not heard of it and Richard had treated them all to a brief discourse on the subject of thirteenth-century fortifications.

He did not hurry back. Terry might catch him up, or perhaps had taken the path through the churchyard and across the fields, though with the water flowing fast so far beyond the river, that was not a good idea.

Not for the first time, Richard wished that he could have afforded to send Verity's boys away to boarding school. It might have given their marriage more of a chance, and the

unemotional, steady framework might have benefited Justin
and Terry. Richard, thinking like this, disregarded the memory
of his own isolation when he was sent away; he had grown
used to the life and had settled down. So would they, and for
those months of their absence, he would cease to feel like an
intruder in his own house.

He sighed. Not long now till Monday morning. He
wondered if Caroline had had a good weekend; perhaps they
could meet on Monday evening, for a drink and a chat, if
nothing else; a touch of kindness, just to keep him going.

Mark could not get rid of Terry. They had kicked the ball
about for a while, and then some bigger boys had come and
snatched it from them, kicking it themselves with so much
force and strength that the smaller boys had no chance of
retrieving it. Terry, whose ball it was, began to snivel, and in
the end the older boys, having succeeded in upsetting him,
grew bored with their teasing and kicked it out of sight, over
the railings and into the road where it bounced off the
windscreen of a passing Renault, causing the driver to swerve
and crash into a stationary car. He missed a slowly pedaling
cyclist by two inches.

Brakes screamed, horns blew, and the bigger boys
disappeared in the opposite direction. Terry and Mark were
still standing on the rough grass, no great distance from the
fence, when the irate Renault driver and the owner of the
parked car, who had rushed out of his house at the sound of
the disturbance, appeared in the park. One of them carried
the offending football.

Terry turned to flee, but Mark stood his ground.

"It wasn't us," he said staunchly when the two angry men
drew near. "It was our ball but those other boys took it."

He gestured in the direction of the far entrance to the park.

Tears on Terry's face were signs of guilt. The two motorists
were not eager to accept Mark's explanation and one of them

had raised his arm, ready to burst into a torrent of speech if not to rain blows on the nearest boy, when a voice came from behind him. The speaker was an elderly woman with a checked tweed hat worn low down over her eyebrows, and wearing a Burberry raincoat. She was accompanied by a golden cocker spaniel on a lead.

"It wasn't these two boys," she said. "I saw it all. There were three of them, all much bigger than these boys. I should think they were fourteen or fifteen."

"Is that so?" The angrier of the two men was still glowering.

"They were teasing these two, snatching their ball," said the woman. "I don't suppose they thought about the consequences when they pitched it into the road."

"Maybe not," said the calmer man, only marginally placated. "Well, we must take your word for it. Would you give us your name and address as a witness? For the insurance."

"I'll write it down for you if you have some paper and a pencil," said the woman.

The man produced a gold ballpoint and a card on which she wrote, resting it against the fence to get some purchase. Then he asked the boys for their names.

"That's not necessary," said the woman firmly. "The older boys, yes, if known, but not this pair."

The second man agreed.

"No one was hurt," he said. "It could have been worse." He turned to the other man. "Let's sort out the details in my house. It must have shaken you up. I wasn't in my car when it happened." He began walking back towards the road, and the second man followed.

Terry, still sniffing, was standing beside the old woman. Mark glanced at him and then·trotted after the men.

"Please, could Terry have his ball back?" he asked.

"Oh, I suppose so," said the angrier man, who was holding it. He threw it to Mark, quite viciously, but Mark caught it.

"Thanks," he said, and added, "I'm sorry."

"Don't push your luck," said the man ungraciously. "You and your friend get off home, and don't bother the lady."

Mark hurried back to Terry, who was being told by their savior to blow his nose and brace up.

"You know those boys, don't you?" she asked Mark.

"They go to the upper school," said Mark cautiously.

He did know them; one was a friend of Steve's.

"Hm. Well, if someone had been hurt, you'd have had to tell the police all about it and there would have been a great deal of trouble," she said.

"It wasn't our fault," said Terry. "You said so," he added.

"No, it wasn't," she agreed. "And those boys were very thoughtless. Let it be a lesson to you two. Think about the consequences of your actions." She'd used that word to the men. Mark had heard her. He knew what consequences were; he'd played the game with old Tom and Steve and he'd enjoyed it, but Steve found it boring. He was no good at thinking of the names, and kept writing down football players and Madonna, or Sylvester Stallone. Even Tom and Mark tired of them.

"Get on home, then," the woman instructed. "Terry, isn't it? And what's your name?" She peered at Mark, eyes screwed up under the brim of her hat. He thought she was very ugly.

"Mark," he answered. "Come on, Terry, let's get going," and he ran off, stopping a few yards away to call back, "Thanks, missus." He'd heard Steve call a woman "missus" when he'd wanted to wheedle money, allegedly for fireworks, from her. Steve had said it was respectful, and certainly the woman had paid up. Mark didn't know what Steve had used the money for; it wasn't for fireworks.

Terry trailed after him. With his tears dried and the ball returned, his fear had turned to anger.

"Sod them," he muttered, kicking at the grass as he followed Mark through the gate by the road through which the two enraged motorists had entered the park.

"That's right. Don't let it get to you," Mark advised. He was feeling calm and powerful. He had taken charge of Terry and had managed to get the ball back. Thanks to that old woman, they'd escaped being blamed for something not their fault. What if the police had been called? It might have been the death of Terry's mum, who seemed to be rather ill as she hadn't appeared for lunch and had been given only soup and fruit.

There was no point in telling Terry this, and besides, he was in a hurry to visit Tom.

"I'm going," he said. "Thanks for lunch."

They parted at the corner of Grasmere Street and Mark walked down it, as if returning home, allowing time for Terry to disappear before retracing his steps to cross into Wordsworth Road.

Terry slouched off, not looking back, but he did not go home. He remembered where the boy who had kicked the ball lived. He was called Greg Black; Justin knew him. Holding the ball under one arm, Terry walked to the square and along the High Street, turning into the more densely populated part of the old market town until he reached the street where, in a neat semidetached house separated from the pavement by a small patch of grass and a parking spot occupied by a dark red Maestro, Greg's sister was now upstairs, doing her homework.

The houses on the far side of the road were terraced, and on one step stood an empty milk bottle. Terry picked it up, crossed over and flung it hard at the downstairs window, which shattered in a satisfying manner.

On a dank Sunday, there were few people about, but one family returning from an outing saw the boy running away, still holding his football. There were shouts and yells, but Terry ran fast, disappearing down an alley before anyone could catch up with him.

4.

Marigold Darwin pulled her tweed hat down more securely over her thick eyebrows and trudged resolutely round the circumference of the park, her spaniel, Sinbad, obedient at her heels. He was a well-trained, mature dog she had found at the Battersea Dogs' home, after her retirement earlier in the year. Naturally, no one there knew his history, but he had not been neglected. She had been lucky to find him: Deciding to acquire a dog had been part of her program, but she had not wanted a neurotic beast, or one given to snapping and whining; she would not have had the patience to deal with temperament.

Walking, she reflected on the incident with the boys. Youngsters had to learn to stick up for themselves, and the bigger boys had been teasing, not bullying; there was a distinction, but where did it lie? It had always been a difficult question, and one that had affected her throughout most of her youth.

She was plain now, and had not been an attractive child—sallow, with heavy eyebrows from a very young age. Given pretty names by her optimistic parents—her second name was Angela—she grew up with her initials spelling MAD, and with neither name appropriate to her looks, so that nothing would be gained by shedding the Marigold and opting for Angela.

No man had ever loved Marigold Darwin. At the children's parties she had reluctantly attended, boys had sometimes been dared to kiss her. Afterwards, they said "Ugh" and went off giggling, the forfeit paid.

In adult life, she had compensated by achievement, doing well at school, getting a good second-class degree at Oxford. Her college, even now, did not accept men, and she had felt safe there, working hard, singing with the Bach Choir as her one recreation. She had a fine contralto voice and hoped, in Haverscot, that there might be a choir which she could join. She had climbed the civil service ladder within the Treasury, working on calculations and analyses, always with figures, undisturbed by personal problems, conflicts and alliances experienced by her colleagues. Avoidance of pain was her aim and on the whole she had been successful. She was efficient and undemanding, determined but unemotional, not a leader. No one felt threatened by Marigold Darwin, and no one needed her as a friend.

She was the only child of her disappointed parents, who had done what they could for her in terms of education and care. Her pretty mother and reasonably good-looking father were proud of her academic prowess.

While at the Treasury, she went home each weekend to her parents, who offered her a refuge and a reason to avoid making independent plans. Later, as they grew frail together, they in turn depended on their daughter. She shopped for them and filled their freezer, and organized help for them during the week. When they died, within three months of one another, she truly mourned them both.

Her inheritance enabled her to move from her modest flat in Pimlico to a small house just off the Fulham Road, which, despite the recession, she had recently sold at a good price.

In Haverscot, she was renting a bungalow while seeking a place to buy. For some years she had been able to afford expensive holidays with a cultural aspect, and had been to music festivals in several cities, and on art appreciation tours. Alert and interested, she kept detailed diaries of her travels, with the relevant costs, and wondered if, one day, she might turn them into a book, but she feared she lacked narrative skill. She read biographies and travel books for pleasure; never fiction. Dreaming, in her youth, had brought disillusionment; it was safer to stick to fact.

In London, lectures and concerts had attracted her, seldom the theater or the cinema; inspecting other people's lives made her uncomfortable. Lectures and concerts would be available to her still, and she would continue to travel; Australia would be a goal, as she could spend more time away now, making longer tours possible. There would be plenty to do in the years ahead; she must not become a recluse, and Sinbad would help her combat such a tendency. She must find some good kennels where he would be happy; he was not to become a tie.

She might get a car. She had driven as a girl, and during her parents' lifetime, but had not needed to in London and was out of practice. Owning one would increase her range, and Sinbad's, though Haverscot was well served by public transport. She would have to take lessons to ensure that she was still competent.

She had come to Haverscot because she had once lived there. Since then, the town had expanded, with an industrial area to the east, and housing estates all round the perimeter. The center, near the town hall and the market square, was little altered, but old shops had become parts of chains and there were parking problems. She had formed a plan to buy Merrifields, which had been her childhood home. In those days, she had wandered about on the banks of the river wondering why she had no friends, blaming her piggy eyes and ugly face. During the war, she had been dispatched to boarding school while her father was in the army and her mother worked for the Red Cross. By then she had already learned that keeping to herself was a way of avoiding persecution. Now, at sixty, she had the habit of self-preservation and enough money to cushion isolation.

Merrifields was not for sale. A local estate agent approached the owner, saying he had a client who might be interested in buying the place, but there had been no response. She had walked past, both along the road and by the river, stepping through the meadows, looking up at it. Places known in childhood always seem small when revisited in later years, and she remembered Merrifields as a mansion; seen now, it was still large, its gables visible above the hedge, a huge willow and a beech tree in the garden. She suddenly had a memory of the gardener planting a beech tree; was this the one? There was a structure in its upper branches, bare now of leaves: a tree house, she realized. There were no willows in the garden in her day.

Her parents had sold the house soon after the war and moved to Woking. They had lived there until they died.

Mr. Phipps, the agent, alert and keen in his sharp suit, with his mobile telephone, worked on commission. He suggested that Merrifields, even if it had been on the market, was perhaps too big for one lady, but he did not waste time showing her inappropriate properties, however desirable, on estates; she wanted a "residence." There were several old houses with beams and with cracked walls that needed repairing on his books, and he showed her some of them, but she took a practical line about the work that would have to be done, and the expense, not to mention the time that it would take, and turned them down. She did not want to pay rent longer than she must, though her capital was earning enough interest to cover the cost. Her present lease, however, ran out at the end of the year.

Those two boys, the weepy one and his sturdier friend, must learn, as she had done, to hide emotion—to reveal neither pleasure, lest its source disappear, nor fear.

She had felt anger when she saw them provoked by the bigger boys, and that was rare for her. Luckily, she had been able to avert injustice.

One of the men had said he was glad she had prevented them from blaming the innocent pair.

"But for your testimony, I'd have dragged them both off to the police station," he had declared.

Miss Darwin knew that he had meant it.

When she reached home, Miss Darwin wrote down a concise account of the incident. Her evidence might be needed if the men claimed from their insurance companies, and time always blunted accurate recollection. She typed it up neatly and filed it, sighing because she had none of her own furniture around her and her papers were in boxes stacked against the living-room wall. The contents of her London house were in store; she might need more furniture when she moved, because she would have larger rooms and increased space all round. Some would think her foolish proposing to expand at an age when most people wanted smaller homes, but she longed to return to her roots, to the comfort and security she had known as a child. She sought, too, to establish her status in the town as it had been defined by the level she had reached in her career.

That evening she decided to go to church. This was not because of any religious conviction; she had long ago shed the beliefs which had carried her through adolescence in expectation of divine revelation. Disappointed by no such experience at her confirmation—and amazed by the weight of the Bishop's hand on her head—she had continued to expect some ray of enlightenment to justify her acceptance of unkindness, because the meek were destined to be blessed, only gradually abandoning this philosophy. Now she knew that it was the tough who survived.

She was restless. The episode in the park had troubled her but she did not understand why; it was, after all, of no great importance; no one had been hurt nor suffered injustice. Perhaps it was the boys—the intent, chubby one and his unhappy friend. She seldom spoke to children and was not used to their ways.

Once, she had wished for children in a vague, undefined way; they looked sweet and were affectionate. She hid her mild yearning, suppressed because confessing to it, even to herself, admitted weakness, and now she had almost forgotten it. As a diversion, church would do; she had not been there since she returned to the town, and there would have been changes. She put on a long camel coat and a felt hat and set forth.

The outside structure of the fourteenth-century church looked as if it had recently been repaired; there were patches of paler stone over some windows, discernible when you walked past in daylight, as she had done more than once in recent weeks. Inside, she found that the wooden pews had been replaced by pale oak chairs. They were more comfortable, she allowed, remembering how she had slipped and slithered on the old shiny seats. The big brass eagle lectern was the same; behind its spread wings her father had sometimes read the lesson. Closing her eyes, she could imagine his sonorous voice, reading without drama but clearly, so that every syllable was audible throughout the building. Such was not the case now, she reflected, listening to the current vicar intoning the prayers and to the man who, this evening, declaimed a section from the latest translation of the Bible. In her head, she recited the Authorized Version. The hymns, however, were traditional, and she enjoyed singing them. A middle-aged man some seats away from her seemed to do the same.

She walked back to the bungalow past Merrifields, and saw a police car standing in the drive.

Tom's house was warm, almost stifling. He'd got the heating on high and his gas fire was alight.

Steve wasn't there. Mark was glad of that; he'd thought Steve might have dropped in on the way home. He liked being on his own with Tom, who had been pleased to see him. He'd been thinking about getting himself some supper. Now, Mark could open a tin of soup, cut bread for both of them and find the cheese.

It was easy to pretend that Tom was his grandfather when Steve wasn't there, but now Tom's son had turned up and Mark didn't want to imagine that man as his father.

"He's gone, then," he said. "Your son."

"Uh huh," said Tom. "Yes."

"How long did he stay?"

"Not long."

"Where does he live?"

"He's on the move at present," Tom replied.

He'd given Alan money, which was what he had come for, and he'd left at once, a great relief to Tom who, seeing the bag he carried, had feared a prolonged visit.

"Is he coming back?" asked Mark.

"I don't know. Not for a while," said Tom.

Alan was on rehabilitation leave from prison. With money in his pocket, he had gone away to spend it while the authorities thought he was at an approved address.

Mark was relieved to hear that the man would not be interrupting their evening. Neither he nor Tom had seemed pleased to see one another, which was puzzling. Why had the man come, if he didn't like Tom? But then, sons did go to see their fathers, didn't they? If they had fathers.

After their supper, they played chess. Mark could sometimes beat Tom, who had taught him how to play. Both of them enjoyed their game and it was half past eight before Tom noticed the time and told Mark he must go home.

"Your mother will be getting anxious," he said.

"She'll think I'm with Ivy, if she's back," said Mark calmly. "But I think she'll still be out."

She was. He let himself in, had his bath—he was grubby after the park—put his dirty clothes in the machine and turned it on. Then he found clean ones for the morning— Mum had done the ironing before she left—and went to bed. He hadn't brushed his teeth, and after a fierce struggle with his conscience—Mum might ask whether he'd done them if she came back before he went to sleep—got out of bed and scrubbed them hard. Then, clutching his squishy green Kermit, he pulled the duvet over him. He tried hard to stay awake, listening for her key, but in three minutes he was asleep.

Tom worried about Mark, after he had gone. The boy was left alone a lot, but what was the mother to do? She was the sole provider and her job demanded that she work a shift system. In his day, mothers stayed at home, at least until the children were older than Mark was, but widows had always had problems. He remembered coming home from school to the smell of baking, tea ready, a fire lit, and a welcome. In turn, he and Dorothy, his wife, had provided a secure background for Alan.

These days, people seemed to have babies to gratify a whim, or because other people thought they ought to reproduce. Tom wondered if they looked beyond the cot and toddler stage to the child like Mark, who needed a framework to his life. Mark, at least, did not have to share his mother with three or four children by different fathers, none of whom took responsibility for them. According to the press and television, there were men who went around scattering their seed at random. Tom thought the Bible had something to say about that sort of conduct.

Despite their care, he and Dorothy had failed with Alan. He had not done well at school, becoming lazy and insolent as he entered his teens and began playing truant. When he was fifteen, he had been caught stealing and since then he had been arrested several times, finally on a charge of murdering his wife. It had been too much for Dorothy. She knew that he was guilty and after he was convicted she had slowly sunk into what the doctor called a clinical depression, and, eventually, had dwindled away and died.

That was six years ago, and Tom had been alone ever since. Most of the time he had been working as a consultant to the firm of accountants where he had been a partner until his retirement. Before his stroke he had been active and had enjoyed gardening, though with less enthusiasm because there was now no Dorothy with whom to share its results. He had been on the town council, and had become interested in local history. When it was clear that he was going to recover, he thought, wearily, "What for?" but did not complain aloud.

Alan's visit had seriously upset Tom, who had persuaded himself that they would never meet again. He was trouble—always had been, and always would be. That poor girl, his wife; Tom had met her only once, at the wedding. She was still so young, and doomed, he had known then, but he had thought to misery, not death. Memories of Alan's childhood flickered into Tom's mind and would not be banished. He was glad when young Mark arrived to impose his own sturdy reality over such unwelcome images.

Mark was independent and self-reliant—just as well, as his mother seemed to be absent more often than not. Sometimes, when he came alone, Mark talked about her, wishing she didn't have to work so hard to keep them both. Tom had asked about his father, and Mark had said she wouldn't talk about him, and that perhaps they had parted because of Mark.

"How could that be?" Tom was horrified.

"Well, maybe he didn't like me. Didn't want me, maybe," Mark had answered, speaking nonchalantly, dealing out the cards, for they were going to play rummy.

"He can't have not liked you if he never saw you," Tom had said, wondering who would not be proud of such a fine little chap. "Maybe he didn't know you were on the way," he suggested.

Mark hadn't thought of that. It consoled him.

"Maybe he'll come and see Mum one day, and have a surprise," he remarked.

"Maybe," said Tom, picking up his cards.

5.

Mark's mother, Susan Conway, arrived home at half past nine. The house was silent, but a lamp burned in the living room; it was operated by a timer, switching itself on automatically, so that Mark did not return to a dark house.

Susan could hear the washing machine churning away. Mark was a good boy, putting his dirty clothes in it. She thought quickly about what he had been wearing; was his sweatshirt red? Would there be pink pants in the final result? It was too late now to alter that; they'd bleach, she decided. She tiptoed upstairs. His door was ajar; he always left it like that if she was out, and by the light from the landing she saw that he was fast asleep, smooth, round cheeks, long lashes like frills. Kermit's world-weary face peered out above an arm. She crept away and went downstairs again. She was lucky that he had such an equable temperament. They managed well; it was easier since she had been promoted, and he was getting older. Her career had taken a slide when he was born.

Before that, she was personal assistant to the manager of an independent London hotel. Earlier, she had worked in various offices improving her administrative skills until a love affair with a colleague ended when he married someone else. She took herself and her damaged heart away on a trip to India before looking for another position.

She had met Mark's father while he was at a conference in the hotel. She knew that he was married, but as their affair developed, he convinced her that it was only a matter of time before he parted from his wife; then they would marry. Their meetings were frequent, but they never lived together.

Her illusions were shattered when one day his wife arrived at the hotel where he was attending a business lunch. Susan witnessed their meeting in the foyer. He was obviously startled, but he embraced his wife with warmth and walked off with her, both of them eagerly talking to one another. Their evident closeness was unmistakable, or was it all an act?

Susan never knew what had brought his wife to the hotel. Had she become suspicious and traced him there? Or was there some important family news she needed to impart? Time passed, and she did not hear from him. When she telephoned his office he would not speak to her, and his firm's next meetings were not held at that hotel.

She contemplated confronting him, demanding an explanation, making a scene. She knew where he lived and could have embarrassed him by challenging his marriage. Half intending to do so, she drove to the Kent village and saw his pleasant house, set in a large garden with a pony looking over a nearby gate. Various scenarios ran through her mind but she banished them all; there was such a thing as pride.

Hers had been seriously wounded. She saw, now, that it, more than her heart, had been damaged, also, by her first rejection; he had never intended to leave his wife at all and once again she had been deceived.

Susan's career was a consolation, but soon she discovered that she was pregnant. She had been a little careless about taking the Pill, playing a sort of Russian roulette, reasoning that if it failed, he would have to marry her. In any case, she was thirty-three; time was passing and she had always wanted children. Otherwise, why get married? Now, hurt and bitter, she resolved not to tell him about the baby. She would exclude him from its life, bring it up single-handed. She could earn a good living for them both. There was no need to go cap in hand to him and thus give him some claim to the child.

In those first, decisive weeks, she thought it would be easy, but time proved her wrong.

At work, she said nothing about her pregnancy, planning to carry on as normal for as long as possible, then take maternity leave and return when she had arranged child care. She had barely begun investigating child-minders and the possibility of shared nannies when problems began. She became quite unwell; her blood pressure fluctuated and rest was advised.

She gave up her job but was able to find a part-time temporary post, lower down the hierarchical ladder, in a country hotel, part of a chain, where the manager was a friend of her former employer. It was close to Haverscot, and she moved there, to a rented flat, for the last weeks of her pregnancy.

The financial loss was severe, but she had some savings, and her rent was far less than for her London flat. However, she had to stop work a month before Mark was born and she did not return until he was six months old, depending, meanwhile, on state benefit.

The hotel was not obliged to reengage her because she had been only a temporary staff member, but a position was found for her as a wages clerk. No more senior opening was available at the time, and the manager was doubtful about her reliability, now that there was a baby to consider. If the child were ill, she would stay away, he reasoned. But by this time she had discovered a reliable child-minder with whom Mark was happy. Now her aim was to make good the lost months and climb back up the ladder. She was capable of reaching top management level, but she must be willing to go on courses and to consider moves to other hotels within the group.

The Golden Accord, where she was working at present, was some distance away, but she was now an assistant manager. She had remained in Haverscot because it represented continuity for Mark and she had discovered Ivy; Mark was too old now for his original child-minder. There might be other moves, a manager's post with a flat in the hotel, one day; it would be soon enough, then, to uproot Mark.

Susan had had no lover since Mark's birth. She trusted no one now and had lost all desire to marry. Her life was too busy to leave her time for a new affair, and one-night stands had never appealed to her. She had a son; the two of them were fine on their own and she owed no one anything.

Susan had no family of her own. Her father had died when she was twelve, and her mother not long before Susan met Mark's father. She had no brothers or sisters, and both her parents had been only children so there were no cousins. Mark lacked the advantages of uncles and grandparents, but he showed no sign of missing these attachments which many children had. His life was simple, uncluttered by complex step-relationships like those of Ivy's son, Steve. Mark would sometimes talk about evenings spent with Steve. Susan had no idea that some of the videos they watched were viewed, not in Ivy's house, but at The Willows. She liked to hear of games of chess and rummy, and she had seen the books Mark brought home—good, old-fashioned stories such as she had read herself. It surprised her that Ivy had this stock; she didn't remember noticing shelves of books when she went to the house. Maybe they were Sharon's. She'd asked Mark if Steve read much, and it seemed that he didn't. He was very keen on cars, Mark said, and could tell you the engine capacity and acceleration rate of almost every make. Mark then proceeded to tell Susan how rapidly various cars reached speed from standstill.

He was enthusiastic when he talked, his eyes shining, his

thick straight hair falling over his brows. He did not look remotely like his father, about whom Susan, now, seldom thought. Her life was disciplined. At the hotel, she had learned to adopt a casual, friendly manner towards the men she worked with, or who were guests. The occasional come-on was warded off almost before it became one. Some of the staff thought she had a lover. She let them carry on with this assumption; it was a sort of protection.

When a police officer rang her doorbell soon after she had come home that Sunday night, she was startled, opening the door to him on a chain, regarding him in the brightness of the security light outside the door. Behind him, she discerned the outline of a woman officer.

They asked if they could come into the house.

Susan was not unused to the police. They had to be called in at the hotel occasionally, when there were thefts or incidents of drunkenness, and they came as a matter of routine at other times.

"What is it?" she asked, admitting them.

If Mark had not been safely upstairs, she would have feared that he had had an accident. But it was Mark about whom they were asking. Had she a son, Mark, who was a friend of Terry Gardner?

Susan had heard Mark mention Terry.

"Yes," she said. "Why do you want to know?"

"Were they together today?"

"They may have been, for some of the time," said Susan. "But Mark spent the day with the woman who looks after him when I'm at work." She must be careful; Ivy was no longer registered as a child-minder, and Susan did not want to get her into trouble.

"You were working today?"

"Yes."

"Where do you work?"

She told them.

"Is Mark at home now?"

"Yes. He's asleep upstairs," said Susan.

"It could have been another boy who was seen with Terry in the park this afternoon," said the male officer. "He's gone missing—Terry Gardner. He was seen alone around five thirty so the boy with him earlier had left him by that time. Your son, Mark, had his lunch at the Gardners' house today."

"Did he?" Susan was surprised. She'd imagined him settling down to one of Ivy's steak and kidney pies.

"You didn't know?"

"No. I suppose he arranged it with Ivy—Mrs. Burton," Susan said. "That would be quite in order, if he was invited." Ivy would not let him accept an inappropriate invitation.

"The Gardners live near the church, at Merrifields," said the woman officer. "But you'd know that, seeing that the boys are friends."

Susan didn't. All she knew about Terry was that Mark had mentioned him as being keen on football, and owning a small snooker table. She knew where Merrifields was, however; she and Mark, walking in the meadows above the river, had looked speculatively and with admiration at the large houses ranged along the ridge, and Mark had said that though they were grand and had big gardens, he liked their small house in Grasmere Street. Susan had bought it as soon as she was able to afford a mortgage; now it represented negative equity because of the fall in value, but they had no need of anything bigger; it suited them.

"Could we speak to Mark, please, Mrs. Conway?" said the woman officer.

"Oh, but he's asleep. I told you. Must I wake him?" Susan asked.

"I'm afraid so. He may know where Terry's gone," the woman officer replied.

"I do hope nothing's happened to him," said Susan, but what she really meant was, oh God, if someone's hurt Terry, it could so easily have been Mark—the kind of thought she never allowed herself to entertain.

A tousled Mark, gently roused and put into his red dressing gown, was brought downstairs. He clutched Kermit under one arm. While they waited, the two police officers noticed the neat, well-kept room, the small sofa and single armchair covered in gray-blue leather, the sensible fawn carpet, the deeper blue curtains, a few framed flower prints on the walls, a bookcase holding a mixed collection of paperbacks and some hardback novels. There was no neglect here. Forming this thought, WPC Dixon heard the washing machine start its spin-dry cycle with a noisy whirr just like her own machine. Susan, coming home late, had, she assumed, put the wash on; clearly, she was no slouch.

Mark, sleepy and bewildered, agreed that he had seen Terry that day, which the police already seemed to know. He did not mention lunch at Merrifields because his mother had not known that he was going there.

"We played football in the park this afternoon," he said. This must be about the two motorists and the damage to their cars. They'd gone to the police, complaining, in spite of the old lady. "We left before it began to get dark," he added quickly. "As we'd been told."

"Separately?"

"Yes," said Mark, yawning. He wanted to go back to sleep but it was nice sitting on the sofa with his mother, who had lit the gas fire so that it was warm and cozy.

"Terry was going straight home?"

"Yes. His mum gets really cross if he's out after dark," said Mark, who did not suffer from this problem with Ivy, as long as she knew he was at Tom's.

"And you came home too?"

He had, but not at once, so to agree did not mean that he had lied.

"Yes," said Mark. He was puzzled. Why weren't they asking

about the damaged cars? "That is, to Ivy's, where I go when Mum's on late," he amended. This part wasn't true.

"Terry didn't get home, Mark," said WPC Dixon. "Do you know where he might have gone instead? Some other friend's, perhaps?"

Mark didn't.

The officers went away without discovering that Mark had been unaccounted for until nearly nine o'clock, and no one, except Tom Morton, knew that he had been at The Willows.

Neither of the police officers who visited Susan lived in Haverscot, which came under the Radbury division of the local force and whose small police station was not manned at night. Several others, though, were from the area and one was the community officer who worked with the various schools. He knew many of the children well, and most of them by sight. His two colleagues lacked this advantage as they started on the hunt for Terry.

He had been seen running off after the incident with the milk bottle, the white globe of the football he was clutching making him stand out, but he could have been any boy of eleven or twelve years old. When Greg Black came home, however, after spending the evening with his companions from the park, and saw the damaged window, he guessed at once who was responsible. His father, who had been visiting friends, had found Greg's sister Mandy very upset after hearing the glass crash inwards. She and Greg had an older brother with some rough friends whom Mandy didn't like. She thought it might have been one of them, but Greg had no hesitation in naming Terry as the likely miscreant. Who else would have been carrying a football through the streets, and was undersized?

"Kid was cheeky in the park. I told him off," he said.

What if Terry gave his version of the episode? Greg would deny it, say Terry was inventing it to cover up his own

misdeeds. It would be Greg's word against his, and Greg
backed himself. Besides, the kid would only get a caution. It
would give him a fright and teach him a lesson.

An officer went round to Merrifields, hot on the heels of
one who had been there taking details because Terry had
failed to come home that night.

It was easy, now, to see why he had not returned. He'd
done something stupid and was afraid of trouble. At least he
was not likely to have been abducted, and he might be found
quite soon. The police took an optimistic line with the
distraught mother and reassured Richard that, when found,
Terry would get off fairly lightly over the broken window.

"If he is the boy who did it," said the constable who had
called to question Terry.

"Bit of a coincidence if he didn't," Richard said.

He had been annoyed, rather than anxious, at Terry's
disobedience. The boy had been told to come back before
dark, but he might have gone to visit a friend. Thinking he
might be at Mark's house, Richard had looked up Conway in
the telephone book; there were several listed, some with
Haverscot addresses. Hadn't Mark said he lived in Grasmere
Street? There was an entry, S. J. Conway, at number 38.

He had rung the number, but there was no reply. This
implied that the boys were still together. Perhaps they were
with the woman who looked after Mark. Yes, that was it, and
she'd send Terry home. Meanwhile, his mother had not
missed him. She had got up during the afternoon and was in
her studio. A Joan Baez tape was playing. Richard left her
undisturbed. To have her in a hysterical state of anxiety would
not bring Terry home. Very likely he would soon return.

Justin, at least, was back, virtuously doing homework in his
room.

Richard had decided to go to Evensong. He did this
sometimes, because it was peaceful in the church and he
enjoyed singing hymns and psalms. He left a note in the

kitchen stating where he was going, exchanged his waxed jacket for a raincoat, and set off.

In church, he sat in the same row of chairs as a grim-looking elderly woman with a maroon felt hat set vertically across her forehead; small boot-button eyes gave him a quick inspection. Richard left some empty seats between them. During the first hymn, he heard her sing; her voice was pure and low, beautiful in tone. She, for her part, noticed his confident baritone. As they sang "Amen" and resumed their seats, preparing to lean forward in a devout posture, they exchanged glances. Marigold Darwin almost smiled; Richard did.

After the service, he had not gone straight home, deciding to take the longer route around the town, thinking he might meet Terry. In fact, he was postponing having to confront whatever situation had arisen in his absence. He was sure the two boys were still together and suspected no more trouble than their simple disobedience.

Meanwhile, Verity had come downstairs, found him out and Terry missing, and Justin with no knowledge of where Terry was.

Verity was angry because Richard was not there and she needed an audience for an emotional scene. Now she had two triggers: his desertion, and Terry's absence.

She asked Justin if he knew where Terry was. He was not the target of her wrath and her manner was still controlled, her voice calm, but Justin saw the gleam in her eye and knew trouble loomed.

"Guess he's still with that little kid. It's early, Mum. I wouldn't worry," he said. He'd finished his homework and wanted to watch a video a friend had lent him. If Mum started to carry on, he would be thwarted.

"Richard's gone out," she said, adding, "to church," in a tone appropriate for a destination of utter depravity.

"Well?" Justin saw no harm in church as long as he was not expected to attend.

"When Terry's missing," Verity said.

"He's not missing. He's just late," said Justin. "Cool down, Mum." He remembered Richard telling the small boys to be home before dark, but did not mention this to his mother. She'd blow a fuse anyway when Cat returned, and another when Terry turned up. "What's for supper?" he decided to ask, and provoked a tirade about how could he think of food when his brother might be lying murdered in a ditch.

"Not Terry," Justin said, laughing at her. "He can take care of himself."

"But you don't know who's out there—perverts—sadists—" Verity began, and soon she was well away, weeping first, a tragic figure. Next, she'd start drinking and the rage would follow. Justin sighed, resigned. Perhaps some food would distract her.

"Let's get something to eat, Mum," he said. "There's plenty of the lamb we had at lunch. I'll put some potatoes in the microwave. Terry will be back before they're ready, you'll see, and he'll be starving," He spoke reassuringly, like a nurse, and took her arm, leading her out of the room.

His tactics briefly worked. She stayed reasonably calm and went with him to the kitchen where she sat at the table while he gave two fair-sized potatoes a token wash, punctured their skins and put them on the turntable, pressing the timer for ten minutes. He thought they would take longer, but by then Terry or Cat, or both, might have come home.

"You're a good boy, Justin," his mother told him. "At least you haven't run out on me. You won't, will you?"

Justin hated talk like this. She'd get soppy and emotional.

"Course not," he said gruffly, going to the fridge to find the lamb. It wasn't quite his choice of supper; he'd rather have a pizza or some chips, but it needed little preparation and he knew his mother had had nothing much to eat that day. If she was going in for a drinking session, she ought to have some food to mop it up. This was one of Cat's precepts which

Justin supported. If she started to moan about not killing little
lambs, refusing to eat it, he'd put a hunk of cheese on her
potato. Sometimes she forgot her vegetarian principles, and
she ate fish, which he thought was inconsistent. Surely fish
had souls and feelings, if sheep and pigs did?

But Verity couldn't sit there idly at the table. She got up
abruptly and left the room, returning with a glass half full of
either gin or vodka; they both looked the same. Justin's heart
sank. He hoped Cat would be back before she was fully
launched into what must surely develop.

It didn't take her long to get maudlin, and in that mood she
telephoned the police. She was still emotional, not yet angry,
when they came to the house. They presented a touching
sight, the weeping mother with the mane of tinted wild hair,
and her attentive son, who had thrust her glass of alcohol,
which she'd refilled after telephoning, into the fridge where
the police would not see it. She'd need it later, after they had
gone. Justin knew there was no point in pouring it away for
she could always fill it up again. Justin liked taking care of
her, but he found it difficult. If it wasn't for the money Cat
provided, they'd be better off without him. Justin had never
liked seeing them together in that big bed. When he and
Terry were smaller, they'd clambered in with Cat and Mum on
Sunday mornings. Cat usually got up almost immediately and
the two boys were left, smug and gleeful, alone in warm
intimacy with their mother.

Cat arrived while the police were there, and Verity at once
turned on him, demanding to know why he had gone out
when Terry wasn't home. Why wasn't he searching the streets
for him?

Richard managed to make the police officers understand
that he had gone to the park trying to find Terry and had
walked round the town looking for him before going to
church. Verity, winding herself up from woe to wrath,
rounded on him for this but one of the police officers, quite a

young man, managed to calm her down, saying, "Now then, Mrs. Gardner, we won't get any nearer to finding Terry if we argue, will we?" in a soothing voice.

Richard said that the boys had been told to come home before darkness fell, but that he thought Terry must be with his friend Mark.

"I rang what I thought was Mark's mother's number," he said. "There was no reply, so I decided he must have gone to the family who look after him when his mother's working. I'm afraid I don't know who they are. Shall I try the number again now?" he suggested, and as the police officer approved, he went off to do so.

There was still no answer.

"Perhaps it's the wrong number, but I thought Mark said he lived in Grasmere Street," said Richard.

"We'll try some other Conways," said the policeman. "But I'm sure Terry's safe. He's just lost account of time. It's easy at that age."

Richard was hoping that Terry had not led Mark into mischief. He thought about the floodwater in the fields below the garden; that could be tempting to a boy. But they had been intent on playing football.

"Perhaps someone saw them in the park?" he suggested.

"Most likely," said the policeman, not adding that it would be difficult to find such a person now, when those who might have been about would have gone home.

At that point in their discussions, the second pair of officers, seeking the vandal, arrived. Immediate concern for Terry's safety disappeared as the reason for his absence became clear.

"That other boy, Mark, must have led him into doing it," said Verity. "Terry's a good boy."

While they were talking, Justin had quietly left the room and gone upstairs, taking refuge in a bath, his radio on. Luckily it wasn't the community officer who had called, and the two police officers had not got in touch with him; when they did, the next day, they learned that Justin was one of several boys suspected of spraying graffiti on hoardings and who had been seen loitering near cars in the station yard, though none had been actually caught in the act of breaking into one.

The police went off at last, and Verity, who had maintained some control until then, turned on Richard with a torrent of abuse. She flew at him, her fingers aiming for his eyes. Richard caught her wrists and flung her away from him. One of these days, she'd fall against a cupboard, hit her head, be hurt and accuse him of attacking her.

"I'm going out," he said. "I'll look for Terry."

He put his waxed jacket on again and found his cap and a torch.

I'm driven from my own home, he told himself, striding off into the night. There must be something about him that provoked this hostility—not that Karen, rejecting him, had been exactly hostile. But Verity and her sons despised him. He was used to Justin's veiled enmity and expected trouble from him; if the police had called to question him, Richard would not have been surprised, and there had been warnings from school, where his performance was disappointing.

What could he do? Was he to turn away from Verity and her problems? Reject them all? If he did, what would become of her and the boys? A divorce would be difficult and expensive. But not impossible. The thought of escaping from his present situation seemed very attractive as he contemplated it, walking along in the now heavy rain.

And there was Caroline.

6.

Richard walked round the churchyard, shining his torch among the tombstones and the somber evergreens which grew near the walls. This was the sort of place where a child might hide; there was cover. It was very wet, however; if Terry were here, he would be so cold. Silly boy! What had made him want to throw a bottle at a window? And why that window? Why that house? The officer hadn't been too clear about why he was suspected of being the guilty vandal.

They might have searched here already. They were making door-to-door inquiries, they said, and they would trace Mark Conway, unless he, too, had disappeared. There was not much that they could do tonight, however, though facts about the missing boy would be broadcast on the local radio station. People might look in sheds and outhouses.

Richard toured the park, trying the doors of the cricket pavilion and the scout hut, but both were securely locked and no windows had been broken to admit a fugitive.

Terry couldn't have run away. He'd had no money on him, as far as was known. He was avoiding retribution.

Eventually, Richard's peregrinations took him along Clement Lane, out of which led Bevan Road and so he reached the end of Grasmere Street. He walked down its length, and passed the house, Number 38, where S. Conway lived. A police car was parked outside it.

So this was the right address. He contemplated calling in; the mother must be very anxious. But the police were there; they'd deal with her, fetch a neighbor in, someone who knew her. There was nothing he could do. He'd better get on home, face whatever situation had arisen in his absence.

Deciding thus, Richard nevertheless walked back by way of the street where Terry allegedly had broken a window. He saw the afflicted dwelling, where boards had been nailed across the broken pane. Was it impossible to get a glazier out to make an emergency repair on a Sunday night? The houses among which this one stood were solid, well built and mostly semidetached, with short driveways in which cars were parked. On the opposite side of the road, much of the Victorian terraced row had been modernized. Glancing across, Richard saw empty milk bottles on several steps; people here still patronized the roundsman. Verity had stopped, saying it was cheaper to buy in bulk from the supermarket, but the result of this was that they were always running out because she forgot to get it or was too wrapped up in her painting to go shopping.

Cold and very wet when he reached home, Richard shed his coat and cap and went in search of Verity, who was in the drawing room, a leatherbound album on her knee, looking at photographs of the two boys when they were very young. She was not crying now but was crooning under her breath; her face was red and blotchy, and Justin, looking terrified, was sitting beside her, trying to give comfort.

"He's dead. I know he is," she said, when Richard appeared. "Justin and I have been planning the funeral. What hymns to have. The flowers." She turned her distraught face up to Richard and sudden color flooded it. "And where have you been when I needed you?" she hissed at him. "Not here, by my side. Oh no! Out you go, seeing some fancy woman while my Terry lies dead and mutilated. Church, indeed! What an excuse! And lasting all this time, the service? You must think I was born yesterday."

In seconds, she had summoned up energy which Richard was amazed she still possessed, considering that she had drunk a vast quantity of gin. Richard picked up the bottle, which stood on the coffee table in front of her. It was empty. A glass smeared with lipstick and greasy fingermarks was on the floor near her feet. He rescued it, wondering if she had been swallowing pills as well as alcohol.

Verity had wound herself up again.

"And now you're going to hit me! I knew you would. See, Justin—he's got the weapon ready—he'll hit me with that bottle," she cried. She was standing now, jutting her hips forward at him, her small, sagging breasts loose beneath her sweater, which was spotted with stains.

Before he could reply, she flew at him, scratching his face, while he was powerless, glass in one hand and bottle in the other, to prevent her.

"Mum, don't," said Justin, ineffectively. "Mum, give him a chance." He caught her arm, but Verity threw it off as if he had no more strength than a baby.

Richard dropped the bottle and the glass and seized her upper arms.

"Stop it, Verity," he said. He shook her, not hard, longing to slap her but aware that she scarcely knew what she was saying. "Terry's missing. He'll be found. What use will you be to him in this state? Pull yourself together."

She was beyond doing that. Suddenly, mercifully, she swayed where she stood, rolled up her eyes and passed out. Richard caught her as she fell. He laid her on the sofa.

Justin looked at him and shrugged.

"She never drank before she married you," he said, and slouched out of the room.

Richard picked up the bottle and the glass again, and took them out to the kitchen. Then he went upstairs and fetched a duvet, which he spread over Verity. After that, he made another trip to get a towel, which he put beneath her face. He turned her on her side, to prevent her choking if she vomited.

He could do no more. He went upstairs to bed where, in unaccustomed solitude, knowing that Verity would not be capable of another outburst for several hours at least, he read for a while. Lately, on the train, he had been reading Trollope, and he had just begun *The Small House at Allington*. It was a soothing read, and, not a witty man himself, he appreciated humor in others.

The whole household was asleep when Terry, cold and exhausted, unaware that he was the subject of a major police operation which was focused on his safety, not his punishment, got out of Richard's car in which he had been hiding until the fuss died down, and let himself quietly into the house, using the emergency key, which was kept in a tin on a high shelf in the garage among jars holding paintbrushes and cans of paint.

He went up to his room, undressed, and climbed into bed, pulling his duvet, which was covered with vivid prints of dinosaurs, over him, and was soon asleep.

Richard woke up in the small hours. Going to bed alone, knowing he was safe from persecution, had been such a treat. Usually he tried to time things so that Verity was already in bed or had embarked on a studio session of either painting or drink, or both, so that he could feign sleep when she came to bed, but often she would wake him, seeking an audience for whatever was her current mood. Now, roused by a feeling of unease, he remembered that she had passed out downstairs and he had left her on the sofa. Was she all right?

Part of him did not care a jot; however, habit and prudence told him he must find out.

He got out of bed, shrugged his arms into his green toweling robe and went quietly downstairs, anxious not to wake Justin, who had had a bad time with his mother the previous evening. If it was heartless to go to bed while Terry was missing, it was also sensible, Richard told himself; wakeful vigil would not bring the boy home. A long day lay ahead, for sure. He had appointments at the office, but could he, in conscience, abandon Verity in order to keep them? Perhaps he could get a friend to keep her company, he thought, padding down the stairs. But had she any friends? There had been a few, from time to time, but, one by one, they dropped her, worn out by her moods.

She was just as he had left her, snoring a little now, her mouth half open, not attractive and not even pitiful, just a squalid sight. He tipped her further over onto her side; she did not stir.

Once he had loved her, or thought he did. Once he had loved Karen, his first wife—and still did, in a sense, or, nostalgically, the idea he had of her.

He glanced at Verity's flushed face, streaked with sweat and tears. She looked ugly, yet a few years ago he had found her pallor—she was seldom pale now—and deep-set eyes, which looked as though they would soon brim with tears, appealing. He had longed to make her smile, but all too often she had wept and wailed. He had never seen her truly happy.

I've failed her hopelessly, he thought, treading up the stairs again. I've failed to give her what she needed. It did not occur to him that Verity's inability to experience pleasure was nourished by her desire to make others suffer.

On the landing, he paused at Terry's door, then opened it, his head full of unanswerable questions about the boy's state of mind. Light shafted into the room and he could see the bed, the rumpled duvet, and, incredibly, the dark hair above it. Blinking, sure that he must be imagining it, Richard went into the room and laid a hand on the firm outline in the bed.

It was no mirage. Terry was back.

Richard did not wake him to demand an explanation. That would mean dealing with what must follow—telling Verity and informing the police. Apart from patrols keeping an eye out for him, there would be no real search until daylight. It would be time enough to discover that Terry had returned in the morning. Richard went back to bed.

At six o'clock, his normal time, Richard woke again. It was still dark outside. He stretched, remembering that he was alone; there was no risk of accidentally touching Verity. Every night he set the alarm, but every morning he woke before it buzzed at him, always determined that Verity should not be disturbed.

He remembered childhood breakfasts—those before he went away to school, and later, in the holidays. His mother laid the table every evening after dinner. Cereal, marmalade and honey would be on the table with the blue-and-white-striped Cornish crockery; butter would appear next morning, and she would fry or scramble eggs, cook bacon and tomatoes, or sausages; perhaps there would be fried potatoes. No one worried about cholesterol then, and, he thought, people were much happier. Every day his father went to the office—on the train, just as Richard did now—with a good hot meal inside him. Now, Richard would have two Weetabix with milk and a mug of Gold Blend, while the boys swallowed fruit juice and whatever cereal was their current favorite. That had to last them until their midday meal at school, which might be good and nourishing, but might, according to their choice, be neither.

If Verity had put eggs and bacon before him, Richard knew he would consume them and would not be pining for coffee as soon as he reached the office, nor ready for his lunchtime sandwich long before one o'clock. There had been a time when he went to a pub in his lunch hour, and drank a pint of beer, which staved off his hunger, but he had begun to put on weight and, with Verity already drinking too much, he saw danger ahead. He had cut out drinking except with Caroline, and an occasional half pint in the evening at the station if he reached it with enough time before his train.

There were other men who did this, some knocking back double gins or whiskey. He saw familiar faces at the bar and would nod to them, perhaps exchange small talk with a few regulars. He wondered if any of them were eager to get home. He saw men buying flowers from the station shop; were these peace offerings or spontaneous tributes? Who could tell? He'd bought flowers too, often enough, hoping to win Verity round from sulks to smiles. It was the same motivation that led him to buy her expensive presents: a brooch, a ring, even an exercise bicycle when she decided, rightly, that she was unfit. She soon abandoned it. He used it now.

Belatedly, he had understood that you could not buy love, but gifts had brought him brief spells of peace.

Now, as he sat up in bed, the events of the previous night came shatteringly back to him. He checked quickly that Verity was not beside him. Reassured, he sighed with relief; much of his pleasure, these days, came from absence of strife, not from any positive experience. Now there was time to shower, shave and dress before he need face her, and time to telephone the police from the bedroom extension before they resumed the search for Terry.

He went into the bathroom, and afterwards looked into the boy's room; for all he knew, Terry had done another flit, though he had seemed, like his mother, to be out for the count.

He was still asleep, one hand now exposed, very grubby, hanging over the side of the bed. A scruffy teddy bear lay on the floor, no doubt pushed out during the night. He was still a vulnerable little boy, thought Richard, and the victim of his genetic inheritance. Richard had formed a picture of his absent father as a violent brute; it had occurred to him only recently that this might not be an accurate portrait of his predecessor and that the two boys' temperaments could have been handed to them by their mother.

He returned to his room, closed the door, dressed, and then rang the police to report the runaway's safe return.

An officer would be round to hear what Terry had to say for himself.

"Don't hurry," Richard said. "He's still asleep, and so's his mother. They need their rest."

He won time, but not much. During the interval before the police arrived, he remembered the other boy, Mark. Was he still missing, or had he, also, sneaked home to bed?

The police were gentle with Terry.

He was asleep when they arrived, but Richard had roused Verity, led her upstairs, and made her have a shower to sober up and regain some control before they came. During this, she managed to take in the fact that Terry was safe. She made a lot of noise, wailing and swearing as the water hit her, and Justin woke up. He hated her exhibitionism and hysteria, but he blamed Richard for them and wove a fantasy in which he saved her by becoming the protégé of a rich patron—sex indeterminate in the dream—sometimes a Michael Jackson figure and sometimes a woman not unlike the Queen, gray-haired and gracious. He had once seen her when she opened a hospital wing near his school before they came to Haverscot and he, with other children, stood in the street waving a flag. Lately, these dreams were fading; he was too old for fairy tales and had begun to think more in terms of becoming a pop singer and making a million, or of major theft. He knew boys who stole successfully. If you took cars, you could sell them for a bomb. Before now, he'd nicked bars of chocolate, magazines, and even audiocassettes without being caught.

The discord at home frightened him. Though he did not want to acknowledge it, he could remember shouting matches between his parents, blows exchanged, his father as well as his mother being bruised and even cut about the face and arms. When he was younger, he had simply thought her unlucky in her choice of husbands; now, he was beginning to recognize, though he did not accept it, Richard's patience, but he still blamed his stepfather for provoking scenes.

He got dressed quickly and went downstairs, where he found there were no Coco-Pops, so he had to have Rice Krispies, Terry's favorite. He took his plate into the playroom and turned on the television, volume up. *The Big Breakfast* program drowned out other noise and he was still watching it when the police officers rang the front doorbell.

Meanwhile, Richard had instructed Terry to get washed and dressed. Verity had put on black leggings and a long black sweater. She brushed her damp, unkempt hair which in certain lights glinted like metal from the rinse she used. She styled it so that it fell over her face, peering out between the frizzy strands in the little-girl-lost mode which Richard knew so well. He sighed. Early in their acquaintance it had deceived him, and it might deceive the police, too. Perhaps that would be just as well. He wondered if they would smell alcohol on her breath; she had brushed her teeth with mint-flavored toothpaste.

The interview had best be conducted in the drawing room. Richard had tidied it, plumped up the cushions and drawn the curtains while Verity and Terry were dressing. He opened the windows briefly, letting in a blast of cold, damp winter air. From the playroom came the sound of Justin's television program; well, that meant he would keep out of the way, thought Richard grimly.

After a good night's sleep, Terry had almost forgotten his adventures of the previous day and thought a mere scolding from Richard for being late would be his only punishment; in fact, Richard had said nothing to him beyond ordering him to wash and dress. But when he was told to go into the drawing room and saw two uniformed police officers, one male and one female, already in the room, with his mother, he turned to flee. Richard, however, stood behind him, barring the doorway.

He looked towards his mother. She would save him and protect him. But she was sitting on the sofa, hiding behind her hair as she dabbed at her eyes with a pink tissue. He thought of running to her, flinging himself against her, wanting to be hugged, as had happened when he was small and she was in a receptive mood; these days, you could never be sure how she would respond, so he did not try it. He glanced at the police officers, both of whom were standing up. Neither smiled at him.

Verity was so used to casting herself in the role of victim that she could not, now, make any effort to imagine what he was feeling. She let her tears brim over.

"Oh, Terry, how could you do this to me? You are a wicked, wicked boy," she sobbed.

"He's safe, Mrs. Gardner, that's the main thing," said Sergeant Dixon, the woman officer. "Sit down, Terry."

Terry gave her another quick inspection. She was the enemy, of course, but she had spoken quietly and didn't seem too cross. The policeman with her was the one who came to talk to them at school, warning them about strangers offering lifts in cars, and drugs, and all that stuff. He was all right, Terry had grudgingly to admit.

"Now, Terry," said PC Withers. "Can you tell me where you were at about half past five yesterday afternoon?"

"Out," said Terry, looking at the ground.

"Out where?"

"I'd been in the park. I had permission," Terry said, his tone now aggrieved.

"Did you come straight home?"

"Er—" Terry hesitated. He remembered the feel of the milk bottle in his hand and the satisfying crash of glass as it hit the window. They couldn't know that it was him. Could they?

"Did you come home by way of Greenham Road?" asked Sergeant Dixon.

"I might have," Terry said.

"Do you know anything about a broken window at number forty-seven, Greenham Road?"

Terry did not answer.

"A boy was seen there, Terry, running away, with a football," said Withers.

"It might have been another boy," said Verity.

"It might have been," Withers agreed. "Was it, Terry? You'd been in the park earlier, with your football, hadn't you?"

"What's wrong with that?" asked Terry. "He said I could go." Saying this, he glared at his stepfather.

"You were told to be back before dark," said Richard.

"Now, Terry, someone thinks it was you who broke that window," Withers said. "OK, you were late going home, but Greenham Road isn't on your way back from the park. Why did you go there?"

Did the police know about the broken windscreen and the other damaged car? Were they to be blamed for that? The old woman had said they hadn't done it but what if those two men had told a different story? Terry felt trapped.

"I can go that way if I like," he said.

"Yes, of course you can, but you mustn't break windows," Withers said.

"It's you says I did it, not me," said Terry.

"Why didn't you come straight home, Terry?" asked Sergeant Dixon.

"I went to see a friend," said Terry promptly.

"What friend?"

"Mark," said Terry promptly.

"Mark Conway?" Sergeant Dixon needed to be clear.

"He doesn't live in that direction, and he says you parted in the park," said Withers.

"He's lying," came the instant answer.

"So everyone's lying except you, eh?"

"Must be." Terry yawned.

"When did you come home? You weren't here when everyone else went to bed," said Sergeant Dixon.

"Later," said Terry, forced to speak the truth at last.

"Didn't you know your parents would be worried? It was dark, and you were meant to be in before dark. What were you doing?"

"I was frightened," Terry muttered.

"What of?"

"They'd be angry. He'd be angry." Terry glowered at Richard, but his lower lip quivered. Justin had it in for Richard, but he'd been decent enough to Terry.

"Why? Because you were late?"

"Yes."

"But why were you late? Wasn't it because you'd broken the window and were afraid of being found out?"

Terry did not answer.

"Where did you go before coming home?"

Now Terry could be pleased with himself, because they hadn't caught him out.

"I hid in the tree house and then in Cat's car," he said smugly. "I came over the fence," he added. "Justin and me sometimes do." It was Justin who had banged strong nails into the fence posts so that it was possible to clamber over the tall fence in both directions. Terry had hidden in the churchyard first, but it had been cold and wet out there, and he'd begun to imagine ghosts. There'd been a service going on, with quite nice singing, a bit of which he could hear, and he'd realized people would soon be leaving. They might find him there, like that boy in that film when the convict caught him. Cat had made them watch it. He said it was a classic. It hadn't been too bad, in parts, but he'd thought the mad old woman stupid. While he was in the tree he'd heard cars coming and going, and knew that he was being hunted; only when all was quiet had he got into the car. Luckily, Cat hadn't locked it, nor the garage, though usually he did.

"Cat?" queried Sergeant Dixon, though she understood who was meant.

"The boys call me that," said Richard, adding, as if it gave the reason, "I'm their stepfather."

"I see," said the sergeant.

"Greg took my ball," said Terry at last. "In the park. Mark will tell you."

Mark hadn't mentioned it.

"So that made you angry, did it?" Withers asked.

"Yeah. He'd no right. He kicked it in the road," said Terry. Let Greg talk himself out of what happened after that; he'd think the men had shopped him. Maybe they had.

"Did he?" asked Withers.

"Yeah—and it caused a crash," said Terry, speaking now with animation. "It hit a car and the driver hit another car. The drivers blamed us. Me and Mark. But some old woman said it wasn't us. All I wanted was my ball back," he ended, looking righteous.

"But you got it back." It was a statement.

"Yeah."

"Where is it now?"

"In my room." During his adventures, he hadn't forgotten it. He'd clutched it all the time, even as he threw the bottle, and had tossed it over the fence before he climbed it himself. It had rolled only a short distance into the wet, tussocky grass under the trees, and was easily retrieved.

"You wanted to get at Greg for taking it, didn't you?" said Withers.

Terry did not answer. He stared at the floor. There was a

dull mark on the carpet, a wine stain. Terry knew well enough what had caused it: Mum at the bottle again.

"Breaking the window meant aggravation for Greg's parents," Withers was saying. "They hadn't been tormenting you. Why should they be made to suffer because their lad had been getting at you?"

Terry shrugged.

"It was there," he said.

"What was?"

"The milk bottle."

"So it was easy?"

"Yeah."

What would he have done if there hadn't been a bottle handy? All the adults wondered, even Verity, and none knew the answer. Maybe he would have been content to mutter curses but he might have found another missile. Round the corner from the house there was a skip containing rubble; if he had been able to climb up and reach into it—and probably he could—Terry might have found a brick.

But he'd admitted his offense, if not in so many words. That was the big hurdle passed.

"I'll make good the broken window, Terry. I'll pay for the repairs, I mean," said Richard. "That will make Greg's parents feel less angry about it. But you mustn't do anything like that, ever again." Through his head ran the notion of docking Terry's pocket money until the job was paid for, but he banished it because of the fuss Verity would make. The same idea was going through the minds of the two police officers, but neither uttered it.

Terry was eyeing Richard from under his lashes; at that moment he looked so like his mother that Richard felt a pang; she had beguiled him when she wore that expression but now she enchanted him no longer, and her cheeks were not soft and smooth, like Terry's, but gaunt.

He made a decision. The boy must not get away with it.

"You'll work it off," he said. "I'll deduct whatever it costs from your pocket money, and you can do some jobs about the place. Wash the car. Do some weeding." The ground would be too wet for weeding for a couple of months, he thought, but the threat could hang over Terry.

Verity needed some attention now. She would save challenging Richard over the punishment until later; meanwhile, she burst into renewed weeping and moaning.

"How could you do this, you naughty boy?" she wailed. "You've disgraced me."

"Now, come along, Mrs. Gardner. It's not the end of the world," said Sergeant Dixon. "Let's go into the kitchen and make some tea." Despite her rank, there were still moments when it was wise to adopt the stereotyped female role, and if the mother was out of the room, Withers and the boy's stepfather could give Terry a proper ticking-off.

They did so, with Withers arranging to show Terry the police cells in Haverscot the following Saturday. It wasn't an offer; he had to be there, and he could bring his brother, if he liked, and his friend Mark Conway. Once the boys saw where suspects were put while being held for questioning, they might be anxious to avoid qualifying. There was always the nearest prison, too; a visit might be arranged, said Withers.

"I trust I'll be able to persuade Mr. and Mrs. Black not to press charges," he added.

As the two police officers left the house, Withers remarked, "I wonder who the old woman was who sorted it with the motorists."

The matter need not be pursued. Once Greg Black's parents had been persuaded to be merciful, the incident could be considered closed.

They would be cooperative. Their own elder boy was no angel; the daughter, though, was a nice girl and quite clever.

7.

Mark, roused during Sunday night to recount his earlier movements, understood that Terry was in trouble for not going straight home after they parted, but was sure no harm had come to him. The police asked about other friends to whose houses Terry might have gone, but Mark could suggest no names, nor did he know of any secret hiding places where Terry might be taking refuge. He had decided not to mention the two angry men and the damaged cars; lots of things were better kept to oneself, and telling wouldn't find Terry. He'd be all right; he could look after himself.

The police had not stayed long, and Mark, back in bed, had soon dropped off to sleep again.

His mother had the next day off, and there was time to chat over breakfast. He liked it when she was there when he left; however, she did not humiliate him by escorting him to school on these rare mornings.

While he was buttering his toast, Sergeant Dixon, the woman officer who had called during the night, telephoned to say that Terry had been found, safe and sound. He had come home.

"Just in case you and Mark were worrying," she told Susan. Susan thanked her. The police had a bad name for following up actions of that kind; they did not always let victims of crime know when the perpetrators had been traced, or even brought to trial, much less the result. Here, at least, some consideration had been displayed—and by a woman officer, noted Susan. Neither she nor Mark knew about Terry's vandalism.

"He probably was with some other friend," said Susan, after telling Mark the news. "Does he ever come back here with you?"

Terry hadn't. Mark never brought friends home, whether or not his mother was there.

"No," he said.

"It's all right, if you want to bring a friend in," she said. She'd told him this before. "I trust you about who you invite."

She'd always trusted Mark; it was the only way.

"I'm usually with Steve," he said, to reassure her.

That morning, Terry arrived late for school.

"The police were round at my house last night asking for you," Mark told him. "Where were you?"

"My mum thought I'd run away or been kidnapped," Terry said. "She acts mad sometimes," he added. "I didn't go straight home. Why should I. I thought it would be cool to scare them."

This explanation had just occurred to him. He didn't think Mark would admire his window-breaking deed, particularly as he had been found out. If you were going to do that sort of thing, you shouldn't get caught. He wouldn't tell Mark about the invitation to accompany him to the police station at the weekend. In Terry's case, the visit was mandatory; Mark might guess that there was more to it than simply going missing for a few hours. The idea that he had caused a commotion was quite satisfying; Terry felt no shame. His mum had been in a right state but that was nothing unusual. He knew his escapade had not earned her approval, but he had won her attention.

"That's silly," Mark responded. He had no desire to scare his mother; quite the contrary. Terry was peculiar, sometimes.

Richard was nearly three hours late reaching his office that morning.

Verity had wanted to keep Terry back from school.

"What? And pamper him?" Richard had said. "Reward him for his behavior? Terry, get your coat. I'll drop you off."

Justin had sloped away at his usual time, anxious to escape from the heavily charged atmosphere in the house. He'd overheard some of the discussion between the police and Terry, and had formed a more or less accurate impression of what his brother had been doing. He'd get the details later. Stupid prat! He needed a few hints on not getting caught.

Justin's friend Bruce had lifted a car from the station yard on Saturday afternoon, in broad daylight. They'd not taken it far, as it was their first effort. Bruce hadn't a lot of experience at driving, and he'd rammed a lamppost when they were trying to turn in Norfolk Road. They'd left the car there, hurrying away, laughing and laughing, on a real high. They'd go further, next time.

They hadn't hurt themselves; they'd been in reverse gear at the time. They didn't look to see how much damage had been done to the car. It was insured, after all.

Justin hadn't been there to hear his mother tell Richard that he'd no right to give orders to Terry.

"He's my child," she'd said.

Richard had not bothered to answer this remark.

"Come along, Terry. You're lucky you're not down at the police station facing charges," he said, ignoring her.

Terry knew this was true. He thought about defying Richard, since his mother was clearly in a mood to spoil him, but if he stayed at home, she'd cry all over him and he'd miss football. He went to fetch his coat.

Richard had telephoned the school to say that Terry would be late; he'd been delayed because his mother wasn't well. The explanation was accepted. He marched the boy out to the car and dumped him at the door of the school, waiting until he had disappeared inside. Then he drove on to the station.

Sitting in the train—less crowded than usual because he was so much later than his normal time—Richard read the paper and mused on the working day ahead. Much would be routine and he had already missed an important meeting scheduled for ten o'clock. He had telephoned earlier, using the same, virtually true excuse he had given the school: His wife was unwell. He had used it before, when she had lightly slashed her wrists and bled all over the bed. He had bound her wounds, changed the bed linen and left her in her studio. If she chose to hurt herself while he was absent, that was her affair.

"Think of the boys," he had admonished, when leaving. "Don't punish them."

She had told him that hers was the temperament of an artist; how could a philistine like him be expected to understand its nuances? But he might at least consider her needs, she would declare. Richard, however, was tired of trying to anticipate her behavior; after some of her wilder extravagances, a mere hangover was trivial and could sometimes be ignored. If Verity intended to swamp her system with alcohol, he could not prevent her, nor could he keep searching every cupboard to find her supply.

He'd failed her, and he'd failed her sons, he thought,

settled in the train, staring at the crossword. If he had been able to meet her emotional demands, to tune in to her moods, she would not need to drink and make scenes. She was a troubled soul, as her paintings demonstrated. Were they any good? He did not care for her dark, dramatic daubs, where occasionally a tiny, shrinking figure lurked in the foreground. Did they represent her own fears and forebodings? Some had been hung at local exhibitions. If she could produce enough to have her own show, maybe a critic would commend her work, make it fashionable, and thus give her a sense of achievement.

After a while, sitting in the peace of the warm train, he dozed.

At work, he was busy, catching up on what had happened at the meeting and making decisions as to future policy. The day passed without a telephone call from Verity, which was a relief. He almost managed not to think about her; time enough to discover her state of mind when he reached home.

He went into Caroline's office at four o'clock.

"You look awful," she told him bluntly. "Had a rough weekend?"

"You could say so," he admitted.

"What's the matter?"

"One of the kids has been in a spot of bother," he said. "How about you? Did you enjoy wherever it was you went to?"

"The weather was foul," said Caroline. "But it was pleasant, yes." She did not tell him any more.

"What about this evening?" he dared to suggest. "I needn't hurry home."

"Sorry, Richard. I've got a date," said Caroline.

"Oh!" For a moment he felt as if she had kicked him in the ribs. A date! But why not? She was a free agent.

"Lucky guy," he said lightly.

"Isn't he?" she replied, smiling.

Disappointed and depressed, Richard whiled away half an hour in the station bar, letting one train leave without him, postponing the inevitable moment when he must return.

It was raining when he reached Haverscot station. He'd missed the thin young woman; she always traveled earlier. Would he ever pluck the courage up to offer her a lift? She might turn round and accuse him of assault. He mused on all the dangers threatening a modern man as he walked back to his car. There, he found one tire was flat, and, in pouring rain, he had to change it, discovering that it had been slashed with a knife.

The car park, on the outskirts of the town, was not supervised, and the station was not manned after one o'clock. Vehicles had been stolen from it; regular travelers kept pressing for more staff or, at least, patrols, so far unsuccessfully. Richard sometimes thought of walking, but it was too far for convenience, and if he took that step, it implied one car would do for the family, and what would happen then? Verity would appropriate it, and, on one of her bad days, might smash it up. Perhaps he'd get a bike, he thought, wiping his hands on some tissues which, luckily, were in the boot.

By the time he reached home, he was soaking wet and in a far from good mood. He found Verity clean and tidy, in black velvet trousers and scarlet tunic, sober—or so it seemed. She and the boys had eaten, as he was so late, but his meal was waiting. It was mixed grill—chops and sausages, mushrooms, tomatoes and peas, with chips. She turned on the microwave to heat it through and mistimed it, but Richard rescued it before it turned into concrete. It was very nearly palatable, an accomplishment for Verity, and this indicated that she had made some effort. He ate it, chewing the hard meat, the peas like bits of shot.

He told her about the car. Justin heard him and smiled. While Verity was busy in the kitchen, he'd taken his bike out of the garage and cycled to the station. His rear lamp was feeble and his front light did not work at all, so that he was a danger to himself and others, but he made the journey safely. A train was just arriving, so he stood apart, beside the fence, waiting till the passengers had gone walking off with umbrellas up or driving away in their cars. Richard was never as early as this.

He did the deed when it was quiet, wanting to slash all the tires, but the sound of another train approaching on the up line made him scurry off.

Never mind. He'd done it once and he would do it again if Cat went on upsetting his mother. He was to blame for everything that kept going wrong.

Verity had planned gratitude; she realized that Terry was lucky not to be in deep trouble and she meant to make amends, although the bullying boys were really responsible for what had happened. Now and then, she had rushes of emotion when she recognized Richard's patience and the security he had provided for them all, but more often she longed to spark a reaction from him. The boys' father, in the end, had hit her when she lashed out at him, and then had left her, but Richard never struck her, even when she hurt him. She wanted to provoke him to violence; then she would have reason to complain. Occasionally, she grew frightened, for what if he decided he had had enough and left her? She'd get money from him—a lot, probably—but she couldn't manage on her own. She'd discovered this, before they met. Other brief relationships had been just that, but Richard was a good man, and in her calmer moments, Verity acknowledged it to herself. So, tonight, to be on the safe side, she meant to win him round again. She'd always been able to do it, with soft words and gestures, and reconciliation was an erotic stimulus.

But not tonight. Richard turned away from her in bed.

"I'm very tired, Verity," he said. "It's been a bad day. Good night."

He heard her crying softly. She didn't scream or yell, just wept. Feeling guilty, Richard drew the duvet around his ears and, exhausted, fell into a merciful, healing sleep.

Early in the morning, drawing close, she woke him, thin arms twining round him. This time, sighing, Richard responded, thus securing temporary peace.

8.

It was Steve who found the old man dead.

A few days after the strange man who was Tom's son called, Ivy asked him to go and check on Tom who had, she said, looked poorly that morning. She had cleaned round and prepared some lunch for him, but he had been very quiet, not even asking about Sharon and the baby, nor joking with her about Bingo which she played on Wednesday nights, her evening out while Sharon stayed at home. But Tom hadn't looked near death.

Steve and Mark arrived at The Willows at around seven o'clock. Steve had had a lot of homework that could not be avoided, and Mark had wanted to finish one of the books about the Secret Seven which he'd borrowed on his last visit; then he could exchange it for another. He'd gone all through the Famous Fives and was well into the other series now. He liked them. The children's lives were comfortable and secure; they had mothers and fathers and a dog and lived in nice houses where money did not seem to be a problem. It was the same with the William books; he enjoyed those, too, and wished he had a friend like William who thought of exciting schemes. William got into trouble, but it was by accident; he wasn't really bad.

Mark was having doubts about Terry. His stepfather had come to see Mum about him disappearing. He'd wanted to explain and to apologize, because she must have found the visit from the police upsetting.

"Mark was no help to the police. He went back to the child-minder after leaving the park," Susan had told him, which wasn't true, and Mark felt very guilty about this part of the story.

"What about the boys who took Terry's football?" Richard had asked Mark. "Who were they?"

"Greg Black was one," said Mark. "They were all older."

"What's this about the football?" Susan had heard only that they'd been playing football, not about losing one.

Richard related what had happened, as far as he understood it, and asked for Mark's confirmation.

"There was the old lady," he said.

"What old lady?" asked Susan.

"I don't know her name," said Mark.

"Evidently she got the boys off the hook as far as the motorists were concerned," said Richard. He filled in the gaps for Susan.

"You didn't mention her when the police were here," Susan said to Mark.

"No one asked me," Mark pointed out. "They just wondered if I knew where Terry'd gone, and I didn't."

"No—it's all right, Mark," Richard reassured him. "That was why they came to see you. We didn't know anything about the other boys and the football till Terry told us the next day. It wouldn't have made any difference to finding him sooner if we'd known. It was why he ran off," he added, to Susan. "He broke a window at the Blacks' house."

"I see," said Susan. "Oh dear!"

"Yes—well, it's regrettable, but there we are," said Richard. "Terry's got off lightly this time."

Susan was thinking of Mark.

"It was lucky the old lady was there," she said. "The motorists might have caused a lot of trouble, otherwise."

"It was," Mark agreed. "She had a dog," he added. "Sinbad, that's his name. I heard her call him."

"That's a good name for a dog," said Richard.

"Wasn't he a sailor?" Susan said.

"Well, Rover's a common name for a dog," said Richard. "It's the same sort of thing."

For some reason, mystifying to Mark, his mother and Mr. Gardner—he knew, now, that this was his name—began to laugh. In the end Mr. Gardner stayed for a glass of wine and some cheese biscuits, and Mark was allowed a Coca-Cola.

"Come and play with Terry anytime," Richard told Mark, as he left, and added to Susan, "Terry and his brother, Justin, are my stepsons."

Now why did he tell me that, she wondered, after he had gone. Perhaps he didn't want to own to having a vandal son. She wouldn't have liked it, either.

It was the next evening that was so terrible.

Ivy had been baking and she gave the boys some homemade biscuits to take to Tom. On the way, they ate one each. Steve unlocked the front door of The Willows and went into the sitting room while Mark hurried upstairs to return the book and choose another, which he would put in the hall to take when he left. The books were kept in the room that must have been where Tom's son slept when he was young. It was strange that his boy's things were still there, now that Alan was so old and didn't live with Tom. Mark wasn't curious enough to wonder where Alan lived now.

He'd been diverted from the Secret Seven books by some others he'd noticed earlier, about four children who went sailing, when he heard Steve shout.

"Mark! Come down," he called. "Something's wrong with Tom."

Clutching *Swallows and Amazons*, Mark came leaping down the shallow staircase. It turned back on itself, with a little landing, and he always jumped the last four steps to the bottom. It was his aim to miss five, then six, then seven steps until the could leap the whole flight.

Steve, ashen-faced, was in the hall.

"He's asleep," he said. "He won't wake up. I think he's dead."

Steve had had a shock. He had entered the room, seen Tom apparently asleep in his big armchair, and had taken the opportunity to look in the old man's wallet, which was in the dresser drawer. He'd taken out five pounds and put it in his pocket, replacing the wallet and sliding the drawer shut very quietly, then turned.

"Evening, Tom. Mum's sent you these biscuits," he'd said, in a bright voice.

Tom didn't answer. It was not unusual for him to drop off to sleep, but as a rule he could soon be roused.

Steve switched on the television and turned up the volume. There was a football match later; it might be a bit too late for Mark to stay and watch it, but he could be sent off home on his own.

After a while, something about Tom's stillness impinged on Steve's consciousness and he felt uneasy. He went over to inspect the old man, watching his chest, which was covered by a Fair Isle sweater. He wore a checked shirt beneath it, the collar points protruding. Ivy saw to his washing and was paid well for doing it.

There seemed to be no movement in Tom's chest. Steve touched his hand, which lay on his lap above the light rug tucked round his wasted, feeble legs. The hand was icy cold. Steve snatched his away.

His first instinct was to flee the house, leaving this for someone else to deal with, but he wasn't alone with the corpse; Mark was here. A faint sense of responsibility for the younger boy stirred in Steve; he mustn't panic. Mark must be impressed.

He adopted a slight swagger as Mark arrived beside him.

"I expect he is just asleep, really," he explained to Mark. "Only he won't wake up."

"Maybe he's had another stroke," Mark said, sensibly. He'd heard Ivy and Sharon talking about the possibility. Old Tom would be all right if he didn't have another, Ivy had told her daughter, and he might improve a lot, as his speech was normal and he had regained so much movement. Mark didn't know what a stroke was. Was it like a fit? Did you froth and foam? He felt a pang of sorrow because Tom wasn't well, but he was interested, too, and marched confidently past Steve into the sitting room.

When he saw Tom, he knew. You couldn't look more dead than that if you had bullet wounds all over you, he thought, seeing the waxy pallor, the total stillness. Unlike Steve, he wasn't frightened, but he was shocked and felt very sad. Tears prickled in his eyes.

"He is dead," he said, and he, too, touched the old man's hand, but he left his own small, warm paw upon it. In that moment, not fully acknowledged until years later, Mark's desire to be a doctor was conceived.

"We'd better get someone," he said. "You go. Or ring up. I'll stay with him."

He had no urge to leave. Death was normal, but it was so sad and he thought he might cry properly quite soon. He didn't want Steve to see him.

"Perhaps we should ring the police? Dial 999?" said Steve.

"They can't help him," Mark answered. "Ring your mum. She'll know what to do."

Steve, in crisis, didn't resent being given orders by the younger boy. He meekly obeyed, picking up the cordless telephone which Tom had found so useful.

His mother did not panic. Sharon was at home and could look after Kylie and Adam.

"I'll come straight down," she said. "You boys go into another room and shut the door."

She rang the doctor, who arrived at Tom's house only a few minutes after she did. Tom had, he thought, suffered another, lesser stroke, followed by a heart attack. His death was not wholly unexpected and, in the end, had come in a merciful manner.

Before he and Steve's mother dealt with what must be done, he praised the boys for using common sense and suggested that they both go home.

Ivy picked up the bag of biscuits.

"He won't need these now," she said, handing them to Steve. "You two might like to eat some on your way home."

The sitting-room door was closed. Old Tom was in there, with the doctor. Mark wanted to say good-bye to him. He saw the door key on the hall chest, where Steve had left it when they entered the house. *Swallows and Amazons* was beside it. Mark picked the key up and slid it under the book, which he tucked inside his jacket. Ivy wasn't looking.

He'd come back later, maybe tomorrow, and say good-bye properly. He'd keep the book until he'd read it.

He ate a biscuit as he walked along the road with Steve. It tasted good.

Mark returned to The Willows the next evening.

As his mother knew nothing about his visits to Tom, he did not mention the old man's death at breakfast. She had waved him off to school; her shift began later in the morning.

After tea at Ivy's, he told her that his mother would be home early, and left.

He didn't like telling lies. Steve did it all the time, and Ivy always believed him; he said it saved aggravation, but Mark didn't feel right about it. It was not the same as having secrets, like his visits to Tom. Perhaps tonight's excuse to Ivy wasn't quite a lie, because he was only going to Tom's house to say good-bye. Then he would go home.

Steve, glad not to be lumbered with Mark, who could be a drag, went to see a friend, an older boy; with Tom gone, he'd need to find another source of income. He'd be lucky if he hit on anything as easy. The two boys left together, and parted at the end of the road. Steve headed off towards the town and Mark slipped away, down Wordsworth Road, to The Willows. It wasn't far; he liked walking alone through the dim streets and he took no notice of the rain. He knew his hair was getting wet, but his anorak was new and water ran off the poplin.

The house was in darkness. Mark hadn't thought of that but of course Tom, being dead, wouldn't notice. It was difficult to find the lock and insert the key; he twiddled about but eventually succeeded and, once inside, turned on the hall light. That was better.

Mark kicked his shoes off. The boys always did that when entering any house, trained to do so by Ivy who did not want them walking mud round her place or anyone else's. Then he went into the sitting room. Tom would be there, surely? He'd be sitting in his chair, his rug over his knees, just as they had left him.

But he wasn't. The room was unnaturally still, and very tidy, the cushions plumped up, the carpet vacuumed. Ivy had cleared up after the undertaker's men. She had not missed the key which Mark had taken because it was a spare, kept for Steve's use.

She'd had another key cut for him because once Tom's key, passing between the two of them, had been mislaid and that had been very inconvenient.

Mark felt anxious. Where could Tom be? Perhaps they had taken him up to bed. Yes, that would be it; he'd seen films with dead people lying in their beds, just as if they were asleep, sometimes with flowers all round them. Mark should have brought him some. Never mind, he would tomorrow, though there were none out in the garden at home; he'd have to buy them.

He went upstairs and entered the big bedroom, but it was empty, the bed neat, the coverlet stretched taut. He looked beneath it; there were no sheets or pillow slips and the blankets were all folded up. Ivy had taken the linen home to wash.

Tears sprang to Mark's eyes. Now he really understood that Tom had gone and wouldn't be returning.

Standing there, he had a little cry, scrubbing his eyes with his none-too-clean hands. Then, reluctant to leave, he wandered slowly through the house, settling at last in the sitting room, where he drew the curtains. It was nice and warm; no one had turned the heating off. He switched on the television to watch the quiz show he'd often seen with Tom, who wouldn't mind, Mark knew. For a while he was able to pretend that the old man was there, that nothing had changed, but when the program ended he felt a deep, heavy ache inside his chest because there was no Tom to talk to about what had happened on the screen and suggest the next occupation for the evening.

He would have to go home.

Leaving the house, he remembered the curtains. He'd better draw them back, leave them as they'd been when he arrived.

He'd come again. He knew he would.

*   *   *

The next afternoon, after school, Mark went to the shop in Haverscot where they cut keys for you while you waited. He'd been there with his mother when she got him one for their house, and a spare to hide in a secret place outside in case anyone got locked out. Only he knew about the spot—and Mum, of course. He wondered what it would cost. He'd taken along two pounds and hoped it would be enough. He didn't get the flowers. As Tom had gone, there'd be no point, and he couldn't have afforded both them and the key. Flowers were expensive.

He was late reaching Ivy's house, but she didn't fuss.

"I had to see Mrs. Williams about my maths," he said, the lie tripping as easily off his tongue as if it had been Steve speaking.

"No trouble, I hope," said Ivy, helping him to baked potato and mince, which was spiced with chili. He liked Ivy's mince; she often gave it to them with various accompaniments such as pasta, beans, or even bread.

"Oh no," said Mark smoothly. "Just something I didn't understand."

He'd put the borrowed key back on its hook and that was lucky, because Steve decided that they'd go to The Willows that night. He'd assumed Ivy had replaced it after clearing up the house, and she, if she thought about it, supposed that Steve had done so.

"I'd like to have a look around," said Steve. "Might pick up a few useful bits. Tom won't want nothing now. Besides, we can watch telly."

Mark knew that Tom wouldn't object to them visiting the house and watching television, but the old man wouldn't want them poking round and prying. He knew what Steve had in mind: stealing. Well, he needn't join in that bit.

They went in together and Steve drew the curtains before putting on the lights.

"Don't want folk getting curious, do we?" he said, but the house, separated from the road by a short drive with trees and shrubs at either side, was not overlooked, and it was in such a quiet road that their presence was unlikely to attract attention.

It was clever of Steve to think of that, thought Mark, who had drawn them for his own security the day before, not from fear of being seen.

Steve lit the fire and Mark settled down beside it, watching television, while Steve went prowling round the house. After some time he came running down the stairs, excited.

"Look what I found, Mark," he cried.

He was carrying a bundle of old newspaper cuttings, yellow and fading, in a plastic folder.

"There were in that room with Tom's son's stuff in it," he said. "In the desk. They tell about him—that guy Alan. He's in prison. He must have escaped. That's why Tom wasn't very pleased to see him."

Mark stared. He didn't understand.

"Go on. Read it for yourself," said Steve, regretting that he had so poor an audience for this revelation. He pulled out a sheet of newsprint and shoved it at Mark, who took it and began to read.

It was a tabloid, more than eight years old, and it reported how Alan Morton, aged thirty-five, had been sentenced for the murder of his wife, June, after he suspected her of having an affair with a local farmer. Alan had shot her with a four-ten shotgun.

"He was on the run," said Steve, excited. "I wonder where he's hiding out?"

9.

Marigold Darwin was not aware that a Haverscot boy had been briefly missing. She did not listen to local radio, but she watched nature programs and discussions on television, and, on wet afternoons, of which there had been many lately, occasional schools broadcasts, which were often interesting.

Because her furniture and most of her possessions were in store, she could not occupy herself with the artwork she had developed as a hobby; on a weekend course she had learned découpage, led into it by a fascination with marquetry in furniture. Decorating plain boxes and tins with detailed cut-out designs from paper, then varnishing them until the ornamentation looked solid, was a possible way of emulating this intricate work. It had become an absorbing occupation, one to which she could flee when no other activity attracted her. Meanwhile, since renting the bungalow, she had learned of a road development scheme which would affect the area. A planned bypass implied later inclusion in a motorway extension and there were meetings to discuss the consequences. Marigold had attended one and concluded that working for the protest lobby might exercise her administrative skills productively; she need not be impartial now. But organizing her future life must wait until she found a house, and her failure to do so was depressing. Not that she acknowledged such a state: Marigold's temperament was equable; she knew no highs or lows.

Walking in the park with Sinbad, after the incident of the boys, she would see youngsters kicking balls about and thought she recognized the two smaller lads on one occasion. She couldn't be sure; children of a similar size looked so alike unless they had red hair or some other distinguishing feature.

She did not need a social life, but it was not wise to pass too much time in isolation. Marigold had no close friends; there had been acquaintances, occasional shared activities with colleagues, but intimacy with anyone was outside her experience. Even her parents, though never unkind and often generous, had been remote and undemonstrative. She had no childhood memories of revealed affection.

As the days shortened and Christmas approached, so did the end of her lease. She was due to surrender the bungalow early in the new year, and if she had not yet found a house, she would have to rent something else, or move into a hotel, which would be difficult with Sinbad. She was on the books of every agency in Radbury, six miles away, and bigger than Haverscot, and daily she received details of available houses within a radius of twenty-five miles, but she wanted to be in Haverscot.

Mr. Phipps was in despair because she was so difficult to please, and then, through a solicitor friend, he heard that The Willows was coming on the market very soon, an executors' sale. Mr. Morton, who had lived there for many years, had died, and his heir was a niece who lived in Canada. She wanted the house and its contents sold; speedy possession could be arranged. The solicitor, who was one of the executors, told Brian Phipps that he could take his potential buyer to see the house at once.

Mr. Phipps telephoned Miss Darwin. Time and money would be saved if she could be persuaded to buy without the house going on the market, which was too uncertain at the moment, and at this time of year, to warrant the risk of an auction.

Miss Darwin showed some interest when he said that the house was in Wordsworth Road, not far from Merrifields. It had a similar outlook over the now waterlogged meadows leading to the river.

"Those houses are all built on a ridge, as you know," he reminded her. "The water never gets beyond their gardens."

She did know. As a child, she had had a canoe, not to be used when the river was up, but once she had taken it out on the still floodwater, and several times, when it froze, she had skated on the flooded fields. It was so safe. If the ice broke, you went through only on to grass. She hadn't skated very well, but she had enjoyed it, and so had many other inhabitants of Haverscot, young and old.

She remembered The Willows. When she was a child, two sisters had lived there, retired teachers. They were keen gardeners; each year they held a party—tea and sandwiches amid beds of lupins and delphiniums, and there were climbing roses. She had gone there with her mother and had hidden from the crowd of guests beneath the concealing tresses of a large willow on the lawn. So close to the river, such trees thrived; there were three of them, she thought; had they survived? If not, one could grow more, very quickly; they were not like oaks, taking generations to reach any size.

Mr. Phipps drew up outside the bungalow. His car, provided by the firm, was a Volvo Estate, large enough to cope with the For Sale signs which he sometimes had to carry and erect. It also had room for the three small Phipps children and their mother, who in her spare time made curtains and chair covers at home. She meant to have her own interior decorating business as soon as all three of them were at school.

He told Miss Darwin about the sudden death of Mr. Morton and the niece in Canada.

"He died in the house," he added. It was best to tell her now, so that if she had any objections on that score, they were declared at once. She was sure to discover, later, what had happened. Most people seemed to die in hospital; it was tidier. Mr. Phipps, who had moved to Radbury from Essex six years ago, knew that there was a son who had inherited nothing. He was some sort of bad hat, Mr. Phipps had gathered, but he did not know any more than that. There was no need to mention him.

"Lucky man," was Miss Darwin's observation. "Had he been ill long?"

"No. I think it was quite sudden," Mr. Phipps replied.

"Lucky again," said Miss Darwin.

She had almost made up her mind to buy the house before she even entered it. It had been built in the 1920s, of brick, plastered over and painted cream. The proportions were pleasing to the eye, and it looked solid.

"It's got a damp course. Houses built after 1924 had to have them," Mr. Phipps told her. "So it's not like your really old places, which can have problems." He was trying to sell such a millstone at the moment, and had shown it to her, glossing over the snag of crumbling beams.

Mr. Phipps turned in at The Willows's gate. The drive was short, but the house was set far enough back from the road to be secluded. He wondered if she would think it too well protected from the passing gaze. Crime prevention theories suggested that a screen of trees and shrubs invited burglars, but all the houses in Wordsworth Road were similarly shrouded. If she bought it, once everything was signed, he might suggest installing an alarm; one lady on her own would thus feel safer. But she didn't look the nervous sort; indeed, he found her formidable.

The house was warm, its heating still turned on, to protect the pipes. As they entered, Marigold had the odd feeling that invisible arms reached out to welcome her. At any moment a smiling woman in a pinafore would greet them and offer coffee. She gave herself a shake; fanciful notions of that kind were not permitted.

Mr. Phipps showed her round. There were four bedrooms. One was small and had been used as a study; there were a desk and filing cabinets, shelves of reference books.

"Mr. Morton was recording local history. He left all his books and papers relating to that to Radbury Museum," Mr. Phipps told her. "They're collecting them next week."

He led Marigold into the largest bedroom, which overlooked the meadows at the back of the house; it had the same view as Merrifields but was closer to the church. Marigold looked out and saw several swans swimming on the gray floodwater. Her heart, seldom disturbed, beat a little faster.

She knew she was going to make an offer for the house, but she let Mr. Phipps describe its merits and display his skills. However, she did not want to risk losing it to another customer by dissembling. He had indicated a price; she proposed another as soon as he returned her to the bungalow and Sinbad's welcome.

"I'll have to contact the executors," he said. "They'll need to consult the beneficiary."

"Of course." Marigold would pay the asking price, if necessary. "You know how I'm placed, Mr. Phipps. I should like to move in as soon as it can be arranged." Surely the beneficiary would view with favor the swift settling of the estate?

She knew she should have the place surveyed. The house might have many flaws—dry rot, a faulty roof—all sorts of problems which an inspection would detect, but she would risk it. Let the worst be discovered when she had painters in to decorate. Mr. Morton—or perhaps it was his late wife's taste—had done the house throughout in neutral tones, and Marigold thought that it would be improved by using more definite colors.

Mr. Phipps was wondering whether to press one of his wife's business cards into her hand but decided that could wait until contracts were exchanged; however, perhaps he should refer, now, to the black sheep son.

"There was a son," he said. "Estranged, I don't know why. Hence, he didn't inherit."

"I see," said Marigold. "That room upstairs was his. The posters. All those books."

"Exactly. Everything is to be sold," said Mr. Phipps. "I shall be arranging it with the executors." There were good local auctioneers, some of whom dealt with whole libraries; unfortunately there wasn't enough to merit a marquee on the lawn; besides, that was too waterlogged at present. Luckily Miss Darwin had been content to stand on the terrace outside the sitting room and look down at the shaggy lawn and the three willow trees while he pointed out the large garden shed.

By that evening, her offer had been accepted. The niece was perfectly content when told the buyer's money was waiting and was not dependent on a survey. She had last seen her uncle some years before Alan's arrest, when she had been the London correspondent of a Canadian newspaper. Her mother, Tom's sister, had married a Canadian soldier during the war and they had always kept in touch. Despite Alan's disastrous history, the bequest had amazed her. She had flown over for the funeral, made the necessary legal arrangements, and flown back again within a week.

In matter-of-fact tones, Marigold told Sinbad that soon he would have a splendid garden in which to prance about and bury his bones. She thought of the roses she would like to grow; she had been to La Roseraie de L'Hay, outside Paris, two summers ago and had been dazzled by the collection. What was in The Willows's garden now, she wondered; all she had been able to discern from the terrace were bedraggled brambly shoots twined round wooden arches, and some withered flowers in a border. She would have to discover what lay buried under the cold earth, whether there were daffodils and snowdrops.

Suddenly there was a future. With that decided, Marigold poured herself a celebratory glass of sherry and as she sipped it, she experienced an unfamiliar sensation, a sort of internal glow.

Though she could not name it, it was happiness.

She had another drink, and then a third. As she prepared her meal, she began to sing.

"I'm just a little tipsy, Sinbad," she declared, aloud. "Well, never mind. Who cares?" and, pouring herself a refill, she danced a little jig, while Sinbad, stubby tail wagging to and fro approvingly, looked on.

Steve had asked his stepmother what would happen to The Willows.

"I'm sure I don't know," Ivy had replied. "I don't know what happened to his son. Tom never mentioned him, but they'd kept all that stuff of his. His mother wouldn't part with it, and after she died, Tom hadn't the heart." She'd thought it such a pity all those books lay there unused, when they could be sold to bring in money for the local playgroup. "Maybe they fell out," she said.

"Are you sure he didn't do the old man in?" Steve asked.

"Of course he didn't. What a thing to say," said Ivy.

"Well, he did kill his wife, didn't he?" said Steve.

But Ivy didn't know that. She had lived in Haverscot only since she married Joe.

"Where do you get these ideas?" she exclaimed. "I think the son's dead. He must be, or he'd have been at the funeral."

Steve didn't show her the newspaper cuttings.

"Why didn't you?" Mark asked. He found it scary. An escaped murderer had come to old Tom's house, and he, Mark, had met him.

"She'd have ticked me off for poking around," Steve said.

He'd put the papers away in his room. Mark thought that was stealing, although with Tom dead, they couldn't be of use to anyone, not like the books and other things. Where was the murderer now? No one seemed to be looking for him. He must have been recaptured.

"If we see him again, we'd better tell the police," he said.

"We'll do that," Steve agreed. "There might be a reward."

Mark knew the son hadn't killed old Tom. There was no blood, and Tom had looked so calm.

He went on going to The Willows. It was easy. He told Ivy that his mother would be home early, and simply left her place when it suited him.

He did not visit The Willows every night, only when he needed a new book. Then he would stay and watch television for a while. Mark could pretend Tom was there. His hat and raincoat hung in the cloakroom, and there were still biscuits and drinking chocolate in the kitchen. Sometimes Mark helped himself, always washing up and putting things away.

Ivy had said that the house might be sold. When that was to happen, a board went up outside, and Mark never saw one at The Willows. Perhaps it would stay empty. If the son was still on the run, he wouldn't move in because the police would be sure to catch him; Mark was certain he was back behind bars, if he had escaped, but Steve might have been wrong about that. People were let out, even if they'd done dreadful things; he'd heard Sharon and Ivy talking about it.

"Free to do it again," he'd heard Ivy say, about a man who'd done something awful to a woman. When Mark asked what had happened, they'd been vague.

Steve sometimes did get things wrong. Mark had gone off him, rather; apart from taking money from Tom, he now went round with a group of boys among whom was Greg Black. Ivy thought he was at the youth club, but he never went there. Mark, however, copied Steve's methods and sometimes told Ivy he was going to see Terry Gardner and would go home from there. Such an explanation was acceptable to Ivy; Susan would approve of that friendship and it was so close; no journey through the middle of town, where the rough element hung out, was involved.

Soon Sharon would be going back to work and Ivy would look after Adam. She had more time, now that she was no longer needed at The Willows.

Ivy paid no attention to Steve's remarks about Tom Morton's son. He'd been reading too many horror books or watching alarming videos. She knew he spent time with Greg Black and a boy called Bruce, but she could not stand over him all the time, watching where he went and what he did; she and Joe had taught him right from wrong; what more could they do? He'd grow out of his interest in morbid matters. While he was at Tom's, he'd been safe from such influences, but those days were past. She missed the old man. The solicitor had sent her a check in settlement of her wages, with a bonus, and that was good; she bought new duvet covers for Steve and Kylie, and Sharon gave her a perm. Sharon had been apprenticed to a hairdresser before she had the baby.

With her new hairdo, Ivy felt ready for the next few rounds life had to offer her. She was growing used to widowhood; it was more respectable, she had found, than being divorced, as she was before; people were surprised and sorry when they heard about it. There was plenty to do each day; she had children to collect from school most days, and there was Mark; other children were left with her occasionally. Tom had paid well for what she did for him but she could find other cleaning jobs if things got tight. At the moment, they were managing.

Sharon's baby's father sometimes came around; he was unemployed and living with another girl who was pregnant by him. Sharon was still fond of him; Ivy feared she might be fond enough to get herself pregnant again. It was all very well for him; he was sure of a welcome from either girl.

"It's no example for Kylie or Steve," said Ivy, after one such visit.

"He's got every right. He's the father," Sharon had replied.

"But he doesn't have any of the responsibility, or the expense," said Ivy.

Jason had brought a soft cuddly rabbit for Adam, but no money. There was nothing to stop him going round giving girls babies all over the country and living off each woman in turn. He was a nice enough young chap who wouldn't hurt a fly, Ivy thought, but what use would he be in any trouble? And what chance had Sharon, now, of finding a man who would be, one like Joe? Though it was true she already had Sharon when they met; that thought consoled Ivy in her bleaker moments, but she had been married to Sharon's father.

She hoped Jason would stay with his new girlfriend and not want to come and live with them.

10.

When Alan Morton went to The Willows, he had been on leave from prison.

He was supposed to be spending the weekend at an approved hostel, but he had never meant to stick to that plan. From the time when he had first been taken on shopping trips to town as a preliminary to his release on license, he had been preparing for his freedom.

He should never have been given life. It was a case of manslaughter due to provocation, for June had been unfaithful to him. She had been having an affair with Phil Wickens, her childhood sweetheart, whom Alan had cut out when he had decided to make a play for June—largely because he wanted to get the better of Phil, who was a farmer. It hadn't been too difficult; he'd simply swept her off her feet, pursuing her with gifts of flowers and boxes of chocolates, and persuading her to have dinner with him at various local restaurants during a long summer when Phil was working all hours bringing in the harvest.

They had met at a young farmers' dance. Alan, at the time, was the manager of a hardware store in the small market town of Billerton, and part of its business was concerned with spares for farm machinery, paint and other such goods. The event was held in the Town Hall; Phil Wickens, not a customer of Alan's store, was a guest, and June was his partner.

Alan had already met her across the counter of the building society where he had his mortgage; he had bought a house on the outskirts of the town and had been living there with a woman who had left him a few weeks before the dance. They had not been together long; none of Alan's relationships lasted, and he had one divorce behind him.

He had been invited to the dance to partner the visiting sister of a customer; they'd had dinner first, at The King's Head in the town square. The customer, a market gardener, had been a generous host but Alan had bought drinks all round and liqueurs later; he had an expansive manner and a booming voice, impossible to overlook. The sister did not take to him and, at the dance, shed him for a quiet man she found standing by the bar. Alan, adrift, asked various women whom he knew by sight to dance with him and was sometimes accepted; then he noticed June, who recognized him and smiled pleasantly. Alan swept her onto the floor as he later swept her off her feet by his pursuit.

How meek she'd been, how sweet, smiling and attractive in her understated way, with soft blond hair and large blue eyes. Even at that first meeting he had wanted to make her cringe and appeal to him for mercy, as he had his wife. He had had that wish, but she had left him, shown her bruises to a doctor and had obtained a divorce as soon as they had been apart for long enough.

At least she hadn't wanted any money.

June left him to dance with Phil Wickens, and Alan realized that they were well acquainted; after the dance, glass in hand, he tagged onto their conversation and, persistent, bought them drinks. Phil was civil; he had not known who Alan was until June introduced them, and he did not want his company, but it was a jolly, social evening and he would not stoop to rudeness. Alan managed to have another dance with June. He was quiet and polite. He knew how to act when he wanted something, and sometimes he regretted the rage that surged within him when the meekness that had at first attracted him began to disgust him.

He waylaid June outside the building society when she was going home, and several times in her lunch hour, inviting her to eat with him at Billerton's new wine bar. In the end his sheer persistence prevailed.

He took it slowly as the summer—hot and dry that year— wore on. June, disappointed because she saw so little of Phil while he was busy at the farm, fell in with Alan's plans to meet, and during that time he never overstepped the mark. He was physically a short, stocky man and she did not feel intimidated, though she sometimes wished he would be less aggressive with waiters and car park attendants. But he spent money on her and he let her know that he admired her. Eventually, one warm July night, he succeeded in seducing her, not forcing himself upon her violently but leading her along with practiced technique and alcohol. They were in his house, after an evening at an inn by the river. To his amazement, he discovered that she was a virgin—almost an extinct species, he believed. To June, this step, once taken, was momentous and it heralded her brief infatuation with Alan.

Meanwhile, Phil, who had always meant to marry her when his future at the farm was secure—his father ran it now—did not realize what was happening. Her engagement to Alan took him by surprise.

June herself was being whirled along on a tide of flattery and sexual excitement, but she thought being married to Alan would be wonderful. He was attentive and seemed devoted to her; he owned his small, pleasant house and he had a good job, with plans, he disclosed, for running his own business in the future, though of what variety she did not learn.

On her honeymoon, she discovered what her predecessor had also learned from harsh experience: Alan was a bully whose gentleness had been a fake. He liked to hurt people, and he was insanely jealous. He took to dropping into the building society at odd hours and if he saw her smiling at a male customer he would attack her, verbally at first and then with blows, as soon as both of them were in the house—she never thought of it as home.

Pride stopped her from telling anyone, at first. Several of her friends had warned against the marriage, telling her that she didn't know Alan well enough, pointing out that Phil adored her.

"He's never said so," June had protested. "He never has time for us to meet."

June's mother and father were disappointed in the match. They and Phil's parents had always hoped the pair would marry. For all of them, the wedding had been an occasion for wearing a brave face, but June was radiant. Later, though, things changed, and June's mother told Phil's mother that she thought the marriage was a disaster. June was looking pale and exhausted, and if the couple went to functions in the town—as they did—Alan never left her side and would glower if she spoke to any other man.

Phil's parents gave a party in the New Year. They asked the Mortons, Alan and June, and at the party Alan saw June talking to Phil. In fact they were discussing the prospects for the new lambs, now beginning to arrive, and Phil had to leave the party to attend to some of them. June went to fetch her coat and followed him, and there, in the lambing shed, she confessed her plight.

Alan saw them leave the house together. He did not kill her then, but he had noticed where the guns were kept, locked in a cupboard in the farm office. He'd have to find the cartridges; it shouldn't be too hard. He went back two days later, when the house was empty, the men out on the land and Phil's mother at a meeting of the women's branch of the British Legion. Alan had known that the house would not be locked; as people were in and out all day, farmers often left their houses open. Even the collie dog was away in the fields, and it was easy for him to break into the gun cupboard and steal a shotgun. After a search, he found a box of cartridges in a desk drawer. Then he went home and sat waiting for June.

Brooding in the quiet house, dusk falling outside, Alan thought about her faithlessness, convincing himself that he had been destroyed, and excited by the thought of vengeance.

Sitting in the darkness, in his big armchair, its back towards the door, he heard her key in the lock and saw the lights come on. She hung her coat up in the hall, then went straight into the kitchen; that would be right, she'd got his meal to cook and would have bought food in her lunch hour or on the way home.

Alan, in stockinged feet, moved into the kitchen behind her. He called her name, stringing it together with shouted obscenities—"Bitch, harlot," and many more. She turned, terrified, and he shot her in the chest. As she sank to her knees, blood gurgling in her throat, he moved towards her and put the second shot into her head.

There was a lot of blood. He hadn't expected there to be so much. He wrapped her up in bin liners, tying the head and feet, and the waist. It was a good thing he hadn't done it in the living room; it would have messed the carpet up, and left evidence. As it was, if she were found, he meant suspicion to fall on Phil, her jilted lover.

Late at night, he put her body in his car and drove off into the countryside, where he dropped her in a ditch a few miles from the Wickenses' farm. Early the next morning, snow fell for several hours and it did not thaw for weeks; the snowplow was out on the roads and this caused heaps of piled-up snow to linger at the roadsides long after the main fall had gone.

Alan told the building society that June had not been feeling well and had gone away for a holiday. He said nothing to her parents, carrying on his normal routine but now forced to cater for himself and deal with his own washing.

The Wickenses reported the theft of the shotgun and a box of ammunition. No one had seen Alan enter or leave the farm; he had left his car in the lane outside and had slipped in quietly on foot. If anyone had come along, he had a story planned about wondering if they wanted to take advantage of a bulk order of wood preservative that he could offer at a bargain rate; when you were the manager of a business, there were always lines that you could push, and you could be absent from the premises without anyone's permission.

The kitchen took some time to clean, but as no one suspected trouble, he did it as his leisure, washing the walls and floor with soapy water more than once.

After a time June's parents wondered why they had not heard from her. She was out, he told them, every time they telephoned, but after two weeks they rang the building society, hoping to catch her there, and learned that she was, allegedly, away. The society was not happy about this long sudden absence, and June's father went to see Alan.

He was ready. He looked downcast and said that they had had a row. June had packed a bag and flounced out of the house, saying she was leaving him.

"I thought she'd run off with that Phil Wickens," Alan said, managing to look distraught rather than aggrieved. "I knew they were having an affair. That was why we quarreled."

June's father could not believe that part of the story, but if June had walked out of her marriage, why had she not contacted her parents? Where was she living? Had she any money?

"Her clothes?" he asked.

They'd gone, said Alan. He had packed them up and taken them to a charity shop, not in Billerton but across the county. He'd thrown away her toilet things. There had been time to see to everything, even to concealing the gun and ammunition. He might need them again.

Her father had insisted on calling the police. At that time, he suspected suicide, though if that was June's intention, why had she packed up all her clothes? Why hadn't she come to them, her parents? Was she ashamed of having failed in her hasty marriage?

She was found when a man walking with his dog along the high road where the snow had melted heard excited barking, and saw his pet scuffling in the ditch where Alan had dumped her body.

Alan acted the part of the grieving widower to perfection. The cold had preserved June's corpse and she was instantly recognizable when he was asked to identify her; her head wound had not obscured her features. There was no doubt that it was murder, and he was the prime suspect, but there was no immediate evidence to link him with the crime, and the gun could not be found.

Alan had, at first, planned to leave it with the body, so that Phil Wickens would be linked with the killing. Then he changed his mind. He had traveled south and buried it beneath the ground in the garden shed at his parents' home in Haverscot, more than a hundred miles from Billerton. Alan interred it there at night, when his parents were in bed; he did not enter the house at all, so that they had no knowledge of his visit.

Because her body was so well preserved, the forensic pathologist found on it evidence of serious bruising. Some contusions had occurred shortly before death; others, yellowing, were healing. There were signs of a rib cracked not so long ago. Colleagues at the building society declared that, since her marriage, June had become jumpy—nervy, said one girl— and another had noticed bruises on her neck which could not be hidden by her uniform shirt. No one had liked to ask about them.

Phil Wickens was given a good grilling. He admitted that he had been devastated when June married Alan, particularly after such a short acquaintance, but if she had seemed happy he would have made the best of it and been pleased for her; however, instead of blooming, she had begun to wither. That was how he expressed it to the detective inspector interviewing him. Alan, at any social gathering, prevented her from speaking to other men, coming up and almost forcibly removing her, he said, and less than a week before she disappeared, she had told him that Alan had forbidden her to speak to him.

"For your own sake, you'd better not come near me, even at work. Go to another desk," she'd warned, and he had said it was ridiculous, they'd known each other all their lives.

"It'll get easier in time," she'd said. "He'll learn to trust me."

In the lambing shed, Phil had urged her to leave Alan. The marriage was a mistake. She could admit that and divorce him. But June had said she must keep trying.

"I still love him," she had declared.

"Do you?" Phil had been incredulous.

"Yes," she had answered. "This is all my fault, you see, Phil. I don't come up to his expectations."

"You come up to mine. More than," Phil had gritted out. "I'd look after you."

The inspector had seen it all before.

" 'Love is blind,' " he quoted. "Its victims don't want to see what's obvious to other people. She was making excuses for him, and for herself. She'd made a big investment in him, hadn't she, throwing you over for him?"

"We'd got no official understanding," Phil said, reddening. "I didn't move fast enough, I suppose. We'd plenty of time, I thought." He was still only twenty-three. June had been not quite twenty-one when she was killed.

At this stage of the investigation, the police had discovered that Alan had been married before and that he had twice been charged with rape. Both times he had been acquitted, alleging that the women had consented. Each had known him slightly; each had been cross-examined in such a way as to imply that they were morally lax. By law, his identity had been concealed. Had she known about these incidents, June might have found Alan less appealing. His first wife, now happily remarried with a baby son, was traced; she described him as a sadist.

"He liked the rough stuff, seemingly," said Detective Inspector Rutherford.

This time, after the wedding, Alan had insured June's life. Rutherford thought June had been doomed from the day she made her vows. The police were sure that Alan was their man but evidence was scarce. The Crown Prosecution Service, and later the jury, must be certain of his guilt.

They had the bruises. These could be explained away by excuses that she had fallen, had been clumsy, even though work colleagues would testify to her altered manner and the marks that they had noticed.

Alan's house was examined minutely. His clothes were taken away for testing. Without the weapon, proof that the gun stolen from the Wickenses had been used could not be found, and in any case ballistic proof from shotguns was notoriously difficult to establish.

It was the string with which he had tied the bundle containing June's dead body that secured Alan's conviction. One of his assistants had seen him take such a ball from stock a few days before June disappeared. He'd watched to see if Alan paid for it, but he hadn't. Typical, the assistant said, and who would get the blame when stocks didn't balance up? The ball of twine was found in a cupboard in Alan's kitchen; it had been cut with scissors, and the frayed end matched the twine tying up the bin bags. In a drawer in the kitchen were the scissors used, and a wisp, extremely small, had attached itself to the hinge between the blades. Taken alone, this was not conclusive; the fragments could have come from an identical ball, but added to the evidence, admitted by the accused, of discord between the pair, and the fact that Alan had no alibi for the evening of the day when June was last seen, it was enough.

He could not plead manslaughter. Theft of the gun proved intent to kill. The insurance policy was further confirmation.

Alan had been found guilty, but though the mandatory sentence for murder is life imprisonment, most killers are let out on license after nine or ten years. His mother had visited him at first, making the journey alone when, after a while, Tom stopped going. Then she, too, had ended her lonely pilgrimages, but she never got rid of his possessions. To the end of her life, she would go into his room and try to recapture the image of the little boy whom she had loved. What had gone wrong? Why had his life turned out so badly? It was only after the murder trial that she and Tom learned the nature of his earlier brushes with the courts and the fact that he had been accused of rape. Dorothy recalled a puppy he had had; it would not obey him, running off, not coming when he called it. Tom had found it with its head bashed in. Alan had denied killing the animal, but his mother had never been convinced that he was innocent for there had been other episodes: butterflies pulled to bits while still alive, toads cut in half. She knew he had a cruel streak, a tendency to violence.

After her death, Tom had not had the will to get rid of Alan's things, though he wanted to turn his back on him, just as if he, too, had died.

But Alan wasn't dead. He had killed one woman and assaulted others—for he had; Tom knew he had carried out the rapes, and there was his cruel treatment of his first wife. One day he would be released from prison and what would happen then? He might kill again. After he came to The Willows, in the presence of Steve and Mark, Tom's physical decline was rapid.

Alan had come to collect the gun. He had plans to use it after his imminent release. With it, he could rob a bank. With money, he could leave the country. Why stay where he had a criminal record? He'd start a business overseas; he'd prosper, making up for all the time he'd lost.

His scheme backfired, however. He had intended to enter the house armed with the gun, use it to terrify the sick old man, and hide it under the floorboards in his room or in the attic, ready for collection later. However, he'd reckoned without the floodwater. Years ago, Tom, to defeat the annual winter sogginess of the garden, had had a flagged path laid leading to the shed. That was not a problem, but inside the shed, where the gun, well greased and wrapped in plastic sheeting, together with the box of cartridges, securely sealed in several protective layers, was buried at least three feet deep, there was now a solid concrete path between the benches.

Digging them out would be a major task. He'd need to break the concrete up. The job would have to wait until a later visit. This time, once the boys had gone, he'd had to be content with frightening the feeble old man enough to get some money from him.

He'd had a night out with the cash, but there hadn't been a lot—less than three hundred pounds, some of it in a drawer in the sitting room, the rest upstairs, an emergency fund, the old man had said, in a bedroom cupboard.

"If I tell you where it is, will you go?" old Tom had gasped.

"Sure," said Alan. "But I'll be back."

As he left the house, Tom's words had echoed in his head.

"You're responsible for your own actions. Everyone is. When they let you out, remember that," he said.

"I'm out now," Alan had jeered. He'd said that he was on official leave.

Tom hadn't been certain that this was the truth. Alan might have absconded from some rehabilitation expedition, and if so, the police would soon be round.

"Don't go hurting other people," Tom had implored. "Not again." There'd been so many—those wretched girls, and his mother.

He was too tired, too shocked by Alan's appearance and his conduct to do more than make this small appeal. Tom suspected nothing about the concealed gun; Alan knew he hadn't found it, or he would have mentioned it. He'd get it on his next leave. By then the water would have receded, or if it hadn't, he would dig the gun out as soon as his release came through; that wasn't too far off now. If necessary, he'd tie the old man up to stop him interfering.

Tom's sudden death surprised Alan; he had realized that the old man was very weak but had thought him merely convalescent. Now he was angry. What right had the old fool to die before he, Alan, had finished with him, wreaked revenge? Forgotten were the rescues of the past, the debts paid, the job found; instead, scoldings and punishments were remembered. Alan did not want to think about his mother's tears, her attempts to mediate between them, to minimize or excuse his transgressions. Finally, even she had deserted him, thanks, Alan convinced himself, to the old man's influence.

There would be compensations, though; he'd get all the money, and the house, in nice time for his release. He was the only heir. Alan made no attempt to attend the funeral, although he would almost certainly have been permitted to attend. Nowadays, his face was unfamiliar in the area, and it was better left that way. He didn't even send a wreath.

It was some weeks before he learned that he had not been left a penny in the old man's will.

11.

Mark hadn't thought much about Christmas yet. Until last year, despite evidence to the contrary, he had managed to convince himself that Father Christmas came down the narrow chimney of their small house, past the gas fire, and plodded silently upstairs to fill his stocking.

For the last three years he'd stayed awake for hours, suspicious about the contents of small parcels his mother had brought home and not unwrapped, taking them mysteriously to her room. He'd thought of searching for them, but it seemed that they were private. He had secrets; she might have some too, and he respected that.

This year, Ivy and Sharon were conspiring. Kylie had written a letter asking for roller blades for herself and a toy garage for baby Adam; she was sure he'd soon be old enough to play with one.

"Have you written your letter, Mark?" Kylie asked him, and when he said no, she pressed him to do it.

Blushing, Mark scribbled something on a pad, folded it and sent it up Ivy's chimney, where a coal fire burned in the grate.

"What did you ask for?" Sharon asked. She liked Mark,

who was intrigued by Adam and would hang over him, making him smile and even crooning to him, promising to read to him when he was older.

"If I tell, I won't get it," Mark replied. His wish was impossible to grant; he wanted a family.

He was often at Ivy's with the younger ones now. He knew that since Tom's death, Steve had been with other boys hanging around cars, looking for any that might be unlocked so that they could steal things. This made Mark uneasy. He didn't think Steve would really steal—but then, he'd thieved from Tom; Mark knew that. Perhaps he'd got a taste for it. He once came home with a camera which he said he'd bought for Ivy; it was going cheap, he'd explained, since everyone knew he couldn't have afforded it at the proper price. He said it was her Christmas present, early. Mark knew that he had stolen it.

Mark didn't want to be a big boy yet. It was enough to be considered old enough to be at home alone. He had no wish to go out in a gang with Steve and his friends.

"Send the kid home," Bruce had said to Steve, who had once taken Mark along, largely at Ivy's insistence; she thought his place was with the boys, not with her and the girls. Adam didn't count yet. But Mark had thankfully returned and played cards with Kylie till it was nearly time for his mother to return.

She would be on duty over Christmas. The hotel ran special breaks to attract people who wanted to escape from one thing or another: their families, the chores, even solitude. Festive programs were arranged, and activities for children. Mark was going with her; he could join in some of the junior treats. He'd spent occasional weekend nights there recently, since her promotion; the head chef had a son much his age and they got on well. Mark liked these excursions; sometimes he sat quietly in the office where his mother worked. She knew he wouldn't interrupt her; he would read quietly or play patience, which he'd learned from Tom. Later, his mother would take some leave and spend time with him. They'd swim, maybe go to the cinema, or skate. They might visit a castle or a museum. Susan always devoted herself to enjoying these days, sharing his pleasure and trying to increase it. He was never wild or naughty, and he was enthusiastic about everything they did together. He was doing well at school and was good company. Much of the credit must be due to Ivy, Susan thought; she'd been so lucky to find her and Joe, whose sudden death was tragic. Susan had thought his influence so good for Mark; he was a solid, decent man who had run the booking office at the station.

His death must have hit Steve hard; now he had no natural parent. In the past, Susan had sometimes taken Steve on trips with her and Mark, but the age gap was becoming more pronounced with Steve in his teens. Perhaps some other boy might be invited, though she had reservations about Terry as a suitable friend, after his disappearance. What had really happened then?

Susan was too busy with the present to think much about the future, apart from doing all she could for Mark. A good education was essential, and the comprehensive school in Haverscot had such an excellent reputation that it was a reason for staying in the area. She had turned down the offer of a job in London; she didn't want to go back there. If she were to take promotion elsewhere, she would have to be sure that Mark's schooling would not receive a setback.

She did not want to marry. In the hotel, she saw couples of all kinds: some were happy, maybe celebrating; others were enjoying one-night stands, or not enjoying them. Many guests were there on business, and if they whiled away some hours with casual partners, it was not her concern. Her work was stimulating and had become more demanding; she often had to sort out problems with the staff, and she wanted to keep her own life simple; she had had enough emotion in it to last a lifetime.

Things would be different when Mark grew up and left home, but she would face that when it happened; meanwhile, there was Christmas. When the hotel festivities were over, perhaps she would take Kylie and Ivy to the pantomime; it would do Ivy good. Sharon was tied down with Adam.

Where would Sharon be without her mother's support? She was little more than a schoolgirl, herself. Susan, much older when she was pregnant, trained and with a good job, had found things difficult enough. It was lucky that Ivy was so fond of babies and small children; Sharon would have more, unless Ivy could coax her in the direction of some effective contraception, and even then, things could go wrong.

Stepfathers could be assets; Joe had been to Sharon and clearly Richard Gardner was a pleasant sort of man; it hadn't stopped the boy Terry from freaking out, however. At least he'd reappeared with no damage to himself. There were no easy answers, Susan knew.

Richard was dreading Christmas, that period of enforced confinement amid one's family. He could spend time in his workshop—but that would be seen as selfish, shutting himself away, not joining in the daily round with three people who were, he now admitted, not really his family at all; no blood tie linked them. He didn't even like them very much.

The confession, albeit made only to himself, was shocking; didn't he love them? You could love people even when you didn't like them; love was visceral, but it could be killed. His love for Verity had died, but not his sense of obligation to take care of her, since she was so bad at doing this for herself.

The two boys were increasingly distancing themselves from him. He recognized in Justin real hostility, though there was tolerance, still, from Terry. What should they do about a holiday next year? Christmas was the time for planning one, and in the past he had taken them and Verity to various seaside places in France, from Brittany to Bordeaux; they had rented gîtes in isolation and in the grounds of châteaux. He had dug sand castles, played beach cricket, financed windsurfing and even sampled it himself. While this went on, Verity painted, substituting clouds and darkness for what were sunny landscapes. Often she destroyed her work when it was done, lapsing into hysteria and self-denigration. Then he would feel pity for her, would put his arms around her, smooth her tousled mane of hair, and try to calm her.

Later, he would find the wine bottles. Even now he did not always connect cause and effect. She still swallowed pills, those calming capsules which her own doctor was now prescribing.

Perhaps next summer they could find an activity holiday, where the boys could spend the day occupied with sports or pastimes—go-carting, he thought, or maybe sailing. Yes, that would be an idea; he could learn to sail, too, if he found somewhere with adult and junior courses, so that they would be separated. Verity would not want to sail; perhaps there would be a painters' group—not a class; she did not consider that she needed teaching—where she could meet like-minded folk, near the sailing school. Trying to find such a location would occupy him. He could make inquiries, scan advertisements, send for brochures.

Following his disappearance, Terry had been subdued for about a week. Richard had given him a real scolding after their visit to the police station, where Terry had been edgy, cracking unfunny jokes about locking up terrorists in the cells. The station sergeant had not found this amusing and had described the offense of wasting police time. Terry had been very lucky not to be charged with committing criminal damage, he pointed out.

Richard understood that some of Terry's behavior had been due to nerves, but a little remorse would not have been out of place, and he said so.

"They couldn't do anything to me at my age," Terry had scoffed.

"They could. You could receive an official caution and that would give you a record, so that next time you got into trouble it would count against you," Richard said. Then he spoke more gently. "There's not going to be a next time, Terry. I know those boys were teasing you and Mark, and maybe if you'd punched them, it would have been understandable, though foolish, but to go breaking windows and giving your mother all that worry is another thing. Aren't you at all sorry for upsetting her?"

Terry was, though he could not bring himself to say so.

"I couldn't punch them. They were much bigger than me and Mark, and there were three of them," was the sulky response.

As the Christmas break began, Richard thought about this conversation. Had Terry learned his lesson? Would he again react in an extreme way at the next attempt to tease him? The other boy, Mark, was a nice little lad. His company might be good for Terry. Richard wondered what Mark was doing over Christmas, with his mother working in a hotel. She was unlikely to have much time off; presumably the child-minder took charge of him.

Anna, Richard's daughter, was at sea, aboard her cruise ship, where there would be gala festivities for the passengers. He hoped that she was happy; she seemed content enough, on their rare meetings. Absent from her, though unwillingly, he felt that he had let her down; however, in the lottery of life, she had not done badly. Her mother's second marriage had turned out well, but another man had brought his daughter up, successfully, while Richard was failing with a different man's two sons. There'd be no Christmas card from Anna. Probably she'd posted one in Adelaide or Sydney and it would arrive eventually. He had sent hers, in plenty of time, to the shipping line's address for the week before Christmas. In it, he told her that he had paid a check into her bank account so that she could buy her own present; this was what he did each year, and for her birthday. It was impersonal but practical; she always wrote to tell him how she would spend the money.

Where was young Mark's father? The boy hadn't mentioned him. Would he see his son during the holiday? Or was he dead?

Verity, who had abandoned her meditation classes after Terry's escapade, had made mince pies. She was having one of her domestic effort spells, which was a good thing as long as it endured, keeping her busy in the kitchen. Richard had bought the turkey and a Christmas pudding, assisted by Terry who had offered to accompany him. This unusual helpfulness was, perhaps, a sign of contrition. They'd stocked up well, remembering fruit juice and Coca-Cola, and bumper packs of crisps as well as all the normal weekly things, enough to withstand a siege. It was a pity Verity's parents had refused to come for Christmas; last year, they'd promised to be there but two days beforehand they had telephoned, pleading incipient influenza. The previous year, during their visit, Verity had wept all through the Christmas lunch, eaten at three o'clock instead of the planned half past one. By that time, her father had filled himself with whiskey and her mother was attempting, in the kitchen, to retrieve disaster, for the sprouts had burned and the potatoes were not done. The turkey was cooked to shreds and dry. Verity had pronounced herself useless and burst into tears while Richard and his mother-in-law feigned jollity for the sake of the two boys. That was when Richard had finally understood the extent of his predicament. He could not walk away from Verity; his task and duty were to try to help her overcome her temperament and control it, instead of letting it rule her and wreck the lives of those surrounding her.

On Christmas afternoon she'd gone to bed, and her father had fallen asleep on the sofa.

"I used to wonder if it was in their genes, this drink thing," Verity's mother had said, as she and Richard washed up. The boys were in their playroom, busy with their presents. "Mind you, I do it, too, at times," she confessed. "If you can't beat them, join them. But it doesn't make Hugh wild, like Vera." Her mother would not play the game of changing names. "He just gets silly," she declared. "Her other husband couldn't cope, and I won't blame you if you can't, either."

Richard liked his mother-in-law, a thin, scrawny-looking woman with hair dyed to match her daughter's—or was the mimicry the other way? She had a sense of humor and was good with the two boys, asking them silly riddles and teaching them card tricks.

"She can't help it," Richard had remarked.

"Yes, she can—we all have choices," said Verity's mother.

Richard was too loyal to answer, but he knew that Verity believed all hurt was aimed at her: The boys were naughty simply to upset her, and Richard came home late simply in order that the meal should spoil. How had this all begun?

He'd hoped Verity's brisk, no-nonsense mother would be at Merrifields this year; her presence would be helpful. But it was not to be. Parcels had arrived from the couple; others had been sent. The conventions were observed.

Richard could escape to church. There were several

services, carols one evening, midnight Mass, and matins on Christmas Day. He could take his pick or go to all of them; no one could legitimately complain.

He wondered what Caroline would be doing. She was spending Christmas with her parents, who lived in Cambridge, where her father had been a history don and her mother a geologist. He imagined that she would have an agreeable and intellectually stimulating time, perhaps visiting her brother, another don, and his family who lived just outside the city in a large house much swept, she said, by icy winds blowing straight from Siberia. Richard wished that he was with her. He imagined going there as her acknowledged lover. But amid those academic types, he would seem so dull, so slow-witted, he reflected.

A shriek from the kitchen brought him back to the present, and he hauled himself out of the deep, comfortable chair in his study where he had been successfully hiding while indulging in his melancholy thoughts. He hurried out. This time, the crisis was not major. Verity had burned one lot of pies because she had gone upstairs to her studio, to do more work on a painting of a Christmas scene she had suddenly felt inspired to create: dark holly, berries dripping blood; a father, mother, infant and donkey all apparently half buried under snow; Richard saw it later. Taking the blackened pies from the oven, she had also burned her hand—not badly, but it was red and painful, and the pies were smoking.

Richard held her wounded fingers under running cold water. When she was able to stand unsupported, he threw away the pies and told her not to worry. Anticipating this disaster, he had bought two dozen at the baker's in the town the day before. They were in the freezer, with some other emergency stores.

Setting off for midnight Mass, he once again reflected on how lucky it was that his employment brought in a generous salary; Verity and her family needed every penny.

*   *   *

Verity was asleep when he came silently to bed. She was breathing heavily, and he caught the smell of alcohol. It seemed she had found ways to pay for all the bottles she consumed.

She was still asleep next morning when he went quietly downstairs to make some tea. The house was quiet, the day not yet begun, the boys not yet awake. He supposed Verity had carried out her role of filling the boys' stockings; she had bought presents for them. Probably she had filched money from the amount he gave her for them to buy drink; he couldn't deprive her of a certain amount of cash, though he had sought every means to limit or define what she spent.

He made the tea and drank a cup in peace, then poured one for her and took it to her.

She was just waking up.

"Oh, my head," she groaned. How she suffered with her daily headache! She was a martyr to pain, she claimed, and Richard did not understand her frustrations; all she wanted was to paint, and, instead, she had to cook and clean. Conveniently, she forgot the cleaning women Richard had gladly paid for, who had come and gone because Verity was always finding fault with what they did, and even with their mere presence in the house.

Now she peered at him as he crossed the room with a cup and saucer in one hand, and a large, ungainly parcel in the other. He put the tea down on the table beside her and drew a small parcel from his pocket.

"Happy Christmas, dear," he said brightly, bending down to kiss her, aiming at her forehead.

She turned her head away and he met a faceful of scratchy, tangled hair. However, she unwrapped the parcels, discovering in one a large azalea, and in the other a bottle of Chanel No. 5.

"Oh, Richard, you know I prefer Diorissimo," she said, though this was quite untrue. Last year Chanel had been what she desired. He could not win this contest, so he abandoned it.

"Don't hurry to get up," was all he said, and left the room, taking the scent with him.

She would not be adopting her housewife role today, so he must do it. He didn't mind—he even liked it—and it was easier to know from the outset that this was his task rather than have to take it over in midoperation. He'd plan the bird for half past one and maybe they would eat it on time this year.

Then he remembered. He'd invited someone to share their turkey.

He must have been out of his mind! How could he have lost his wits to that extent! Too much Christmas spirit in the church porch; that was the trouble.

Some of his acquaintances from the choral society were among the congregation. He had sat next to a couple whom he knew slightly from this contact, and on his other side had been an elderly woman who seemed vaguely familiar. As they sang the hymns she revealed a lovely clear contralto voice, and he remembered that she had sat near him at evensong the night Terry disappeared. She was a forbidding-looking woman, with a felt hat pulled down over heavy graying brows, and wisps of iron-gray hair just showing round its edge. Last night she had not taken Communion, and nor had he; they'd exchanged a calm, unsmiling glance as the others in their row of chairs filed out, and each had looked about the building as the long procession of communicants wove back and forth to the altar.

After the service, he stood back to let her precede him down the path. There were little groups of people chatting as they made their way towards their houses or to their cars.

Richard exchanged greetings with those people whom he knew, and who were near him as he left the church, but they were few, and he soon caught up with the woman in the hat, as he now thought of her. She had a very efficient torch, which she shone to light her way down the flagged path.

"Yours is better than mine," he said, indicating the weak beam coming from his own pocket torch.

"I expect you need a new battery," she said. Her speaking voice was mellow, too.

"You're right," he said.

"I like to carry this at night," said Marigold Darwin. Her own torch was a considerable instrument; useful as a weapon, Richard thought. Was that what she meant? He remembered a shocking case a year or two ago, when an elderly woman had been attacked and raped walking home from church in some country town. Where was it? Was no one safe?

"Have you far to go?" he asked.

"To Shelley Drive," she said.

"That's some distance. Have you a car?"

"I'm on foot," she answered.

"Would you allow me to escort you?" Richard offered. "Let me introduce myself. My name is Richard Gardner and I live at Merrifields. It's just along the road."

"I know Merrifields," said Miss Darwin. Her voice altered, deepening and growing stronger. "I lived there as a child."

"No! Did you?" Richard asked. By now they had fallen into step together.

"Yes," said Marigold. "I was so sad when we moved away."

She had never told that to another soul.

"It's a lovely house," he said. "And it has a lovely garden."

They talked about it as they walked, the strong, icy wind

cutting into them as they left the shelter of the yews around the churchyard. Marigold explained how she had rented her present bungalow while she was house-hunting, and about her acquisition of The Willows.

"You'll be a neighbor, then," said Richard.

"Yes." By now Marigold had learned that he was married with two stepsons, and an older daughter by an earlier marriage, and Richard had heard more about Marigold Darwin than people she had known for years. "I suppose your family is quite excited about Christmas," she said.

"I suppose so," he replied. Then he remembered that she was new to Haverscot, and alone. "What about you? Have you friends visiting you?"

"No," she said, adding, "Not this year."

He had noticed that she referred to the family as singular; she was a pedant and he liked her for it.

"Why don't you join us for lunch?" he invited. "You must come and see your old home, in any case. Why not tomorrow? No formality," he added, "Just us. Please do. I won't let you refuse."

Marigold thought of the chicken she had bought. Sinbad was to share it with her. It would keep till Boxing Day; he could have his usual Chappie.

"I'd like that very much," she said. "Thank you."

By this time they had reached her gate.

"One o'clock," he said. "See you then. Merry Christmas."

"Merry Christmas," she replied, as they parted, Richard making a gesture to remove his hat. A polite man, she thought, and sad.

Now why had she thought that?

She went into the house regretting her swift acceptance of his invitation. In daylight, she would have refused the meal but asked to see the house and garden another time. In daylight, she would not have told him of her grief at leaving Merrifields. In darkness, not looking at the other's face, one's defense was down.

Richard, walking back with long, swift strides, was also regretting his impulsiveness. What had made him do it?

It was the night, he thought; it was the night.

12.

In the morning, Marigold resolved to excuse herself from keeping the engagement. She could plead a diplomatic cold. She woke early and made coffee and toast, listening to carols on the radio. Then she put on a recording of the *Messiah* and was so uplifted by it, by the blue sky outside and the sudden sunshine, that she felt more confident. Why not go round to Merrifields? She longed to see the house again, to walk round the garden and discover how much of it remained familiar. She would soon be the Gardners' neighbor and she must not be aloof, though she did not expect to be liked. She knew that people found her hideous, but as she grew older she had developed from being a gauche girl into a competent, impersonal administrator; efficiency and intellect could carry one through a professional life; procedures and protocol dictated action. By the end of her time at the Ministry, she had earned respect, if not affection, and early timidity had long been overcome.

She did not intend to be a complete recluse in Haverscot. Richard Gardner's invitation was kind, and at Christmas, when turkey and plum pudding were the fare, one extra meant nothing—another potato peeled, a few more sprouts prepared. In a family, it was simple. Marigold had been asked to families before; she was godmother to some colleagues' children, not because the parents prized her but because they knew she was reliable, and they pitied her without a family of her own; they were doing her a kindness. She had never yet forgotten a godchild's birthday or neglected one at Christmas; that was all the parents wanted from her, and the comforting knowledge that if anything were to happen to them—some fatal accident— she'd be there, a background figure of stability. Marigold had attended the weddings of her two eldest godchildren and learned, sadly, of one's later divorce; the second seemed to be happy, living in Notting Hill, a journalist married to a video editor. They never asked Marigold to visit them and she had stopped sending her goddaughter presents after providing a dinner service when she married. But she still sent cards, though none came back.

She had received some Christmas cards; they came from a few former colleagues, and one was from a widow met on holiday last year, when Marigold had been to the opera at Verona. Next year, the widow would exclude her from her list; this was what happened after such chance meetings. Marigold knew she had been included only because everyone in their group was exchanging addresses. A row of robins, sacred scenes and wintry landscapes was spaced out across the bright wood of the mantelpiece in her bungalow. Marigold looked round the room: It was so tasteless, with the tiled hearth, the lozenge-patterned carpet, the beige dralon-covered chairs. Merrifields must be a better place to spend the day than Fairways.

She went to matins; it would pass the time. After that, she took Sinbad for a walk.

When Richard rang to put her off, intending to use the

excuse of his wife's indisposition, there was no answer. He tried again half an hour later; still no reply.

He gave up. Perhaps the presence of a guest would prompt Verity to produce some better manners; she used to try in front of other people, but he hadn't tested her for more than a year.

Marigold drew a deep breath as she walked through the gates of Merrifields. Well-trimmed bushes bordered the drive, which curled round in front of the house. Today, the air was crisp with frost; if this continued, the flooded fields would freeze and there might be skating. To the left, trees bordered the property, many more than she remembered, or perhaps they had simply grown larger; no, some were young. They formed a barrier between Merrifields and the house next door. A boy and girl had lived there; they had taunted her across the wall and would not let her climb into their tree house when their mother invited her to tea. They'd hauled the rope ladder up and left her below. She hadn't made a fuss, nor cried. She'd sniffed and found a tree at the end of their garden, which she'd climbed, and had remained in its branches until dusk, when the grown-ups had come searching for her. By then she was cold and stiff, but she was the victor, for the brother and sister had been punished for neglecting her. She'd forgotten all about it till this moment.

What had become of those two? She would never know.

The house, built of brick, bow windows in front, a garage round the back, was covered now with climbing plants: roses, she observed, approaching, and was that a wisteria? Berries on a cotoneaster glowed against one wall. She didn't remember such a covering; hadn't her father said that plants harbored insects, beetles and flies, which would invade the building if encouraged?

The front door was startlingly unaltered: solid oak,

buttressed with iron studs and a heavy knocker, the letter slit narrow, no doubt causing problems for the postman now but in those days he used to ring. He came on Christmas Day, she recalled. Hadn't the milkman come, too? She couldn't be so sure of that.

Marigold had left Sinbad at home. He was a well-trained dog and would be content, after his walk, for several hours. She rang the bell.

There was some delay before it was answered and she almost turned away, wondering if she had, after all, misunderstood the invitation, reluctant to press it a second time. She had just stepped back, preparing for retreat, when the door opened and there stood Richard, looking harassed, wisps of graying brownish hair standing up round his head. He wore a shiny plastic apron decorated with a Snoopy motif, and a swift, artificial smile.

"Hallo! You came," he cried, effusively. "Welcome. Do come in."

Marigold knew at once that he had repented the arrangement, but it was too late now for either of them to withdraw. She must exert herself to be a perfect, unassuming, helpful guest.

"So nice of you," she murmured. "Happy Christmas once again."

"Indeed, indeed," cried Richard, falsely merry.

He took her camel coat and laid it over a chair which stood against the wall. "Perhaps I should hang it up?" he asked himself, aloud.

"No, no. It'll be splendid there," she assured him. She was wearing a hat, this time one made of flecked tweed, not unlike his own, and now she removed it, laying it and a pair of brown leather gloves on top of her coat. Then, with short, stubby fingers, she briskly plumped up her wavy iron-gray hair.

Entering, she had set down a basket full of packages covered in Christmas wrappings. Now she picked it up.

"I brought you these," she said, tentatively. "Nothing exciting. So last-minute."

"You shouldn't have bothered." Richard had not thought of finding a present for her. There might have been a box of chocolates among their own presents; perhaps he could contrive to find one. Then he looked at what her basket held. "Do I espy a bottle?" he cried, extracting a parcel shaped unmistakably. It might contain some nonalcoholic concoction—elderflower wine, for instance—he warned himself.

But it didn't. It was a bottle of a very good Chardonnay. How fortunate, because as he had stopped buying wine or spirits, he could not have produced anything with the meal, unless he tapped Verity's secret supplies, and he would not ask her where she had them hidden. He knew there was some sherry; he'd put a bottle in his study, in case of seasonal callers such as carol singers.

He took her into the drawing room.

"I expect you feel a little strange," he said. "Coming back like this after so many years."

"I don't know how I feel," she said. "Not yet."

She looked around her. Near the window was a large fir tree, more than six feet tall, decorated with painted glass baubles, mainly red and silver. There was tinsel on it, and tiny starlike lights.

"How lovely," she exclaimed. "Our tree was always in the hall."

It had seemed immense to her, reaching up to heaven, though it must have been about the same height as this one.

"Sherry?" he offered, adding, "Verity will soon be down. She's changing." Dressing, he meant. She'd not yet surfaced for the day.

"Thank you." Marigold accepted the sherry, in a pretty glass—Georgian, she suspected, of some value. She had been thinking about the rooms the house contained in her day: drawing room, dining room, study, and a room the maids used as a sitting room. There had been two maids, living in: amazing! One had been the cook. Upstairs, there had been six bedrooms and her father's dressing room, and a single bathroom. Leading off the kitchen, in a sort of extra scullery, had been a bath, covered with a board by day, for the maids, who shared an attic bedroom. "How many bathrooms have you got?" she asked abruptly.

Richard laughed.

"Three," he said. "One en suite, as they say. Four bedrooms on the first floor and two in the attic. The boys have those; they're both a good size."

When they moved in, frequent guests had been expected, at least by Richard, but none came except, occasionally, his daughter, Anna, and, still less often, Verity's parents.

"So many!" marveled Marigold. If there were two attic rooms, why had Doris and Mabel, the housemaid, not had one each? She would never learn the answer.

"I expect you'd like to look around," he said.

With Verity still upstairs, this was not the moment, and Marigold demurred.

"Another time," she said, but he showed her the ground floor.

Here, the kitchen had been entirely redone when Richard bought the house. Its design was modern but its wood fitments retained the older character of the house. In the center was a vast table.

"It's got a heat-resistant top," said Richard. "I had it specially made. We eat in here most of the time."

In Marigold's youth, Doris, the cook, had operated at a large scrubbed deal table—not so very different. Marigold had been allowed to put pastry leaves on pies and cut out circles for jam tarts.

Today, the dining-room table—mahogany, a good reproduction, Marigold decided—was laid for five people. Red candles rose from swags of holly and there were scarlet paper napkins set beside each plate. Silver gleamed. Heavy cut-glass tumblers sparkled.

"How lovely it looks," said Marigold.

"My wife's artistic," Richard loyally declared, but it was he who had done all this. Verity, the night before, had painted large black streaks across her Christmas scene and turned it to the wall after Terry had said it looked too sad for Christmas. "She paints," Richard added.

He led his guest on, showing her his study.

"It was my father's study, too," said Marigold. "It's still dark."

Even on this sunny day, the room was dim. Marigold remembered that in the summer, her father always had the light on when he was in the room. She entered it sometimes, to read to him. He wanted to be certain of her progress.

"Verity uses one of the bedrooms as her studio," Richard said. "It's much lighter. I've got a workshop in the garden."

Marigold had noticed the large wooden hut as she walked up the drive.

"What do you make?" she asked.

"I do a bit of carving," he replied, opening the playroom door.

The two boys were in there, one intent before a television screen, obsessed with his computer game. The other one was reading a book with a fearsome cover; he had a headset on, pumping rhythm into his head as he read. Neither glanced up. This room, Marigold recalled, had been the maids' sitting room.

"Forgive them," Richard said, leading her out again.

"They're deaf to the rest of the world. You'll meet them properly when we eat. Now, if you'll excuse me, I must just dish up the bird."

Marigold did not offer to assist; the wife, Verity, would be doing that. She sat down in the drawing room and closed her eyes, trying to refurnish it as it had been more than fifty years ago. The curtains—green now—had been a sort of coffee color and the chairs and sofa had worn coats of flowered cretonne—yes, that was what it had been called. Wasn't it really printed linen? Blue, it had been, with large pink sprawling blooms like peonies all over it, quite pleasant. There had been several casual tables here and there; ornaments had stood on some, and photographs on others. The room, in winter, had been extremely chilly unless there was a roaring fire, though there had been central heating, with a coke boiler in the cellar. Today, there was a log fire which looked much the same as she remembered, but the room was very warm; a more efficient heating system must have been installed when the house was renovated. She wondered which of the bedrooms had been turned into bathrooms; how luxurious it sounded.

She was still lost in the past when she heard a sound and opened her eyes. A thin woman had entered the room; a tragedy queen, she thought at once, observing Verity's haunted expression. She was dressed in peasant style, with a flowing skirt of some eastern printed cotton, and a long black sweater which clung to her meager breasts and bony elbows. Dark hair, glinting with copper shades, tumbled abundantly about her shoulders, but it did not hide her scrawny neck and it emphasized her somewhat raddled—yes, that was the word—face. Her dark eyes were large and staring, slightly unfocused. She did not speak, but gazed down at Marigold, uncomprehending.

Marigold stood, levering herself out of her chair with powerful arms. A stocky figure in a burgundy-red woolen dress, she was a surprise to Verity, who expected to see an old, frail woman in her eighties, not this resolute-looking person who could clearly play two rounds of golf, straight off.

"Marigold Darwin," said the visitor. "Your husband most kindly invited me." She extended a small, square hand.

Verity advanced and touched the outstretched fingers. Her own were icy, and felt fragile. Marigold did not clasp them.

Silence fell.

"I'm shortly moving to The Willows, just along the road," said Marigold, at last. "It's a delightful house—just as yours is, though much smaller of course. I lived here as a child. Did your husband mention that?" Why should he, she reflected, as soon as she had said the words.

"How nice," said Verity vaguely, then, brightening, "Ah—I see you've got some sherry. Where did Richard put it?"

"It's over there." Marigold gestured towards the bottle which was on a table by the window.

There was no spare glass. Verity made an impatient sound, became more alert and hurried from the room, soon returning with one, which she filled, tossed the contents down her throat, filled again and swallowed half, topped it up once more and then sat down on the sofa, opposite the hearth. She spread herself across it, skirt fanning round lean thighs.

Marigold thought, not for the first time, that love was very strange. What had attracted this ill-assorted pair to one another? Or were opposites, like magnets, inexorably drawn together? Before another silence overwhelmed them both, she spoke again.

"A lovely day," she said, in her low, rich voice.

"Is it?" asked Verity. "I hadn't noticed."

"Very cold." Marigold persevered. "Maybe it will snow." It

wouldn't; the sky was too clear. "I expect your boys would enjoy that."

"I daresay." Verity had finished her sherry. She refilled her glass and, as an afterthought, waved the bottle inquiringly in Marigold's direction.

Marigold shook her head.

"No, thank you," she said.

With the sherry, Verity was relaxing; her tense expression softened but her focus was now even less acute. She's had something already, Marigold decided, but was it drink? She felt a flicker of concern; that nice man, Richard, had a problem here.

At this point in her speculation, he appeared, smiling warmly and announcing that the meal was ready.

"Where are the boys?" asked Verity. Her voice was harsh, in contrast to her drowsy appearance.

"Waiting eagerly for nourishment," said Richard. "They've been helping me dish up."

Hunger and greed had driven Justin and his brother to the kitchen, where they had hopped about in some excitement, not too sophisticated to be unmoved by the sight of a large turkey, roasted to a perfect golden brown. One had stirred the bread sauce; the other had drained the sprouts. There were carrots, too; some people—Richard among them—did not care for the traditional sprouts.

On the sideboard in the dining room stood the bottle of wine which Marigold had brought. She wondered whether to ascribe this to his tact and then remembered that when they visited this room on their tour, she had noticed only tumblers at the place settings. Now, everyone had a wineglass.

"This is Justin and this is Terry," Richard introduced, as the two boys waited by their chairs, Richard having sharply told them to stand up when they had already seated themselves, Terry brandishing his knife and fork around in anticipation. He replaced them, crookedly, as an old woman entered with his mother, and he knew immediately that she was the woman from the park. He'd seen her there a few times since that episode, always in her hat and with her dog. She recognized him, too; he saw it in her face but, to his amazement, she gave no sign that they had met before.

"Happy Christmas, Justin. Happy Christmas, Terry," she said, her stern features creasing into what was, for her, a smile. She identified the smaller boy at once, but did his parents know about the incident in the park? He had done nothing wrong; the bigger boys were the miscreants. In her experience, it was best not to complicate matters, so she did not mention their earlier encounter.

Somehow, Richard kept the talk going while they ate. There was quite a lot to do, what with serving everyone and passing round the vegetables and all the trimmings.

"Miss Darwin lived here years ago," Richard told the boys, in between carving and seeing that Justin was handing round the gravy and bread sauce. Verity sat silent, and idle.

"Did you?" Terry looked at her directly.

"Yes. Until I was about your age. Then we moved away," she said.

Terry was intrigued by her hair. It was so thick and curly, like a wig. Perhaps it was a wig.

"Did you have a tree house?" he tried out. "Did people then?"

"I didn't, but the children next door did. I envied them," said Marigold.

"Cat made us one," said Terry.

"Cat?"

"The boys call me that," said Richard. "Because my name's Richard—Dick Whittington, you know."

"I see," said Marigold. Somehow she did not think the name was intended as a compliment.

"Willy would have been better," said Terry and began laughing wildly.

"That isn't funny, Terry," said Richard. "Mind your manners and pass Miss Darwin the cranberry sauce."

Marigold had, after a second, understood the boy's remark. Why were the two of them hostile to their stepfather? Why was Verity so obviously miserable? Despite his apparent geniality, was Richard really a domestic tyrant? It was possible. Malevolence could lurk behind benign facades, despots could beam kindly upon children, and the mild man next door could turn out to be a murderer or a rapist.

Verity contributed little to the conversation. Richard had given each boy what he preferred to drink—Coca-Cola—after offering them some wine.

"You're not too young to have a taste," he told them, but they both declined.

Marigold noticed that he only half-filled Verity's glass while being generous to her and to himself. Verity drank hers rapidly, and when he did not top it up, she asked for more.

"In a minute," he replied, and rising, filled all their tumblers with water.

She drinks, Marigold thought; she really does, and if I hadn't brought that bottle, it would have been a soft drink meal for all of them, though Richard might have been embarrassed by not offering wine to a guest.

"It's a very nice wine," he told Marigold, topping up her glass and his and just covering the base of Verity's. "Thank you. Miss Darwin brought it," he told the company.

"And I'd like some more of it," said Verity distinctly. "Richard doesn't like me drinking," she told Marigold.

"I got it at the wine merchant's in the town," said

Marigold, smoothly ignoring this observation. "Where it is, there used to be a draper and haberdasher. The money went in small screw-top containers on an aerial pulley to a cashier, who put the change in it and sent it back by overhead wire. It used to fascinate me as a child." She thought of purchases made from the Miss Morrises, who kept the shop: knicker elastic, lisle stockings, linen buttons for the dreadful liberty bodices.

"It must seem very different," Richard said kindly.

They talked about the changes she had noticed while the boys ate without comment and Verity toyed with her food, abandoning the meat and barely eating any vegetables. Then Marigold, rather daringly, inquired if the boys liked football.

"Don't ask," said Justin. "Terry got himself into a fair old row in the park while playing, not so long ago."

Marigold could see by Justin's expression that he had said this to cause trouble.

"We don't want to discuss rows on Christmas Day, do we, Justin?" Marigold replied.

She was surprised to see Terry, his mouth full of roast potato, gaze amazed at her and then almost grin. Was that gratitude because she had blocked his brother's attempt to reveal the incident, presumably not mentioned to their parents? She sent another diversionary remark on its way.

"Do you enjoy swimming?" she asked.

Yes, they did. They wanted Cat to install a pool.

"Do you skate?" she asked, and learned that they had roller blades and skateboards, and went occasionally to the ice rink.

She told them about the floods freezing in her youth and how she had skated in the fields. Richard fed her questions. The boys concentrated on their food and, when the pudding, which had flamed effectively while it was carried in, was being eaten, she questioned Verity about her painting, wanting to know which medium she preferred.

Verity ground out responses about oils and gouache. She spoke with such reluctance that Marigold wondered if it was her own presence which had provoked this sour mood. Had there been a fearful quarrel before she arrived? She began to fear this was the answer. Richard would regret his friendly act.

After lunch, the parcels she had brought were opened. There were sweets for the boys—nothing exciting, but she had some toffees left from those she had bought as an answer to Trick or Treat children over Halloween, and had bagged them up in polythene and tied them with ribbon. There was a box of chocolates for Richard and Verity. It was her own Christmas indulgence; otherwise she would not have had a present. There was nobody to give her one, now that she had left the office and was not part of the ritual gift exchange between colleagues.

Then Richard astonished her by handing her a parcel. When she opened it, she found inside an expensive bottle of Chanel No. 5.

She did not see the look of pure hate which Verity directed at him.

"Oh, how lovely!" she exclaimed. "Oh, thank you. I shall enjoy using this." Her opinion of Verity did a turnaround; how generous of her to let this bottle be thus redirected.

"I think most women like that fragrance," said Richard lightly. "I do, certainly," said Marigold, who, when younger, had sometimes sprayed herself with samples. Why shouldn't she enjoy it now, just a tiny dab to add glamour for herself alone?

He took her around the garden after that, and while they were out there, the boys appeared and began kicking Terry's football about. They were showing off, making a lot of noise, heading the ball to one another and toeing it as far as each was able.

Marigold admired their tree house.

"They don't use it much these days," said Richard.

"How old are they?" asked Marigold, and he told her.

"Terry gave us an awful fright a few weeks ago," he said. "That's why Justin was needling him at lunch. He and another boy, Mark Conway—he's about a year younger than Terry—went to the park one Sunday and got into some scrap with a few older boys. It seems they took Terry's ball and kicked it into the road. It caused damage to some cars and the boys might have been in trouble with the police, but luckily there was a witness who had seen what happened. Terry flew into a rage afterwards and didn't come home. He was missing for hours. We had to call the police."

"Oh dear," said Marigold. She was horrified. "What a fright you must have had."

"Yes," said Richard. He did not tell her about the broken window.

Briefly, Marigold considered confessing that she was the mystery witness, but if she did so, what explanation could she give for not admitting to recognize Terry earlier? She and the boy had already connived at a deception. It had better stay that way.

While they were outside, Verity was in the drawing room, finishing the sherry. She stood at the window gazing out over the garden where the two boys romped, cooperatively for the moment, and where her husband, in his waxed jacket, was walking towards the end of the garden with that weird old woman in her camel coat and speckled hat. They were talking animatedly.

He never talked like that to her. There he was, turning to look down at Marigold, and laughing.

Richard, remembering Marigold's fine singing voice in

church, had mentioned the choir of which he was a member and had asked her if she would like to join. They were giving a concert in the town hall the following Thursday. She should try to come.

Marigold promised to do her best, though her house move was taking place the following day.

"I'm so lucky that they're letting me move before completion," she said. "Everything's signed, of course, and the solicitor will hold the money. I'd be very glad to join the choir if I'm found suitable."

Watching them, Verity felt her anger rising. It was ridiculous, she knew, to feel jealous of a woman old enough to be her mother and who looked like a suet pudding, but she was.

13.

Christmas passed relentlessly in prison. In the new year, Alan Morton would be released on license. To aid the process, he had been obliged to express remorse for killing June, when all he really felt was rage at his conviction. It wasn't fair for him to be punished when she was the offender, deceiving him with Phil. Alan had convinced himself that she had meant to leave him. While serving his sentence, he had been a model prisoner, determined to avoid any action which might hinder his return to life outside, but he had made plans for the future. First came vengeance; next, total freedom, which implied escaping from the country.

While his mother was alive, he had bled her with emotional blackmail, painting hopeless prospects for the time when he got out unless he had some money put away. She had opened a building society account for him and had regularly paid in as much as she could put aside from her housekeeping allowance and the savings she had made when, after he grew up, she had returned to work. Before her marriage, she had been a secretary; she had revived her skills and found a post with a firm making furniture, and there she had stayed until his arrest. After that, she lost all heart, and soon, in any case, she reached retirement age.

Each time she came to see him, she told him what the sum now totaled, reminding him that he could adopt a new name easily; there was no need for any legal action. He could start again, wipe the slate clean and make amends in the years ahead. No one need find out about his past.

Her visits bored him, but he placated her with the assurances she sought and said he was following an educational program, aiming at GCSEs in subjects which had eluded him at school. She chose to believe him, but it wasn't true, though he did make an effort to learn Spanish. He was going to live in Spain after his release—Spain, or South America. When he had retrieved the gun, he would kill Phil Wickens who had seduced his wife and so caused Alan's present plight; then he would rob a bank and with the proceeds go abroad. He had planned the bank raid with another man who would be freed soon after Alan; they'd met at the open prison where the last part of their sentences were being served.

It would have been so easy if the old man hadn't died. A visit, a quick trip to the garden after dark, then bingo. After that, if the old man turned his toes up, not to worry: Alan would be on his way and somehow his inheritance would follow him. He hadn't worked out yet how that could be arranged but there would be an answer. As he would not have been responsible for Tom's death, there would be no ban on his inheriting the estate, and though he might have left the country illegally, he would not be a wanted man because he would not be connected with the bank robbery. He and Mick would leave no traces.

Before his last leave expired, he had been to Billerton, spying out the land. He'd stolen a car to drive there, one he'd found parked in a street near the school. He'd learned a lot in prison, and how to steal cars was among his new accomplishments. He'd picked an old one; newer models weren't so easy to lift.

Phil Wickens was married. He had two children and was making a success of running the farm. No doubt his father had died. Well, learning his habits and picking him off with the shotgun would be easy. Or maybe he'd kill the wife and cripple Phil; that might be a better punishment. He'd have to catch them separately as he might need two shots for each of them. That would leave plenty of cartridges for the bank job. They'd saw the barrel off the gun for that; Mick knew more about guns than Alan and he'd regretted that it was not a more powerful weapon. Alan toyed with the idea of shooting him after the raid and going off with all the stolen money, but Mick knew about false passports and where to hide; he was more useful as an ally than a corpse. But perhaps all he needed was a visitor's passport, obtainable over the post office counter on production of some documents. The solicitor acting for his cousin had told him that the house was to be sold and that such papers were safely in his office. They could be collected at Alan's convenience. Soon, it would be most convenient.

How dared the old man leave it all to Penny! What a stab in the back that was, a blow to a man already down. And to think that she would sell the house! He could have settled there, become a respected member of the community, found a new wife, started a business, had the chance he needed to get his life organized. Plenty of people prospered after a spell inside.

Alan had spent hours brooding, turning it over in his mind, working up his anger.

He'd get the gun, whoever had bought the house. No one was going to stop him.

*   *   *

Mark had enjoyed Christmas. His mother and he had left home very early, arriving at The Golden Accord in time for breakfast. He'd already undone his stocking, and had given his mother some soap he'd chosen on Sharon's advice; it was a success and she was delighted. His present, which was waiting at the hotel so that he could ride it in the grounds, was a mountain bike. Peter, the chef's son, already had a good bike and they had ridden round together. The whole day was a festival. There had been a conjuror and there were games Mark and Peter and some other staff children had joined in. The new manager was more tolerant than the last; he said he wanted people to be happy. Mark rather liked him. His name was David and he'd given Mark and the resident staff's children presents. Mark's and Peter's were tool kits for their bikes, so he must have known that Mark would need one. The bike was exactly the right size.

Peter told Mark that David was sweet on his mum.

"P'raps they'll get married," said Peter's older sister, Hazel. It was she, hearing her own mother talking, who had identified the situation. Mark was too young to work out that this accounted for his own presence in the hotel over Christmas, and the freedom he had been allowed.

Once or twice there had been men who had called at the house, given Mum flowers, all that stuff, but none had come more than two or three times. Mum didn't have a boyfriend, like, for instance, Sharon.

"We're all right, the two of us," she'd often said.

He'd agreed with her, but occasionally he felt the burden of responsibility; Mum had no one else. Of course he would look after her when she got old and feeble, and he meant to work hard, get a good job and earn lots of money so that she could take things easy, but it would all depend on him. Some help might be a good idea. He thought about it a bit, in bed that night; it would mean David being with them all the time. Would he mind that? He didn't know. David seemed quite nice.

But Mum hadn't mentioned it at all; she was no different. He decided to forget about it, which was easy when they went home after the weekend. They'd gone to see *Scrooge*, just him and Mum and Kylie in the end; Ivy was too busy. He'd enjoyed it; it was a sad story with a happy ending when the horrid miser saw the error of his ways. They'd had several days together before his mother had to go on duty once again.

He'd finished *Swallows and Amazons*, which he'd taken from The Willows, and had exchanged it for *Coot Club*, which he must return; the house would still be empty so he could go on borrowing books. Ivy said she'd heard The Willows had been sold but she didn't know who had bought it.

"They won't be moving in yet," she had said. "These things take time."

Ivy was worrying about Sharon. She had a new boyfriend, a young chap no older than herself, not working at the moment but intending to become a lorry driver. You had to have a special license for that and Ivy thought you needed several years' driving experience before you could apply, which he hadn't had. He'd spent several nights in Sharon's room with her and the baby, which wasn't right. Ivy had spoken to Sharon who had lost her temper and said she was entitled to some fun and that Keith cared about her. Ivy thought he cared more for her own good cooking and for rent-free accommodation. The next thing would be another baby and a second absent father. Sharon was so careless. What if Keith and Adam's own father, Jason, coincided on a visit? Then the sparks would fly.

Ivy was too busy with the present to dwell on these difficult problems. Two of the children she used to meet for school had moved away, but she had a new toddler to take care of all day. He had to get accustomed to her, be made to feel safe and happy. Sharon's baby fitted in with him, but where was Sharon's help? She was often out now, alleging she was job-hunting. Maybe she was.

Young Mark scarcely seemed to need her, except for eating up his tea with gusto. Susan might save herself some money by cutting down the time he spent, officially, with her. She was working more conventional hours now, and spent fewer nights away from home. Most days, she was back by eight at the latest. The new manager and her promotion had made a difference in her timetable. Still, Mark could get into mischief if he was on his own, free to run wild, though even now he had a busy social life; after his tea he often went to various friends such as Terry Gardner.

For Justin and Terry, once the novelty of their presents had worn off, the holidays dragged. Their stepfather spent hours in his workshop, sculpting away at his wood, or reading in his study, emerging at intervals to see about food if their mother was not functioning. Unlike many offices, Richard's opened between Christmas and the New Year, to his relief. How her children spent their time then was up to Verity; she should make plans for them and take them out. She knew he would provide the cash.

Justin thought Terry's trick of running off that night had been stupid. There were other ways to harass people and cause them grief. You could make bogus telephone calls, pretending there were bombs in shops, or that you'd seen a thief in action, or you could light a fire, run away and come back to watch the firemen put it out—just a little fire, not one to cause a lot of damage. It would be a breeze.

When his mother had set Cat's books alight Justin had found it first frightening, then exciting. Cat had dealt with it quite quickly, but she must have been so cross with him to do a thing like that. It would have served Cat right to lose the lot. The older boys Justin had started to go around with in town got up to various tricks. They not only stole cars to drive for thrills, but lifted things from shops. Justin admired their daring.

Richard had been looking forward to seeing Caroline again. He hoped to spend a few hours in her flat one evening soon, not specifically to make love, though he'd be happy if things worked out like that. He simply wanted to be in a place where he felt easy, to enjoy domestic minutes free from wondering what the next crisis would be and how best to handle it.

Caroline told him she had enjoyed the Christmas break but soon disappointed him.

"I'm sorry, Richard—I'm busy every evening," she declared, on the first day back.

People were, of course; it was the time for entertaining. Even he had his concert, hurrying home on an early train on Thursday. Miss Darwin should be in the audience. She had written a prompt letter of thanks to Verity; her handwriting was small and angular, like that of a classical scholar. Perhaps she was a classical scholar. It had been delivered while they were out.

He worried that Verity might stage a drama to prevent him going to the concert; a wrist-slitting had stopped him on a previous occasion. This time, though, she had forgotten about his plans and he was able to come home, have a quick shower, shave and put on his dinner jacket without alarms, then make himself a sandwich. There was still plenty of ham left; he had bought a huge piece of cooked gammon which, with the remains of the turkey, should keep the household going till he shopped again.

Ready to leave, conscience made him look in at the studio. Rapt, Verity was busy painting. On her easel stood a canvas depicting willows bending in the wind and stormy clouds above troubled gray waters where a small boat tossed; in it, threatened by alarming waves, a female figure lay, Ophelia-like, her head thrown back, reeds clasped in her hand. What troubled thoughts had prompted this? How allegorical was it? When he first met Verity, some of her work had been garish in tone, gaudy colors used for clothes and buildings, and for landscapes, like tropical scenes; now everything was somber. Perhaps this represented her change of mood from hope to despair. Was he responsible for that? Surely, at first, they had shared moments of joy? Now, they seemed to bring out the worst in one another; there were times when he felt like strangling her and he could understand the rage that led to violence. So far, he had always managed to walk away.

She did not look up when he entered the studio. Perhaps she really hadn't seen him. He left a Post-It note on the fridge to say where he had gone; then, banishing his gloomy thoughts, he set off to the concert. Tonight, he would think only of the music.

He saw Miss Darwin sitting in the audience. She had on the maroon dress she had worn on Christmas Day and her serious hair was regimented across her forehead, going into frizzy curls around her head. Was it a desperate perm, he wondered, or had nature dealt her this grizzled wire? He smiled at her as the overture began, the choir in echelon above the orchestra, which was composed of local amateurs and the best players from the school. She nodded in acknowledgment. After that, he forgot her.

Marigold enjoyed the concert. The singers were, she knew, heedless of everything except the music, voices blending, surrendering to the sound they were creating. It was a sort of rapture; she imagined sexual love might be like that. It was the only way in which she had ever let herself go, and even then, the mingled voices were under the rule of the conductor.

The crisp, cold weather had broken and it was wet again. She put up her umbrella as she left the town hall and set forth homewards. Tomorrow she was moving. The Willows was empty now, with everything removed except a few items which it had been agreed that she could buy, notably the contents of the gardenshed; she would need a full set of gardening tools and these had looked to be in good condition. She was taking the existing curtains and carpets; changes could be made later. She was excited; she admitted it, just to herself.

Richard, driving slowly out of the market square where he had parked, saw her trudging along. That determined stride, the rather flat feet in low-heeled shoes, toes turned out, the sober raincoat and the plastic hood over her head under the umbrella which the gusting wind was catching, could belong to no one else.

He slowed down and offered her a lift.

"You are kind," she said, accepting gratefully.

"Half a mile can be a long way on a night like this," said Richard. "Did you enjoy the concert?"

"Yes. It was glorious."

He was surprised to hear her use such an extreme word; moderation, he had sensed, was her mode.

"I'll let you know when rehearsals for the Easter concert begin," he said. "I'm sure they'll love to have you, if you want to join. Something to plan for, eh?"

"Yes," she said again. "I'd like to."

"You move tomorrow, don't you? What weather for it. I hope it clears up by then."

"At least they haven't got to load," said Marigold. "Everything's in store. I've only got a few things at the bungalow."

"You'll soon get straight," said Richard heartily. Had she anyone to help her? The removal men would do it all, he supposed.

"Can I offer you a nightcap?" she suggested, when they drew up at her gate. "Though it's not too orderly inside," she added.

He could not imagine this controlled woman being anything but organized. Probably there were some packed boxes waiting for the van.

"No thanks—I'd better get home," he said. "I'm going to the office tomorrow."

"Perhaps you and your wife will come to sherry one Sunday at The Willows," she said.

"Thank you. We'd like that," said Richard, though Verity would not. She had had plenty to say after Christmas Day about his choice of guest: A boring old crone, had been her verdict. Even Terry had objected, hearing that description.

"She's all right," he'd said. "Rather hideous, though," he conceded.

As she let herself into the bungalow, Marigold reflected that now, in her retirement, she had twice within a week been escorted home by a pleasant man. She could not remember this ever happening before in her adult life, not even by a colleague. Everyone had known that Maddie would get home safely; the old nickname coming from her initials had followed her into the civil service.

Well, she was not too old to enjoy this belated courtesy; she appreciated Richard's kindness, which was not the patronizing false solicitude displayed to older people by some brisk shop assistants. It could be that her time in Haverscot would be the best years of her life; she would be accepted as she was, a plain elderly woman with a good career behind her; she would not be competing in a world where she had never been a starter, the world of the good-looking and attractive.

The next afternoon, at The Willows, as she stood among her packing cases, a bouquet of spring flowers, sent by Interflora, was delivered. They were from Richard. No one—male or female—had ever sent her flowers before. And flowers, too, not a pot plant; she was overwhelmed.

Richard did not quite know why he'd done it. Caroline was going away for the weekend and she left the office early. He had meant to send her flowers to welcome the New Year but as she was not at home, he had been foiled. Perhaps that was why he had chosen Miss Marigold as the recipient. Well, he was sure that she would like them; she had been a tactful guest on Christmas Day when the tensions in the house must have been apparent. She had not made a fuss of the boys but she had not ignored them, and her presence had prevented Verity from making a scene. The holidays were nearly over; soon the boys would be back at school and the country would tick into action once again. It was amazing how one managed to negotiate each obstacle as it came along, learning not to look too far ahead—unlike the world of insurance where anticipating disaster was part of the job.

In the train, he began to think about Caroline. It was more than a fortnight since his last visit to her flat. At the office they maintained a certain distance, not wanting their colleagues to divine their relationship, and that had not changed; she was friendly but cool. However, there was no special look for him when they were alone, which occasionally had been the case in the past, though only ever for an instant. The secret had, to him, been quite exciting.

She wanted it to end; he knew it, with a sense of desolation. She had met someone else and she had not summoned up the courage to tell him. Perhaps she never would. Perhaps she meant it just to fizzle out.

He'd let her go without a struggle. He had enough of that at home. He'd wish her happiness, if he heard she had a new partner. Perhaps she had met someone who wanted to marry her, a man free to do so, and to whom she could respond.

Would he have liked to be that person?

Sitting in the train, Richard admitted that he would. He loved her gently and sincerely; yes, he did, and he had lost her.

Further down the coach was the thin, dark young woman who traveled regularly on this line, the one who walked away from the station. He looked at her as she read her book. What was it? He could not tell. It was a hardback, perhaps from the library. He'd never met her there—he often called in on a Saturday.

He tried to think about her instead of Caroline or Verity. Where did she live? What did she do in London? He might get to know her, if he tried.

But he didn't want to; he didn't want a new entanglement, even if she could be persuaded to enter into one. Besides, she was so thin, like Verity. She might snap, like a twig.

He should be bringing flowers to Verity. Perhaps he'd get some in the morning; the shops were opening tomorrow.

Verity was in the kitchen when he reached home. A savory smell came forth: She'd chopped up ham and turkey and made a spicy sauce; there was a pan of water boiling on the stove, ready to receive the pasta that was waiting to be cooked. She'd washed her hair and wore clean patterned leggings and a white sweater. She even had some scent on; not Chanel, of course. He caught a whiff of it as she came towards him, smiling grimly, lifting up her face to receive a kiss.

He brushed her cheek with his lips. So this was to be her role for the next few hours—or minutes. She was playing the devoted wife. Such intervals never lasted long. Was she sober?

He decided that she might have had one or two drinks, but no pills. That meant she would soon be manic, tearing round, wanting to rearrange the furniture or play charades or some other noisy game. Such ventures always ended in a scene.

"How was your day?" he tried, and heard that she had cleaned the house from top to bottom and remade all the beds with fresh linen.

"And the boys?" he asked, when she ran out of breath. He was longing for a drink. Perhaps he could slip out to The Red Lion after supper. Maybe he could copy her and start keeping a bottle in his workshop, which he always locked because of his tools; the boys might hurt themselves if they went in there and began messing about.

They'd been out all day, she said. She didn't know where. She supposed they'd been down to the river as they'd come home soaking wet.

Richard thought about their safety in the flooded fields. He wondered if they'd had any lunch. Well, they were her children, not his, if she chose to let them drown or starve. He wouldn't provoke her by suggesting she should have some idea of where they spent their time. They were here now; the beat of Justin's pop music was redounding dully in the background.

"Terry had that friend of his, Mark, over for the morning," said Verity. "They came in and got crisps for lunch. Then they went out again."

"And Mark's gone home now?"

"I suppose so." Verity shrugged.

Richard went off to the playroom where he spent some seconds trying to get the boys' attention and an answer to his question.

Mark had left at about five, they said. They'd been to the river doing nothing much but splash about, all three wishing they had a canoe; that would have been brilliant today.

"It would have been dangerous," said Richard, sounding

like a killjoy to himself as he added, "The water is flowing very fast; you could have been swept away or tipped over."

"Well, we can swim," said Justin. "Anyway, why are you steamed up about it, Cat? We haven't got one."

Richard thought he should check up on Mark. He dialed Susan Conway's number, and had an answerphone response. That was new; there had been no reply when he rang the night Terry was missing.

He gave his name and said that he hoped Mark had got back safely; he was simply checking.

Mark saw the light blinking when he returned and he listened to the message. It was therefore not revealed to Susan when she came back later.

Richard had been rather hoping that she would return his call, but she didn't. While he was telephoning, Verity had a few quick slurps from a bottle hidden behind cereal packets in the store-cupboard. This caused her to let the pasta boil too long and the sauce to catch. Even so, her husband and her sons found the meal much more palatable than was usual when she undertook the cooking.

Afterwards, they played Monopoly. The game became rowdy but even Verity seemed to enjoy it; perhaps they could find some contact after all, thought Richard, if only through these sorts of activities. His head began to ache, but he played on doggedly, doing his bit for the cause of domestic harmony.

When the boys had gone to bed, Verity accused him of being patronizing.

"You weren't enjoying it. You looked bored to tears," she said.

"I did enjoy it. I thought it was good that we were all getting on so well," said Richard.

"You kept looking at your watch. You couldn't wait for it to be over."

"It's a long game," he said. Then, suddenly, he lost his

temper. "I've had a hard day at the office, I'm tired and I've got a thumping head, but I've done my best to be a good stepfather—a role model—that's what's thought so necessary today, isn't it? I might as well save myself the effort."

He had been going to pack the game up and put it away, a small task he'd told the boys to do, only to have their mother countermand the instruction and tell them to hurry off to bed, she'd see to it. Now, he pushed the board away from him, leaving the scuffed piles of money on the table, walked out of the room and found his coat. Verity heard the front door bang behind him.

She burst into tears. She'd intended to be nice tonight, to be the good little wife and mother, not to quarrel. She'd played the boring game as well as she was able and hadn't lost her temper. The sherry she'd had before dinner had helped to calm her down and Richard hadn't made a fuss about the meal, though the boys had complained that it tasted burned. She'd woven a fantasy in which she and Richard made rapturous love; surely it had once been like that between them? Yet again it had all gone wrong and he, this time, had been angry, at last reacting to the provocation she applied whenever she had the opportunity. She'd thought him like a piece of dough, impervious to needling; tonight, he'd proved otherwise, and the discovery unnerved her. Where was her safety now, if even Richard had a point at which he might explode?

She'd say that she was sorry. She'd done that before, when she'd gone too far and been frightened that she would lose him, and then what would happen to them? He had stroked and calmed her, then made love, silencing her tears with kisses. The last few times, however, he'd simply said, "I accept your apology," and left the room.

This time, she'd really make him listen; she'd cry and

even go down on her knees. He'd have to turn to her, after that.

But he didn't come back. She waited up for a long time, feeding the fire with logs, sitting by it, shivering. In the end she went to bed, where she swallowed several of her pills, recklessly, with no firm intent to harm herself beyond vaguely thinking, "If I die, that'll show him."

But she didn't die. She sank into a heavy sleep and did not hear Richard stumble in, late and rather drunk. He had been in The Red Lion until the bar closed.

14.

Mark had had a good time with Terry. Later, he and Mum were returning to The Golden Accord for another weekend, with a New Year's Eve party and a big wedding on the Saturday. His mother was quite pleased for him to go to Merrifields that morning, after Terry telephoned to see if he was free. She let him ride his new bike round; David had brought it back for him in his Mitsubishi Space Wagon. Mum had been in a happy mood, but then she was nearly always cheerful, though often in a hurry. She didn't sit about in tears. Mark didn't associate tears with mothers; Ivy never cried, not even—or at least when he was there—after Joe died.

So when he saw Terry's mother crying, he was most surprised.

His own mother had made him promise not to join in any mad schemes Terry might be planning, and if it began to rain hard, he must come home, unless he sheltered in the house waiting for it to stop. In any case, as they had to leave at three o'clock, he must be back well before then.

"That's all right," he said. "I won't forget." He had his watch, which Mum had given him for his birthday.

The boys had climbed into the tree house to survey the area from its branches. Terry did not tell Mark he had hidden there the night he ran away; he didn't want to hear Mark tell him he'd been stupid. From their high perch, the water-covered meadows looked inviting, like a lake.

"Let's go down there," Terry suggested.

Mark agreed. He was wearing his rubber boots. This was not a silly scheme. Terry had his football with him; he seemed attached to it. Mark hadn't noticed that it had been in the tree house, lodged in a corner, when they clambered up. Terry threw it over the fence before crossing himself. There were strong nails to tread on to climb the solid structure.

"Cat doesn't know about these," Terry said. "He doesn't know we go across like this. He thinks the fence is strong enough to keep intruders out. Mum knows. She saw Justin banging them in. She goes over sometimes; she likes walking in the fields."

Mark thought that Cat would find the nails one day. He didn't say so; it was handy to get across like this instead of walking down the road to the path near the church. The two boys kicked the ball about, aiming to send it near the water, and then Terry began throwing it in at the edge, to make a splash. It was a good game, and while Mark found bits of stick which he flung out to float with the tide, pretending they were boats on their way to join the Thames, Terry went on doing it until the ball dropped rather too far out, and he fell in when he collected it. He got drenched.

"Your mum'll kill you," said Mark unsympathetically.

"We need a canoe," said Terry. "I'll ask Cat to give us one."

That sounded good to Mark.

"Will he?" he inquired.

"Of course," said Terry. "I've only got to ask." If Cat said no, he'd make a scene, like Mum and Justin did, and Cat would soon give in.

After his ducking, Terry decided he was too uncomfortable to stay longer in his sopping clothes, so they went back to the house. He left his boots and jacket in the rear lobby by the kitchen door. Mark put his boots there, too, and hung his jacket on a peg. Then they went into the kitchen, where Verity was sitting at the table, crying. She looked at them as they entered but she did not speak, not even commenting on Terry's dripping jeans and socks. Mark thought she had not noticed them; she simply went on crying.

"Oh, Mum," said Terry. He did not ask her what was wrong but picked up a roll of paper towels, pushing it over to her, and tearing off a sheet which he thrust into her unresponsive hand. "She does this," he told Mark, turning away from her and heading for the store-cupboard. He left a trail of water as he crossed the floor. "Come and help yourself," he hospitably invited, opening the cupboard to reveal packs of crisps and canned soft drinks.

Mark did as he was bidden. He was hungry. Glancing at his watch, he saw that it was two o'clock. He'd have to go soon. There was just time to have a little meal. Laden with his selection, he followed Terry to the playroom. Wet footprints marked the polished floor on which were several handsome rugs.

"You're soaked," Mark said. "Hadn't you better change your jeans and socks?" He'd make such a mess if he didn't.

"I suppose," said Terry. He put down his can of Tango and, carrying a pack of crisps, went upstairs eating them and leaving crumbs.

Mark settled on the sofa, eating his. He wondered briefly where Justin was. Out writing on walls with Greg Black or his friends, perhaps. Mark had seen him doing just that, with an aerosol near the scout hut. They'd written a lot of words which Mark knew were very rude; he understood what most of them meant. Ivy, hearing Steve use some of them, had got extremely cross and said that saying them was silly. Mark knew his mother wouldn't like to hear him say them, either.

Poor Mrs. Gardner seemed so sad. What could be wrong? Perhaps she had a pain. He spared her quite a lot of sympathy before turning on the television to watch till Terry came downstairs again.

She was still in the kitchen, sobbing quietly into a wad of paper toweling, when he went past to get his boots and jacket before rescuing his bike from where he'd left it, leaning against the wall of Richard Gardner's workshop. She never noticed him pass by, and Mark decided she'd be most embarrassed if she knew he'd seen her crying. He crept out on tiptoe, almost silently.

Marigold was very busy in the house. The solicitors had employed a firm of cleaners to go through it after the contents were removed, and it was spotless, but she could see where the paintwork was flaking, and the walls were marked where pictures had hung and furniture had stood. The whole place must be redecorated, but meanwhile nothing was offensive to her, and she had slept soundly in her own bed, released from store, the mattress warmed through with an electric blanket.

Sinbad was enjoying the garden. He flapped about in the flood puddles and got very wet, the long feathery hair on his legs saturated. Marigold fussed over him and kept a special towel in the back porch to dry him.

She found some vases where the men had left them on the dining-room floor after unpacking their boxes, and arranged the amazing flowers in two of them. There were so many! Instantly the place seemed brighter, more her own. A glow of pleasure lifted her spirits, which, when she was in the bedroom where the children's books had been, had fallen. Empty, it looked so bleak, though bright patches marked the walls where posters had been fastened. It seemed the disinherited son had been interested in aviation; the posters had shown aircraft, she remembered. What had happened to him? Why was he disowned? Had he vanished?

If she were to disappear, who would notice?

The sudden thought made Marigold shudder. When she died, there would be none who mourned, no one to lament. Oh, a few old colleagues might put on a show of respect, if they knew, but who would tell them? Not her godchildren, who would wonder only what she had left them in her will. She had divided everything between them; what else should she do?

A charity, she thought, but what? One that aided children? Famine relief? Battered wives? A mixture of good causes? She'd think about it, after she was settled in.

Sinbad would miss her, and he needed feeding. She gave herself a shake, pushing away bleak thoughts as she had sought to do throughout her life. The main thing, now, was to look outwards, while getting the house organized. She must join in one or two local activities to give structure to her days; the choral society, as Richard Gardner had suggested, would be a start. There was probably a charity shop where she could be usefully occupied, she thought, depressed at the very notion. And she'd get back to her découpage; now she could unpack everything—the plain wooden boxes waiting to be embellished, the varnish, the glue, the small neat scissors. She'd use the dining room as a working area; her large table, covered with a protective cloth, would make a perfect surface. She'd keep her desk there, too, for all her business papers and her files. She would eat in the kitchen which was large enough to hold a good-sized table and six chairs, but she did not expect to entertain. She could not see Verity Gardner coming willingly to lunch or dinner, and whom else would she ask?

On Sunday she would go to church, and if the Gardners were there, she'd invite them back to sherry. How many other people went to church, as she did, to punctuate their lives, with no particular belief to support? A good few, she guessed, including Richard, who would find peace there.

Why did she know he needed that? Marigold was not perceptive about other people and interacted with so few; at work, contact with her colleagues had been superficial, for which she blamed herself, knowing her brusque awkwardness did not endear her to them. Already, though, in Haverscot, she had sensed Richard's sadness. Why did his wife drink? Why had the silly small boy gone into hiding? Why had he and she forged a secret bond between them? What was wrong with that family? Was it Richard's fault? Could he be a villain in disguise?

Surely not. He must be what he seemed—a decent, ordinary man, such as many she had met, on superficial terms, at work.

If there were any chance that they might come so soon, she must get the sitting room in order. Spurred on, she plugged in the vacuum cleaner to sweep up behind the removers.

When everything was arranged as far as she could manage, and there was no more that she could do, silence fell at The Willows. Even Sinbad had gone to sleep in front of the gas fire. At the bungalow, there had been the distant buzz of traffic; even, when the wind was in the right direction, the sound of a train. Here, as she listened, she heard the rain begin again, a swishing sound, and the spattering it made on the flagged terrace beyond the windows. She knew a moment's desperation; then her gaze fell on the flowers. She would not give way to dread; instead, she would go out to dinner, have a meal at The

Red Lion. During her weeks at the bungalow, she had been there several times. A good steak and some burgundy would set her up. She was used to dining out alone in unassuming places; it was one luxury she could afford and which had become easier to handle as she grew older. She did not need the restaurant staff to like her, merely to respect her.

Respect was lacking nowadays. She meant to command it, where possible, for herself.

She did not hurry over her meal, enjoying the steak, followed by an excellent crème brûlée. She sipped her wine and drank her coffee. The hotel was small; it had two stars, and she had stayed there while she found the bungalow, sleeping in a comfortable room with an uneven floor, a beamed ceiling and a small mullioned window overlooking the market square. She'd occupied a double bed—the hotel had only one small single room, without a bathroom of its own—and she'd wondered what it was like to have someone lying there beside you, touching. Years ago, when she was young, she'd expected the experience; she knew no one would fall in love with her, but she thought she might experience a flirtation or a holiday romance. Neither had ever come her way. Yet she could have loved someone. Children could have followed. She'd known none well, not even her godchildren in their youth.

Perhaps she would get to know Richard Gardner's stepsons, now that they were neighbors. But they didn't like him, calling him Cat in a tone that held no affection. She had been astounded by Terry's escapade; what had made him behave in such a way? The boys were not in any trouble; he should have gone straight home. What about the other boy? Children could be very naughty and act unpredictably; some were even wicked. Perhaps, by having none, she had been spared a lot of worry. Those two weren't Richard's own children; did that make a difference?

Could you love the child simply because you loved its mother?

She paid her bill and rose to leave, passing the bar on her way out. Something made her glance inside. The room was busy, but not so crowded that she did not see Richard, who was standing by the counter, a brandy goblet in his hand. She paused. He was not talking to the people near him; indeed, he looked morose, almost desolate.

Marigold very nearly went to speak to him, to thank him for the flowers, but she held back. She wasn't good in crowded bars and there was something so dejected about his appearance that she felt he might not want anyone he knew to recognize his misery.

Though of course, as a longtime resident of Haverscot and member of the choral society, he must know others who were in the bar.

Perhaps he came here often in the evening, but she had never noticed him when she was staying at the inn.

15.

Marigold had not looked inside her garden shed since moving into The Willows. Water lapped around it, a large pool in a hollow of the lawn around a bare weeping willow, the rest of the lawn soft and saturated. She liked the pool; birds fluttered on it; she had seen a wild duck and there were several moorhens, but keen gardeners might suggest that drains should be sunk under the turf. She would consider it, she thought, at last stepping down the garden to inspect the collection of tools which she had bought. She wore her wellingtons, ones with strong ridged soles in case the ground was slippery, and an old raincoat, with a rainproof hat. As she walked along the brick path which wound its way towards the bottom of the garden, she saw bulbs thrusting through the ground on either side: daffodil spikes, and the greener stems of grape hyacinths. Discovering what lay beneath the ground would be exhilarating, Marigold decided, still reluctant to admit excitement, though she had felt it several times in recent weeks.

Inside, the shed smelled damp and musty; the window glass was grimed and masked with cobwebs. It must all be cleaned up, but not now. At least the floor was solid concrete, dry under her feet, and the tools were tidily arranged, a spade and several forks in different sizes suspended by their handles, a besom brush upended in a corner, various rakes. The mower was an old Atco. Did it work? If not, she'd have to get a new one. She might have to pay a man to come and cut the grass; there was a lot of it and it would take more than an hour to do, she estimated. She'd often done the mowing for her parents and had enjoyed walking up and down behind the machine. Her parents' mower had been tricky to get started and temperamental when in action; doubtless modern ones were easier to operate. She need make no decision about what was best until the grass began to grow, perhaps in March.

Flowerpots were stacked neatly on a bench, some old earthenware ones and newer ones made of plastic. Trowels and other implements were well cleaned; there were few signs of rust. She'd made a good purchase.

She closed the door and left. There was no bolt, but, not visible from the road, the shed would surely not attract a thief, and its contents were of small value. If she bought a new, expensive mower, though, perhaps she ought to lock it up. She'd heard no talk of local burglaries, but nobody was immune to predators.

Richard had not been in church on Sunday, so she had been unable to invite him and Verity back to sherry. She had written him a note of thanks for the flowers and posted it—cowardly, in a sense, since if she had delivered it, he would have received it promptly, but she did not want to risk meeting his prickly wife without warning. She'd ask them round another time.

Mr. Phipps, the estate agent, had suggested a painter who could come and tackle the redecorating. Her own bedroom would be first, and she must decide what to do about that sad room where the children's books had been. For some reason she felt uncomfortable in there, as though an unhappy ghost lingered in the shadows. It was a fanciful idea: Instead of speculating about the estranged son of Mr. Morton, she should think of the happy spinster sisters who had lived here in her childhood. Even so, her thoughts kept returning to question marks about the Mortons. How would the niece use her windfall? Had she been kind to her beneficent uncle? Had he been to visit her in Canada?

Marigold's own income was assured; her pension was a good one and, with some investments she had made, she had no financial worries. Thanks to her own inheritance, she had seen her capital increase; the London house had financed the purchase of The Willows. She had never known material insecurity and that gave her a form of confidence, but she had also had a successful career; if she had done less well, her pension would have been less generous. She was lucky; things that worried other people did not apply to her.

When she had seen the painter she felt optimistic. He could start almost at once; in winter, work fell off, and these days many people did their own decorating, especially indoors. They discussed colors and the order in which the rooms should be tackled. Marigold thought she would probably have the kitchen completely refitted but that could wait; she wanted to test its layout before deciding on a plan. As it was, the inoffensive cream worktops and pale green cupboards were, though showing signs of wear, pleasant enough. Her fridge from London fitted into the slot where Mr. Morton's smaller one had stood. It was relatively new, solid, with a freezer on the top which held enough emergency supplies for one person. If she grew soft fruit, perhaps she would need a larger one, but that was for the future.

"We'll be busy, Sinbad," she said, when Mr. Samson, the

painter, had agreed upon a date to start. He would have a
mate to help him, he had said, which reassured Marigold,
for he was very small and thin, unlike his namesake.

She would have company, too; it might stimulate her.
Since stopping work and having no particular timetable for
her day, she had slowed up. Until a few months ago, she
had risen early and tidied up her London house before
leaving for the office. There, she had made decisions and
written directives, all to a prescribed policy with which she
did not necessarily agree but which was customary in her
department; her mind was working actively. Now, visiting
the supermarket was a major feature in her life, and
choosing furnishing fabric rather special.

She still took Sinbad to the park, which was drier than
the garden; besides, he needed more exercise than it
provided. She knew several other dog owners by sight, but
was too inhibited to greet them unless they first spoke to
her. Unaware that she appeared forbidding, with her hat
drawn down over her brows and her face set in an
expression which reflected not ill-humor, but determination,
she seemed to discourage friendly greetings, and any
tentative approach some walker might have made was
stillborn because she never looked at those approaching.
Marigold walked firmly onwards, eyes to the front, like a
guardsman on parade.

She wrote inviting Richard and Verity to sherry on a
Sunday in the middle of January, but received no reply.
Richard had not even seen her letter, which Verity had left
lying on the table in the drawing room. Later, she had
picked it up with a pile of magazines and it was
sandwiched between them. Verity forgot about it.

Though she found it odd that they had not answered,
Marigold prepared for them. She'd bought flowers to
replace those Richard had sent her; she had provided tiny
toasts spread with cheese or fishy mixes; she had cut thin

squares of brown bread and butter and laid smoked salmon on them. No one came.

She thought of telephoning to see if there was a misunderstanding, but if it was their error, they might be embarrassed. If they'd simply forgotten, they'd remember later and would telephone. But they didn't.

She felt obscurely sad. Richard would not have been deliberately rude; she knew that. Verity, however, was unpredictable, at least to Marigold.

Three sherries cheered her up, and she began to sing while putting Sinbad's meal in his bowl. She ate most of the smoked salmon herself; the rest, she saved for supper.

Mark wanted to return *Coot Club* to The Willows and exchange it for another sailing adventure. He was sure Tom would want him to go on borrowing books. One evening, when Steve had gone into the town to meet his friends and so could not be curious about Mark's activities, he told Ivy he was going to see Terry, and set off.

Soon he was marching down The Willows's drive, in pitch darkness. He'd forgotten his torch. Never mind. He'd find the door.

He fumbled about seeking the lock, and managed to insert the key. Once inside, he located the light switch and turned it on. He was surprised to find that things were different. There was a new carpet in the hall, and an unfamiliar table, a chair with a tapestry seat, other pictures on the walls. He examined one which showed a square-rigged ship in full sail; he liked the look of that.

Not apprehensive, simply intrigued, he went into the sitting room. Sofa and matching chairs, covered in blue fabric, stood on Tom's carpet. The television was a small modern one. There was a CD player and he inspected that with interest. Steve had acquired enough money to buy one and Mark, though happy with his own ghetto blaster, thought it great.

He touched nothing, walking carefully round the house in his socks. He had left his shoes by the front door, as he and Steve had always done. Finally, after a thorough inspection of the ground floor, he went up to the room where the books were kept.

It was completely empty. Even the curtains were gone and the window showed dark against the sky. Smeared, faded wallpaper was marked with squares where posters had hung. The bookshelves, which had been put up by Tom many years before, were in position, scratched and chipped, but bare.

Mark's heart began to thump. He couldn't exchange the book, which had been his plan, but he could replace *Coot Club.*

He laid it sideways on a shelf and then turned towards the door.

A figure stood framed in the doorway. It was a woman in an overcoat. She held a heavy torch in her hand. Miss Darwin had picked it up in the hall on her return from taking Sinbad to the vet. He had suddenly developed stomach trouble, writhing round in pain, and they had traveled to the surgery in a taxi. She had had to leave him there, for he might need an operation. They had left the house well before dark, and she had not expected to be long. Returning, she saw lights on in the house. She had let herself in with care, making no noise, and had almost fallen over a pair of sturdy black lace-up shoes, not very large, by the front door. She had expected to find several vandals in the house, small ones, breaking the place apart. Instead, she saw one boy, not five foot tall, staring at her, terrified.

Miss Darwin was the first to recover, and she recognized him.

"You're one of the boys from the park," she said. "You're a friend of Terry Gardner's. You're Mark." At that moment she could not remember if she had ever heard his surname. He looked anything but menacing, standing by the bookcase, gazing up at her. "What are you doing in my house?" she asked.

Mark had retreated towards the window as he realized who she was. She had on the same grim hat, pulled down, and the same coat. He saw the big, heavy torch she held. Her attitude was threatening, but when Miss Darwin saw his fear, she took a backward step.

Mark swallowed.

"I didn't know anyone was living here," he said. "I brought back a book old Tom—Mr. Morton—lent me." He gestured towards *Coot Club*, lonely on the shelf.

"Hm." Miss Darwin crossed over, scrutinized the book and saw written inside, *Alan Morton, from his mother*, and the date, in 1958. "Did you enjoy it?" she asked.

"Yes. I was going to borrow another," Mark said, courage seeping back. This old woman wasn't a witch, though she looked so fierce; she had saved him and Terry in the park.

"I'm afraid you can't," she was saying. "As you see, all the books have gone and I've moved in. I live here now. How did you get in?"

"I had a key," said Mark. "I used to come and see Tom. Me and Steve did. Every night, mostly. We played chess and watched telly with him."

"Who's Steve?"

"Steve Burton. Ivy's son. Well, not her real son. His dad died but he stayed on with Ivy. I go there after school till my mum gets back from work."

"Aren't you meant to be at Ivy's now?" queried Miss Darwin.

"I'm on my way to see Terry," Mark said promptly, but it wasn't true, though he'd told Ivy that was where he was going. He had planned to stay at The Willows till it was time to go home.

"So late?"

"It's not that late," said Mark. "Six o'clock?" he hazarded.

Miss Darwin checked her watch.

"Nearly half past," she said. "You'd better come downstairs," she added. "Leave the book."

She led the way, Mark following, watching the sturdy shoulders under the coat. In the hall, she took it off and crossed to hang it in the cloakroom. She removed her hat, not glancing at her hair in the mirror; she knew it would be orderly, compressed for hours beneath the hat. Then she returned to look at the small miscreant who was standing on the Indian carpet in the center of the hall. He wore his school trousers, rather baggy, bought big to cater for his rapid growth. His socks were gray. Except for the slightly different clothes—instead of a blazer and shorts, Mark's trousers were long and he had on a navy anorak—he might have been William Brown incarnate.

"Have you read about William and his friends?" Miss Darwin asked. "Henry was one, and Ginger," she remembered.

"Oh yes. I borrowed them from Tom," said Mark. "They made me laugh."

"They made me laugh, too," Miss Darwin said, gravely.

She looked less alarming without her hat. She couldn't help being so ugly, he thought kindly; she was old.

"Would you like a drink?" she suggested. "Milk? Or orange juice?" She could not send him off abruptly and she must decide how to deal with him. In his own eyes, he had not transgressed.

"Orange juice, please," he said promptly.

"Take off your jacket," Miss Darwin instructed. "Hang it in the cloakroom. Then come into the kitchen. I'm sure you know your way around this house." Better than I do, she reflected. Perhaps he had already helped himself from her stores, she thought, but saw at once that he had touched nothing. She took a carton of juice—she always had it for breakfast—from the fridge and poured some into a glass, then found a packet of chocolate biscuits. "Would you like one of these?" she said.

"Yes, please," said Mark, and added. "Thanks."

He'd stood his ground, Miss Darwin recollected, when the two motorists had been so angry. Terry had been about to flee, but Mark had denied their responsibility for what had happened.

"Terry will be expecting you. Perhaps you should ring him up and say you've been delayed," she proposed.

"No—it's all right," Mark assured her. "I only said I might come round. It wasn't definite."

"I see." Miss Darwin did not think another hunt for a missing boy who had not really disappeared would be desirable. "Very well. Come and sit down and tell me about the books you've read."

She had arranged three chocolate biscuits on a plate, which she put, with the juice, on a tray, just like at Mum's hotel, thought Mark admiringly, used to drinking out of cans and tearing open packs of crisps; then she led the way to the sitting room. Mark ate his biscuits very fast and neatly, careful not to drop crumbs on the floor, though some landed on the front of his gray school sweater. He noticed them and spiked them with a damp finger, then conveyed them to his mouth. He looked quite composed, setting his glass back on the tray which Miss Darwin had put on a coffee table in front of him.

"Where's your dog?" he asked her.

While he was drinking his juice and eating his biscuits, Miss Darwin had poured herself a stiff whiskey, adding soda water. Bottles and glasses were in a cupboard built into a corner of the room. Tom had kept tapes and videos in there, and the games.

"He's at the vet's," said Miss Darwin. "He's not at all well, I'm afraid. He's probably got to have an operation. He'll be there a day or two."

"Oh dear," said Mark. "That's sad. But he'll get better," he assured her, bracingly.

Miss Darwin knew that this was far from certain.

"I hope so," she said.

"When he is, I could come and see him," Mark offered. "I could take him for walks for you."

"Thank you," said Miss Darwin, taken aback but touched.

"I miss coming here," Mark confided. "It was so sad about Tom, but he looked quite peaceful."

"You saw him?" Miss Darwin was astonished.

"Yes. Steve and me came in as usual, and he was in his chair, not moving, like asleep," said Mark. He blinked, and Marigold, in some strange, visceral manner, knew that he had suffered a big loss and was grieving.

"And you've been coming in since then." It was a statement.

"Not many times," said Mark. "But it's nice here. It still is," he added politely.

"Do your parents know you come here?"

"There's only my mum. I haven't got a dad. I never have had one, not like Steve. His died, as I said," Mark answered. "Mum works at The Golden Accord. That's why I go to Ivy's."

Miss Darwin had not heard of The Golden Accord. She imagined a pub, with his mother a barmaid.

"And where do you live?" she pursued.

"In Grasmere Street," he said. "Ivy's house isn't far from there. I see myself home at night now."

"As you've changed your mind about going to see Terry, perhaps you should be thinking about doing that soon," said Miss Darwin, though she was reluctant to part with her unusual guest.

"I needn't go yet," said Mark, expansively. Tom had enjoyed his visits; this old lady might, too. But she wasn't a bit like a gran, he thought, not at all cuddly and spoiling, as they were meant to be. Some of his friends had them, but Mark rarely met one. "Can you play cards?" he asked.

Miss Darwin had neither cards nor a chess set, nor anything Mark thought might provide her with a pastime. She was about to question him about his tastes in literature when he asked her about her activities in the dining room.

"I saw you'd got some paste and stuff in there," he said. "What's it for?"

She showed him, and he was impressed, unstintingly admiring the small boxes she was decorating. She showed him how she grouped the neatly cut-out flowers, and explained that they needed several coats of varnish to harden it all off.

"Very nice," he said, then, graciously, he took his leave.

She watched him go down the drive into the darkness. The nearest street lamp was twenty yards away. She thought he turned to wave to her before he vanished, and, not certain, she waved back.

She must have security lights put up, she decided: one at the front and another at the back. If he could get in so easily, so could a thief, who would not need a key.

He hadn't given his back to her. He could still get in. Did it matter? Perhaps she ought to change the locks. She'd think about it in the morning.

Marigold poured herself another drink; soon a warm glow of fleeting pleasure filled her, until her thoughts returned to Sinbad. She forgot about the key.

16.

Sinbad did not recover from his operation. Marigold missed him and understood that by growing fond of him, she had become vulnerable in a manner she had not permitted herself for years. She would not get another dog; at least, not yet.

Without him, she was freer. She could go to London for the day; to leave him for so long would have been impossible. She made several expeditions, enjoying them, though drenched one night when she returned in pouring rain. Surely this was the wettest winter for very many years, she thought, plodding flat-footedly towards home. Haverscot station was on the very limits of the town; its booking office closed around midday and there were no taxis on the spot; to get one, you must telephone. She should pursue her plan of buying a car and refreshing her ability to drive. There had been a car in Mr. Morton's garage, a well-kept Ford Escort; he hadn't been able to drive it since his illness, she'd been told. Like all his other possessions, it was sold.

She'd need something small, just a little box on wheels to get about in. With one, she could visit stately homes and study famous gardens. It must be in good condition, so that it would not let her down.

She went to the Fabergé exhibition and to several matinées, a muted figure in the audience, responding to the drama in a manner she had not enjoyed before. The audience was the fourth wall of a room, peering in. She had peered briefly through the fourth wall of life at Merrifields, she thought one night when she noticed Richard Gardner sitting further down the coach on her returning train. He was reading, and did not notice her until they climbed the steps to cross the bridge at Haverscot station. She wondered what his book was, to insulate him from the journey so successfully.

When he recognized her, he offered her a lift home and, gratefully, she accepted. She told him not to take her to the door; she would soon walk the short distance from Merrifields to her own house. However, he insisted.

"It's a foul night. You'll get soaked," he said. She would have, if he hadn't come along. He'd seen the thin young woman, too, striding off, umbrella raised, wearing boots today. She looked a bit like Verity had done when he first met her: pale and anxious.

Miss Darwin, though, was very different, and a safer case to transport in his car. She told him she had seen him in the train, intently reading, and he said that he was catching up with Trollope. She'd read none of the novels.

"I go more for biographies and travel," she confessed.

"I was never one for the classics," Richard answered. "But I like the gentle pace of these. People behave very badly but on the whole everyone's so civil."

He turned in at the gateway of The Willows, drawing up outside her door. She had turned the porch light on before she left that morning, but no light showed.

"Oh dear—the bulb must have gone," she said. "I knew it would be dark when I got home, so I left it burning."

"Have you got a spare? Let me change it for you," Richard offered.

"Oh—that's very kind of you," said Marigold, who would have needed to perch on steps to reach the socket. "Yes. I know I've got some bulbs."

While he changed it, she told him she intended to have security lights fitted, and he suggested an electrician she could use.

When the job was done, she offered him a drink, thinking he must be eager to get home and would certainly refuse, but he accepted a large whiskey. She poured another for herself.

"I'm almost home. No Breathalyzing bobby will be waiting in the road," he said, and sank back in a big armchair while Marigold lit the fire. "Gas—how wonderful," he said. "No work or ashes."

"It was already here. It's very convenient," she said. "But you don't get mysterious shapes and patterns in it, like you do with ordinary coal or logs."

For someone who professed not to read fiction, this was an illuminating comment; she would enjoy it, if she tried it, Richard thought.

He had gulped down a large amount of his drink almost as soon as they were seated, facing one another. Marigold saw, with concern, that he looked dreadful. He was very pale, with dark patches underneath his eyes.

"I needed that," he said, indicating his glass. "Thanks."

She remembered her sight of him in the bar at The Red Lion. Drink, she had learned, could alleviate despair, could bring a sense of ease and even joy. Until lately, she had never let herself experience this; only now, in her retirement, where there was no witness, had she discovered this pleasure, one which could be easily abused.

"A hard day?" she asked.

He nodded.

She waited in case he wanted to enlarge on this, but instead he seemed to give himself a shake and began talking about the choral society. He knew when it would meet again and said that he would take her.

He couldn't really want to do that, she reflected, looking at him, a middle-aged man, perhaps attractive—she did not really know about that—though, tonight, his face looked ravaged. Something terrible must have happened; perhaps his wife was leaving him, though would that be so awful, since their relationship was clearly, even to a stranger and one not well versed in such matters like herself, far from easy? Perhaps he was simply lonely.

So was she. Marigold had been lonely all her life but she had never admitted it to herself before. She rose, refilled his glass and her own, and went out to the kitchen, returning with some crisps in a small dish. She had bought them in case that boy, Mark, called again. Children lived on crisps, she had heard.

"A little blotting paper," she suggested. Her father used to use that phrase. "For us both," she added, offering them.

While she was out of the room, Richard's thoughts had left the present, returning to his interview with Caroline that lunchtime. She had asked him to meet her at an Italian restaurant they had been to before. She was looking very well, he saw; there was a glow about her and she was fuller in the face.

"I've got something to tell you," she had said.

She was getting married; that was what it was, he felt certain, and he prepared himself to hear the news.

She insisted that they order their meal before she told him anything, then asked about Verity and the boys, trying, he bristlingly decided, to remind him of his own responsibilities before mentioning her plans. It was not until they were drinking their coffee that she made her announcement and then he was, literally, dumbfounded; he could not speak for quite two minutes, simply sitting there, incredulous.

"I want to tell you before it's all round the office," she said. "I'm pregnant. I'm not sure if you're the father, or another man I've been seeing for some time. He lives down in Wiltshire. He's married, too—a former boyfriend." She'd paused to sip some of the house red wine, a Bardolino. He'd noticed that she drank very little of it, asking for some Perrier. "I decided I wanted a child before it was too late. I don't want a husband, though," she added. "I was meeting the other man—let's call him X—from time to time, with this in mind, but nothing happened. He'd got some children, so I felt sure that he was fertile. Anyway, I decided to try someone else." She was looking at him all the time she was talking, and Richard was staring at her, aghast.

"Me," he managed to croak.

"Yes." She smiled at him, a maternal smile, he recognized, with horror. "I'm so fond of you. You're a nice man, and bright. Suitable," she said. "That makes it sound so cold and calculating, but we had some happy times together, didn't we?"

They had. He could not deny it, but it had been false, simply for a purpose: to acquire his acceptable genes.

"I don't know which of you is, in fact, the father," she repeated, smiling still, a Judas smile. He had never heard of anything so cold-blooded. "I don't want any money or support. I can take care of my own child." She smiled again. "A test could prove paternity, but who wants that? It's better to leave it vague, don't you think?"

"Are you going to tell this X?" Richard asked at last.

"Not specifically. We have mutual friends. He'll hear like that," she said. "Just as you would have, in the office, but I didn't want you to be alarmed."

Richard was profoundly shocked. That was his chief emotion. His sperm had been hijacked. He'd been robbed.

"Won't this child need a father?" he managed to inquire.

"Oh no. There'll be men around. My brother, and my father's very fit. He'll have grandparents for quite a while, I hope," Caroline said calmly. "I'll get a really good nanny and send him or her to a first-class school."

She could afford it. He knew that. The child would be well cared for, was wanted, and would probably be loved.

"Will it thank you for giving it no father and no siblings?"

"It might have siblings," Caroline replied. "There's time."

"You'll have to find another sire, then. I'm not going to be used like this again," said Richard. "Maybe X will oblige, or you'll find someone else to play this game with. A younger man, perhaps."

"Don't be bitter, Richard," Caroline reproved him. "It's not like you. Remember, I needn't have told you anything."

"No," he agreed. "I suppose not."

He finished his coffee, then, before she could do so—it had, after all, been her invitation—he secured the bill and paid it, tipping lavishly.

"I've upset you," Caroline observed. She looked surprised. "I thought you might feel flattered that I chose you."

Richard managed not to say that she had exploited him; somehow, he succeeded in leaving the restaurant without losing his temper or his outward poise. He had a wretched afternoon, accomplishing almost nothing in his office, and, in the train, had found it impossible to concentrate upon his book, reading the same page over and over again, not absorbing anything.

People were going mad, he thought; young girls in poor areas got pregnant in order to obtain a flat and so leave home, or more practically, to have someone to love and to love them: a living doll. What emotional demands did single mothers make upon such children? When they turned from toddlers into ten-year-olds, some went out of control.

Caroline would have expectations from her child: love and loyalty, maybe to excess.

Young Mark Conway's mother was alone. What was her story? She might be a widow. Whatever her situation, she was making a success of the boy, and she seemed pleasant. He suspected Mark's conception was not the result of feckless conduct.

Sitting in front of Marigold's gas fire, staring at the flames which, as she had said, made no new patterns, simply repeating their own formula, he felt an impulse to tell her what Caroline had done, but he refrained. She would not want to hear it, and anyway, what could she do? She might not even understand.

But she had news for him.

"I had a visitor a little while ago," she said. "Young Mark Conway, Terry's friend." She did not say that he had entered the house uninvited. "He came to return a book he'd borrowed from Mr. Morton, the previous owner of this house."

"Oh yes? What was the book?"

"A good one. *Coot Club*," said Marigold. "Arthur Ransome. I loved those books when I was young. Mr. Morton had the whole set, it seems, and dozens of other children's books. Mark had been visiting him and borrowing them."

Richard hid a smile. Here was someone who eschewed fiction, yet she had read it in her youth.

"What happened to them? The books, I mean," asked Richard.

"They were sold, with all his other things," said Marigold. "If I'd known about the boy, perhaps I could have bought the children's books."

"I wish Justin and Terry read Arthur Ransome," Richard said. "They barely read at all, and when they do, it's horror stories."

"Did you know Mr. Morton?"

"Not really. By sight, before he had his stroke. We said good morning, that kind of thing," said Richard. "He went to pieces after his wife died."

They went on talking about Mr. Morton and his sad decline, and the pathos of selling someone's possessions after their death, then moved to Marigold's plans for the garden.

Richard left at last, feeling much calmer, but Marigold knew that inside, he was screaming with pain.

She poured herself another drink, and after a while she put a disc on her new music system. Soon she forgot Richard, and even Sinbad faded from her mind.

17.

Though he was desperate to retrieve the gun and store it safely, Alan did not visit Haverscot during his next leave. Instead, he found a flat in a part of Reading largely occupied by transients, an anonymous area where people came and went unchallenged as long as they paid their rent. He paid for two months in advance, telling the landlord that his job involved traveling and he would be away a lot.

"No problem," said the landlord, happy with the cash. His new lodger looked respectable enough, clean, with trimmed hair and wearing dark trousers and a corduroy jacket. Alan had always been a sharp dresser.

He spent the weekend in the flat enjoying sybaritic pleasures such as lying in a steaming bath, and sleeping late. On Saturday night he went out to dinner in an expensive restaurant, eyeing the other customers; in this place, many were middle-aged, enjoying what they ate and drank, living in the moment. Alan looked at the women, most of them well dressed, some overweight, some pretty, prepared, in his opinion, to lie and cheat to get what they wanted from their dupes, the men. He scorned them all, but later, in the bar, he picked one up, a smart tart who had a room not far away. He'd boast of that to Mick, when he went back, make a good story from their short encounter. He felt nothing for her; that was not her function. Still, she was better-looking than some and he soon showed her who was in charge. Sex was not important to Alan; power was.

The flat was barely furnished, but it was adequately equipped for what he and Mick would need. There were two bedrooms, a tiny kitchen and a bathroom, and a sitting area. It was spacious after what he was used to. He could hide the gun here, once he'd got it out. He examined the floorboards; they could be prized up and it could lie there safely. So could the cash; he'd remove the rest from the building society as soon as he was out for good.

Alan stayed in bed for most of Sunday morning, but then he went out looking for a bank to rob, one that was well placed for leaving promptly, where a car could be left nearby. He marked down several, and disqualified others. Mick, he knew, had contacts, people who would make it easy for them to go abroad once the job was done. There was nothing for him here, in England, not now. He'd find it hard to get a worthwhile job with status, after what had happened, but if he'd inherited The Willows and the money, he could have started up a business of his own, gone straight. He had been unlucky; June had spoiled everything for him in Billerton. Alan conveniently forgot that until he went there, he had never stayed in one place long because an action of his own had always ended in some sort of trouble.

All women were traitors, even his mother. On her final visit to him in the prison, she had told him that he was not Tom's son. She was pregnant by another man when they were married, and Tom still didn't know the truth, but she could bear her secret no longer; after telling Alan, she was going to reveal the truth to Tom. He had been her childhood sweetheart and, while he was a prisoner of war, they had corresponded. Meanwhile, she had met someone else. Then Tom returned, just as she and the other man ended their transitory romance when she discovered that he was going out with another girl. Later, by chance, she and the man had met again and had spent their only night together; he had cajoled her, and she had given in, knowing at once that she had made a terrible mistake and that Tom was the man she really loved. They were married within a few weeks, and by then pregnant, she resolved that Tom should never know that he was not the father. In those days, abortion was illegal and difficult to arrange. Saying nothing was the easiest way out and anyway, perhaps she would miscarry; but she didn't, and on Alan's infant face she saw a likeness to his natural father. This recurred throughout the years that followed, but it was more a facial expression than a physical resemblance. Both of them, though, were selfish individuals; no one mattered other than themselves. That was why she had succumbed, that night; she could not say that she was raped, but she had been a most reluctant lover.

She had spent her whole life trying to make up to Tom for her deception. She'd hoped for other children, but none had come along, part of her punishment, she told herself. Tom, meanwhile, had never failed Alan, always there, trying to mitigate the consequences of his actions, always a good example of what a man should be.

She would not tell Alan who his real father was.

"I heard he'd died," she said. "We're all old now."

After this revelation, Alan had brooded on his new knowledge, wondering if he had half brothers and sisters, other relatives, curious about the man himself. Was he successful? Was he rich? Since his mother knew that he was dead, she would know the answers to the questions crowding in his mind. Alan mentally ran through his parents' circle of friends; was any of those men his father? Was there one in whom his mother showed interest? Did he look like any of them? He was not in the least like Tom, and now that was explained.

Dorothy Morton knew that Tom had blamed himself for Alan's failings. Now, at long last, she would release him from unnecessary guilt. If heredity had any bearing on the matter, Tom was not culpable.

After her confession, she gave up on life, eventually dying more of despair than any precise illness, and then Tom changed his will. He owed Alan nothing, and it was a relief to know that he was not the father of a murderer, but was a tendency to kill inherent? Surely not, and surely upbringing could counteract a leaning towards violence? Every family had its black sheep; all that might be needed to trigger a latent impulse was a certain situation, and perhaps poor June provoked the worst in Adam, by default. Tom's sorrow was immense. Now he understood Dorothy's gentle fading through their life together; all the sparkle she had had when young had gradually disappeared, but she had loved the boy; there was no doubt of that.

Alan, in prison, concocted various stories which satisfactorily removed responsibility from himself for any misfortune, large or small, real or imaginary, that had occurred during his entire life. For want of another villain— he would not cast his mother in that role—his wrath was concentrated on Tom. Punishments were remembered: pocket money docked; chores enforced; his bicycle locked up, its use forbidden for a period. That was a favorite act of retribution, imposed because it curtailed Alan's freedom. By the time he reached The Willows in November, all Alan's old wounds were reopened, raw, and he was eager for revenge.

He supposed his mother had carried out her intention of telling Tom the truth. She might have chickened out; there had been no reaction, no angry letter or irate visit, simply silence from the pair of them, although his mother had continued paying money into his building society account. After she stopped coming to see him, he had no visitors; she had been his only one. He hadn't requested an official prison visitor; he did not need a stranger prying into his affairs. When, at last, he reached the open prison, with its rehabilitation program, including shopping trips and work experience outside the premises, life expanded for him and he saw there was a future.

In spite of his mother's revelation, it never occurred to Alan that when Tom died, he would not inherit; after all, there was no other child. He'd barely known his cousin and it did not cross his mind that Tom might prefer her, a blood relation and without a criminal record, as his heir. If he'd known that there would be nothing for him after Tom's death, he might have killed him in November. But those two boys were in the house, those tiresome kids who seemed to have made themselves at home. They'd say that he'd been there. Of course, he could have killed them, too, but even Alan drew the line at killing children, and they had not annoyed him, personally; it was their mere presence that was the nuisance. Besides, a visit to an invalid parent plausibly explained his presence; a beaten-up or dead old man would end all chances of parole.

While the boys were in the house, he'd suppressed his rage, but after they left, he had watched the old man shrink back into his seat as Alan taunted him.

"I'm glad I'm not your son," he'd sneered. It wasn't true. He'd been proud of the man he had thought was his father, boasted to his schoolmates about Tom's war record and had taken a genuine interest in aviation until, in adult life, he had rebelled.

"I'm glad, too," Tom had answered. "You've shamed me, and your mother."

Alan had hit him then, hard, in the stomach, where bruising would be hidden, and the old man, winded, winced, but made no sound beyond a tiny groan. He'd surrendered his immediate funds without protest.

"You've destroyed everything you've touched, Alan," he'd said, when he was able to speak. "Yourself, as well as your mother and your poor, unhappy wife. What do a few pounds matter after that?"

Alan had not taken his credit card; using that could cause problems. It had taken Tom a few more weeks to die.

He'd go to The Willows when he got out. He had to find the gun, and make sure it worked. Mick had said the ammunition must be checked for damp.

"You could use a hair drier on it," he'd suggested. Alan didn't know if he was joking; you couldn't always tell with Mick.

While Alan was finishing his sentence, the days began to draw out; you always noticed this in January, said Ivy. She was worrying about Steve, who, as the weeks went on, was coming in too late at night.

He told her that he'd been with friends watching videos, or at the resurrected youth club. Sometimes these replies were true but Ivy was suspicious about a new pair of trainers he'd acquired, and a smart navy donkey jacket. How had he paid for them?

He said he'd bought them from a friend, that they were misfits, bad buys.

Then Sharon, who had a part-time job at the supermarket now, saw him pocketing cans of lager in the store. She did not tell her mother, but she tackled him.

"You were lucky not to get caught," she told him. "How do you think Mum would feel if she heard you were down at the nick?"

Like most thieves, Steve didn't expect to be caught, and he said so.

"If you go on with it, you will be, one day," Sharon said. "I'll have something to say about it, if you bring trouble on us. Your dad was good to us and Mum's treated you like her own son. What a way to act, after all that."

"He shouldn't have died," Steve muttered, scuffing the ground.

"Well, he did. People do," said Sharon. "I don't think much of some of your friends," she added. She had seen him with a group of tough-looking, slightly older boys, a few of whom she remembered from school, which she had left only two years ago herself.

"You should talk. Look at you—a kid with no father," Steve retorted.

"Adam has got a father. He's an absent one, that's all," said Sharon. "No one thinks anything of that these days. Besides, he's got a good home, and so have you."

Steve paid no attention to her advice. He had had an idea. The Willows's key still hung on Ivy's dresser; now that the place had been sold, there'd be stuff there to steal. There'd be money, probably, and a television and video. He could enter without breaking in, and take whatever he could carry. Greg Black's brother had a mate who sold things on at boot sales; he asked no questions about where they'd come from.

Steve asked his stepmother who had bought the place and Ivy said she'd heard it was a retired lady, Miss Darwin.

She'd be old, Steve decided. Perfect.

He'd never burgled a house before, but people did it all the time and got away with it. Once he'd off-loaded the goods, he could brag about it; no one could pin it on him then. He dreamed about large sums of money: hundreds of pounds which he could spend on trips to London or to Birmingham, where there would be amusement arcades and clubs, bright lights and excitement. Steve was bored. He was lazy at school, scraping through his tests and sometimes playing truant, though not yet often enough to have been in big trouble. The group of boys he'd fallen in with couldn't wait to leave, despite an uncertain future. Though there were jobs in Haverscot, the town had suffered in the recession and factories on the perimeter had had to cut staff. However, there was work for those who really wanted it and did not expect to start out as managing director. Steve saw no point in working for peanuts when you could lift things for nothing, and either use or sell them. After all, he had no living expenses; Ivy fed and housed him, and clothed him too, though not in the style he'd choose himself, and some of what she bought for all of them came from jumble sales. He never thought that this would end when he left school; that it might be reasonable, then, to contribute to the household budget.

Steve took the key one Thursday night. He walked along the street in his new stolen trainers, and turned into Wordsworth Road, continuing past the first houses till he reached The Willows. It was so isolated, just asking to be done, he thought. If this went well—and it would—he could return, once there'd been time for the insurance to pay up so that the old lady could replace what he'd taken, and do it again. After all, she wouldn't lose; he might be doing her a favor as she'd get the latest models for her replacements, each time he visited.

He'd brought a holdall with him. Without wheels, he wouldn't be able to take away a television unless it was a portable. Steve didn't feel confident about lifting a car yet; he needed practice.

Turning in at The Willows's gate, sauntering up the drive, just as if he were about to call on old Tom, Steve had a sudden memory of his father and of Joe's wrath if he could see him now. Joe had never beaten him, but he would for this, Steve knew for certain. He felt a squirm of indecision but he shrugged it aside. His dad had left him, so he must do what he could to help himself, and thieving brought him things which Joe, if he'd been around, would have provided.

Was the old girl in? The place looked quiet, but there was a light showing in the hall. Old people went to bed early, so she'd be upstairs by now and he could move about below without disturbing her. Maybe she'd forgotten to turn out the light. He walked on, more confidently, and as he approached the front door a security light flooded him in sudden brilliance. He halted. Tom had had no lights like this.

He changed his plans, dumping his holdall under a nearby bush and striding firmly to the door. He would ring the bell, and if she answered, he would ask if she had any jobs for him—he'd come back and do them on Saturday, he'd say.

He rang the bell, but no one came. Marigold, now a regular member of Haverscot's Choral Society, was rehearsing for a performance of *Elijah*. Steve opened the door, and entered.

While he was there, Steve took a look around the house. Painters were working in the bedroom at the front; trestles and dustsheets were in position and the walls were bare, rubbed down. In Tom's old room, overlooking the garden and the river at the back, there were sea-green curtains patterned with tiny flowers, and the single bed was covered with a quilted matching spread. The room where all the books had been was now painted a warm primrose color, and there were bright curtains at the window, printed with some sort of plant, each with its name below in funny writing. They were herbs, but Steve did not investigate that far. There was a table and a small, neat desk against one wall, and a chair. It was a sort of study, he supposed, not looking at a few books stacked neatly on the freshly painted shelves.

In what had been the dining room, there was a large table covered with oilcloth and spread with heaps of varicolored paper, pots of glue and tins of varnish, and a row of wooden boxes, differing in size. On it, there was also a cylindrical tin; it looked like a wastepaper basket and it had bits of mottled paper stuck to it. She was pasting paper on it, prettying it up; what a waste of time.

Then he saw a decorated box. It stood on a small table with some other objects Marigold had nearly finished. This one, hinged, was covered in flowers, matched and patched, darkly varnished; it looked like a sort of captured garden, Steve thought. It had a catch to hold it shut. It could be used for storing bits and pieces—costume jewelry, love letters, photographs. Ivy would love it.

When Marigold returned, her portable radio had gone; so had her new toaster, and the video. Steve had taken her jewelry; there wasn't much, just some things that had been her mother's. He hadn't touched the silver; he was still a small-time crook. She did not discover the burglary until the next morning when she could not make her breakfast toast.

She called the police, but the thief's mode of entry was not obvious. No window had been broken and no door was forced. She knew she had left nothing open, not even a fanlight; it was too cold for that. Then she remembered Mark, for whom she had equipped the haunted room and where he sometimes came to do his homework. She hadn't had the locks changed, and he still had a key; she'd never got it back from him.

Could he have taken the video? Was he big enough to carry it and the other things that had gone?

Perhaps he'd brought an accomplice with him: Terry?

18.

The police sent a detective round to dust for fingerprints. He made a mess of Marigold's clean surfaces, and, as she expected, threw up a child's handprint here and there, though not in her bedroom, from which the jewelry had been taken. She did not mention whom she suspected. A child had visited her, she said; adult prints might be those of the two painters working in the house. The thief had not ransacked the place; Steve had been a tidy pilferer when he stole from Tom, and this time he had been restricted by what he could carry away. There was no second set of child's prints but Terry, taller than Mark, might have larger hands and his, Marigold thought, could have been one of the unidentified sets revealed. He would have known that she was out, with his stepfather, at the choral practice. Mark knew there was no dog to see them off—not that Sinbad would have deterred a burglar; he was more likely to have welcomed an intruder with a wagging tail and friendly licks.

All the stolen property could easily be sold, but Marigold had marked the television and the video with the postcode at her old address, using the recommended pen which would show up the writing under ultraviolet light. She had been wearing, on her right hand, as she often did, her mother's ruby and diamond engagement ring, and her pearl necklace, but she was sorry to lose a gold locket which contained a lock of her grandmother's blond hair; such things were common in Edwardian times. There was a garnet brooch, too, and some other things. She hadn't photographed them. The police were not optimistic about her chances of regaining them.

She notified the insurance company immediately, but she took no steps to replace the larger items. If her suspicions were correct, she might recover them.

The thief had taken one of her decorated boxes. Mark, she remembered, had admired it.

Dealing with all this occupied her throughout Friday. In the evening, she telephoned Richard and asked him if he could spare the time to come and see her the next morning. It was important. When he arrived, she described the burglary and said that the police, so far, had no clues.

"But I've a suspect in mind," she said. "Young Mark. I didn't say so to the police because I hope to deal with it myself, perhaps with your aid." She explained her theory, based on Mark's possession of a key.

"You think he had help," said Richard, when he had heard her out.

"I don't think he could have carried all those things by himself," she said. "Do you?"

"Not really. You've got Terry in mind, haven't you? And you think we might find the things they took?"

"If it was those two boys, yes. Before they try to sell them," she answered. "I don't want to believe that they're the culprits, but I've good reason to suspect Mark."

"Yes, you have," he agreed. "Terry gets plenty of pocket money. I know, because I provide it." He pondered. "Shall we go and see Mark's mother? If he confesses and Terry's involved, then we'll tackle him."

Marigold understood that he wanted to approach the possible culprits in that order because he did not want a confrontation with Terry if he was not involved.

"Yes," she said. "I'm sorry about casting Terry as an accomplice but I don't know any other friends of Mark's."

"No offense taken," said Richard, who thought Terry, if he knew about Mark's key, could well have been the ringleader.

Together, they set out. The rain had eased off and the gray, dank day was raw. Richard had come by car as he was on his way to do the shopping. They drove round to Susan Conway's house and rang the bell, which was answered promptly.

"Yes?" Susan stared at the pair, the elderly woman with a felt hat pulled down above her sallow face, whom she had never seen before, and the tall, sad-looking man whom she recognized but could not identify. Susan met so many people in the course of her work that she found it difficult to place those she came across only rarely.

Richard saw her problem.

"Richard Gardner," he reminded her. "And this is Miss Darwin who lives at The Willows."

"Yes?" Susan said again. She was busy cleaning the house and they were a tiresome interruption.

"The Willows," Richard repeated. "Where Mr. Morton lived."

"I don't know Mr. Morton or The Willows," Susan said, using professional calm to hide her impatience. She had remembered who Richard was: stepfather of the disappearing Terry.

"Mark knew him," Richard said.

"Mark and he were friends," said Marigold, intervening. "I bought the house from Mr. Morton's executors. He lent Mark books," she added. "*Coot Club*, for example."

"Oh!" Susan still looked puzzled, but here was a ray of

light. "I thought he borrowed them from Ivy—the woman who looks after him when I'm working," she said. "How did he get them from Mr. Morton? How were they friends?" Then, facing the inevitable, for she must discover what had been going on, she stood aside. "Won't you come in?" she said.

She was an attractive woman. Richard had thought so when they met before. Her fair hair was cut short, almost like a boy's, and she had very blue eyes; he could see that she was irritated by their visit and had had a major surprise about Mark's activities. She led them into her sitting room, which was functionally furnished; the chair and sofa looked like those often seen in a hotel bar, covered in soft gray-blue leather. Perhaps they came from a hotel supplier; maybe she got a discount through the trade.

They all sat down, and Susan, who wore narrow black trousers and a long pink sweater, leaned forward, looking intently at Miss Darwin.

"You said Mark knew a man called Mr. Morton, who lent him books," she said. "I want to know about him. What sort of man was he?" All sorts of possibilities were passing through her mind.

"He was an elderly invalid who died just before Christmas," said Miss Darwin. "I never met him. He'd had a stroke. He was unable to walk far."

"And?"

"He wasn't a child molester, Mrs. Conway," Richard said. He had followed the direction of her thoughts.

"Did Terry know him? Why are you both here?" asked Susan.

"Mark's been to see me, too," Miss Darwin told her, adding, "I've been pleased to make his acquaintance."

Clearly, he hadn't told his mother about his visits. Miss Darwin did not want to get him into still more trouble than he might be in already; there had to be a reason for his secrecy.

"Where was he last night, Mrs. Conway? Between eight and ten o'clock," asked Richard.

"At Ivy's—Mrs. Burton's," Susan answered. "I was on late duty and he stayed over. He does sometimes." She colored up suddenly. She had spent the night at The Golden Accord, with David; it was the third time this had happened, made possible by Ivy keeping Mark. Susan was not quite sure where this was leading her, but she had let herself stray into it. "Why do you want to know?"

"Someone entered my house last night, while I was at a choral society rehearsal," said Miss Darwin. "They stole my video recorder, a portable radio, some jewelry, and other items."

"Are you accusing Mark?" Susan's anger rose. "How dare you!" she exclaimed. "He'd never do anything like that."

"He has friends you don't seem to know about, like Mr. Morton," said Miss Darwin. "And he could enter the house. He has a key."

"He wouldn't steal!" Susan was insistent, and still furiously indignant, but a doubt was entering her mind. How could she be certain? She knew so little about Mark's daily life, trusting him to Ivy, who could not watch him all the time. She'd agreed that he was old enough to play in the park and visit his friends, and come home alone. "You think Terry did this with him," she said, turning to Richard. "That's why you're here."

"He couldn't have carried everything himself," said Richard. "If it was Mark, he must have had some help."

"Then it was Terry's idea," said Susan. "Mark would never plan such a thing—and Terry's been in trouble before."

"That's true, but not for theft," said Richard, admiring her spirited defense of her son. "Why don't we ask Mark about it?" he suggested. "Where is he now?"

"He's still at Ivy's," Susan said, more calmly. She had been back only half an hour herself. "I'm due to fetch him soon."

"Suppose you do that straightaway," suggested Richard.

"I will," said Susan. "But what about the police? You must have reported the burglary. You said it took place on Thursday night. A whole day's gone by."

"I have reported it," Miss Darwin said. "But I didn't mention Mark. I thought, if it was him, we might recover what was taken and no more need be said, as long as he is made to see the error of his ways."

She did not want to believe that Mark was a thief. They'd grown so friendly and she looked forward to seeing him. He always rang the bell and waited to be admitted. Once or twice she'd asked him for his key and he had said that he'd forgotten it. She wasn't sure if this was true. She had bought some books she'd hoped he'd read, and she had taken him along to the library one evening, getting the librarian to enroll him. It seemed that no one else—not his mother, nor Ivy—had thought of doing this. Then she'd had the melancholy room redone in a way that he might find appealing, equipping it with a table and chair so that if he wanted to, he could do his homework there. He'd used it several times and said that it was brilliant.

"I'm sure Mark's completely innocent," said Susan. "But we must get to the bottom of this now. I'll ring Ivy and tell her I'm coming round for him at once. Please wait here for us. I'll only be a few minutes."

But Ivy said that Mark was out. He'd gone to Merrifields to see his friend Terry.

"We didn't see him when we were on our way here," said Richard. "We could have missed him, though, while I was picking you up, Miss Darwin."

Inconsequentially, Marigold wondered if he would ever use her Christian name.

"It's possible," she said. "Shall we go and see?"

* * *

Verity had planned, that Saturday, to go to an exhibition of watercolors at a gallery some twenty miles away. Nowadays she plotted to avoid Richard, either by shutting herself in her studio or by going out. His long, lugubrious face was a constant reproach, and for some weeks they had shared an unacknowledged conspiracy to escape from one another. He went to his choral society on Thursday nights and had just joined an amateur drama group which met on Tuesdays. Verity had taunted him about it.

"You'll make a fool of yourself. You can't act," she said.

Richard thought he acted all the time. At work, he played the part of an efficient executive; at home, he adopted the role of benign parent and caring husband. Sometimes he wondered if he ever felt a genuine emotion or uttered a spontaneous word.

"I shan't be acting," he informed her. "I'm helping the stage manager."

To his amazement, the stage manager proved to be the thin woman from the train, who was a solicitor with a city firm. She was getting married in September.

What if Verity, in one of her sudden fits of togetherness, offered her services as a scenery painter? But she didn't; since Christmas there had been no such lightning impulses.

She rarely went out at night, sometimes talking about joining another evening class but never doing so. Lately, she had often been in an alcoholic haze when he came home, and that was better than the belligerence which usually preceded that stage. For her own part, Verity could not bear to contemplate the plight that would have been hers and the boys' if Richard had not rescued them, and by inference, her debt to him. At that time, she had been popping pep pills as well as drinking; she was heavily in debt; the two boys lacked confidence and Terry had been bed-wetting. All that ended when she and Richard married.

For months she had limited her drinking, and, in the euphoria of her new romance, had given up the pills. When this wore off, she turned to tranquilizers instead of winding herself up artificially; that happened now without a stimulant because Richard irritated her so much. He was too patient. He suffered all her provocation as she tested him to see how much he would take before he hit her, but he never did. The boys' father had not lasted any time at all.

Verity, in her calmer moments, knew that her conduct was indefensible, but she never blamed herself; it was all Richard's fault. He was so weak. He simply walked away when she was wound up for a quarrel.

That morning, she drank two cups of black coffee and ate a piece of dry toast, in her dressing gown, then went upstairs to have a bath before the exhibition. She'd dress up, pull out all the stops, become the painter lady; maybe she'd meet people she knew and be encouraged to mount an exhibition of her own. That was her world, the world of art; if she hadn't saddled herself with a family, she could be having a successful career by now. She often thought like this, dreaming of the might-have-been. She lay in the bath, her hair pinned on top of her head, a few damp wisps trailing over her shoulders. Her body made islands in the foam: thin breasts, bony knees when she bent her legs. Her ribs, masked now, stood out against her white skin. Verity did not want to believe that she was unattractive; slenderness was desirable, wasn't it? But Richard didn't want her, not like that.

Tears of self-pity began to run down her cheeks as she lay there in the water, almost forgetting her plan for the day ahead, and then, breaking in upon her miserable wallowing, she heard voices.

Terry was talking, and there was another voice she did not recognize until she heard her son call his friend by name. It was Mark.

"We've got no dad, either," Terry was saying. "So what?"

"Don't you ever see him?"

"Not really. Not for years," said Terry. "But he will come back," he added confidently, reassuring himself, not his auditor.

"And you've got him—Mr. Gardner—" Mark persisted.

"Cat's his name," said Terry.

"Him," Mark repeated. "He's like a dad."

There was a rustling sound, paper tearing. The boys were eating crisps.

"He's not our dad," said Terry. "Our dad's an artist, like Mum is."

Verity, by this time, was lying motionless in the cooling water, listening intently. The voices, she realized, were being transmitted to her up the bath overflow pipe; the boys must be sitting near the outlet.

She had met the boys' father when they were both art students and he had gone on to become a graphic designer with a promising career, which he abandoned when he left her and went abroad. She did not know what he was doing now. It was so unfair that he had gone away and left them all; look what had become of them—her talent wasting, her sons dependent on an unfeeling man who loved none of them.

At this point in her thoughts she craved a drink, but the boys had resumed their conversation and she was compelled to listen.

"If your mum died, he'd look after you," Mark was saying. "Mr. Gardner, I mean."

"Well—yes," Terry admitted, such a thought never having crossed his mind.

"And you've got a gran and granddad, haven't you?"

"Yes."

They had two sets, in fact, though they never heard from

the pair belonging to their father. There were some aunts and uncles, too, also invisible.

"I haven't," Mark said, cheerfully. "Only my mum. I sometimes wonder what would happen if she got run over. Perhaps Ivy would look after me, like she does when Mum's away."

"I expect so," Terry said, not really interested. "There's always the social," he added. They'd come to see his mum once or twice before Cat came into their lives.

Mark didn't want to think about the social. They were all-powerful and could whisk you off without you having any choice. Dreadful things could happen to you in their care, he knew; he'd seen it on the telly, Ivy and Sharon clucking about it, while they thought that he was too intent upon his book to take in what was being said. Now and then, the dread of being left without his mother rose up like a nightmare in his mind. If that were to happen, there was no human soul responsible for him. He used to think that Tom would see that he was safe; more than once, when assailed by this rare panic, he'd mentally moved into The Willows. But Tom had gone now; there was no safety net for him, unless Ivy took pity on him, but without Mum to pay for him, how could she afford to?

He seemed a long time answering. Verity wondered if the boys had moved away, and she sat up in the water, wringing out her sponge, ready to soap herself. Then she heard Richard's voice.

"Ah—Terry—Mark—there you are," he said. "I want a word with both of you. So does Miss Darwin. Come into the house."

He sounded very stern. Richard was never angry, only annoyed, severe, reproving; these moods scarcely varied in degree.

Now what had the boys been doing?

Verity did not want to know. She sank down again,

submerged her ears beneath the water and turned on the hot tap with her long, thin toes.

After a while, when all was silent, she stepped out of the bath and dried herself. Her hair had got quite wet and needed blowing dry. This took time.

She still had her own car, a small Fiat; Richard allowed her that and paid for it, including the petrol bill at a local garage.

Let him deal with this latest escapade, she thought, leaving the house quietly while voices droned on from behind the closed drawing-room door.

She did not ask herself where Justin was; sometimes it was better not to know, and it was not until hours later that she began to feel aggrieved because whatever had happened concerned one of her sons, and Richard had not thought fit to see that she was told.

19.

Miss Darwin became certain, very early in the discussion, that Mark was not the thief. He hadn't understood, at first, what he was being accused of having done.

"You've been going to The Willows," his mother had pitched in, before either Miss Darwin or Richard could open the bowling. She'd stated it as fact. She knew.

Mark, looking at Miss Darwin and Mr. Gardner, saw them regarding him with very serious expressions on their faces. He was not afraid of either; in fact he liked both of them and was accustomed, now, to Miss Darwin's grim features. She could smile; he had seen her do so, especially when she'd had her glass of whiskey. Besides, grown-ups were often hideous; children too, sometimes. He could name a few.

"You've still got a key, haven't you, Mark?" Miss Darwin intervened.

"It's on my ring," he said, patting his waist. Beneath his anorak, he had a key ring snapped to his belt. While he answered, he avoided looking at his mother. Mounds of explanations lay ahead. He knew that she was not just annoyed, but puzzled.

"Did you go into my house last night, Mark?" Miss Darwin pursued.

"No. I was at Ivy's. Me and Sharon played cards and then I went to bed," he said. He'd read in bed, a book borrowed from the library, by Terry Pratchett. It was good.

"What time was that?" asked Richard.

"Nine, about," said Mark.

"What's all this about you going to The Willows?" Susan demanded. "What's been going on?"

"I used to go and see Mr. Morton," he said. His lip trembled. Why were they all so angry? His mother was furious, he could tell; he'd seldom seen her really cross, and though she was sometimes short with him when she was tired, she was never unfair.

"He lent you books," his mother stated.

"Yes." That wasn't wrong, surely?

"I thought Ivy lent you those," his mother said.

"I never said so," Mark replied.

"Why didn't you tell me about Mr. Morton?"

"You might have stopped me going there, and I liked him," answered Mark.

"He was an old man, and he was your friend," said Miss Darwin. "You told me that, Mark." She turned to Susan. "Mark had a book Mr. Morton lent him just before he died. One by Arthur Ransome, wasn't it, Mark?" She looked at him, her gaze steady behind the dark-rimmed glasses which she did not always wear. Mark had worked out that she put them on when she was concentrating very hard, and when she did that work of hers, with the cut-out flowers and patterns.

"Yes," he agreed, warily.

"Mark came to return the book, believing that the house was empty," she told Susan. "I was out at the time, but I returned while he was replacing it, and we made friends." Miss Darwin spoke firmly; she had directed women like

Susan in her working life. "We'd met before, hadn't we, Mark? In the park when you and Terry were having trouble with some older boys."

Mark nodded. "Yes," he muttered.

"I was living in a rented bungalow then, Mrs. Conway," said Miss Darwin. "While I looked for a house."

Now Richard was the startled listener. Miss Darwin had not, on Christmas Day, mentioned meeting the boys, and nor had Terry. She might not have recognized him, but surely he would not have forgotten her?

Susan remembered that it was from Terry's stepfather that she had heard of the old woman who had told the motorists that Mark and his friend were not responsible for damaging their cars. What else had he been doing that she didn't know about?

"You missed Mr. Morton, didn't you, Mark? You were sad when he died," said Miss Darwin, firmly leading her witness.

"Yes."

"But you knew you should return his book."

"Yes." Mark spoke more confidently now.

"Miss Darwin's video and her portable radio and some other things were stolen last night, while she was out," said Richard, thinking it was time they got to the point. "You didn't take them, did you, Mark?"

Susan began to bridle but before she could defend her son, Mark answered for himself.

"No. How could you think so?" he said, on a wail, and the tears began to fall, though he tried hard to blink them away and did not sob.

Miss Darwin frowned at Richard.

"We didn't, Mark, but we needed to hear you say so," she said. "You see, you had a key, and whoever was the thief didn't break in. There was no sign of a forced entry."

Mark knew then who was guilty. It was Steve.

"I shall change the locks," said Miss Darwin. "And you will still come and see me, if you want to, and if your mother says you may."

She glanced across at Susan, who knew herself outmaneuvered.

"Of course. It's kind of you," she managed.

While all this was going on, Terry had sat there silently, but now it was his turn.

"So you knew nothing about this either, Terry," Richard said.

"No." Terry was completely mystified.

"I didn't think so," Richard said, not altogether truthfully. Terry could have been an accomplice of whoever did it, if it was a youngster—one of Justin's dubious friends, for instance. But it could have been someone connected with the painters; he was unable to think of anyone else who would have been able to enter the house without leaving any signs of how it had been done. He had seen Miss Darwin lock up before she left; he'd even asked her if she'd checked all round, so used was he to Verity's slapdash ways. Miss Darwin wasn't careless; she would not have left any window insecurely latched. He hoped having an aura of suspicion, however fragile, directed at him would not make Terry disappear again. Mark was the one in possible hot water, for visiting without his mother's knowledge. He saw that she could not wait to pitch into him. He'd take them home; then she could get it over.

But Susan didn't give him the opportunity.

"We'll be going now," she said, standing up. Then, turning to Miss Darwin, she added, "Thank you for not mentioning Mark's name to the police."

Richard stood up too, looking at her with some admiration. She was thin—not scraggy, like Verity, but slim; her expression was alert. She was a capable woman with a lot to manage, a strong person much the same age, he

guessed, as Verity, though she looked younger. He
wondered idly if she had some man in her life.

"I'll drive you back," he said.

"No—please don't bother," she said. "It's not far, and it
isn't raining."

They let her go. Richard saw her to the door, Mark
following behind her, head cast down. Terry seized his
chance to escape, and when Richard returned to the
drawing room, Miss Darwin was alone.

"She can't wait to give that child the telling-off of his life,"
she said.

"No," Richard agreed. "Poor kid."

Mark still hadn't returned his key to The Willows, but his
mother would soon take it from him; that was certain.
There must be another one elsewhere, or someone with the
skill to enter undetected; whatever the answer, Marigold
knew she must call a locksmith in without delay. Mortice
locks, she thought regretfully, like she'd had in London,
with security catches on all the windows. She believed
Mark's story, but he would have a nasty time when he
reached home. His mother should have known about his
visits to Mr. Morton; they had been frequent, over quite a
period of time—some months. Mrs. Conway had been
shaken by today's revelations, and was angry; there must be
a way to smooth her down, make things easier for Mark.
Marigold resolved to try.

Susan did not speak to Mark until they arrived home. She
held him by the arm all the way, and he was frightened. He
always tried so hard not to be a nuisance, and she knew
she could trust him.

But this was exactly what Susan now accused him of
betraying: her trust.

When they reached the house, she sat him down
opposite her in the sitting room and began.

"Now, Mark, what else have you been doing that I don't know about?" she asked. Ivy would have to answer some important questions, too, but Mark must first tell her everything.

"Nothing. Ivy knew I was at Mr. Morton's," Mark said, his face averted as he studied his sturdy shoes.

"Every time?"

"Yes." Mark knew she hadn't known he was at The Willows after Mr. Morton died, but that wasn't what his mother had asked. Until then, he and Steve had gone there with her blessing and often on her instructions. "She looked after him," he added.

"Looked after him?"

"Cleaned the house. Left meals for him. He couldn't hardly walk," said Mark. "Steve did shopping for him," Mark went on. "He couldn't, you see. He could only go out in a wheelchair. He was going to get one with an engine in the summer. They run on batteries like some milk vans."

He hoped she wouldn't ask about the time when Mr. Morton died; he knew she wouldn't like to hear that he and Steve were there. Susan, however, was calming down.

"Why didn't you tell me about him?" she persisted.

"I don't know."

Because there wasn't time, she was thinking guiltily. She was always in a rush. She asked him about school and homework, gave him messages for Ivy, but seldom sat down and heard about his day.

"You were lucky Miss Darwin believed you about last night," said Susan.

"I'm not a thief," said Mark indignantly. "She knows that."

"Even so, if she'd told the police about you having a key, we'd have had them round again," said Susan.

"I'd done nothing wrong then, either," Mark protested.

Susan's head was ringing with propaganda about the children of single mothers being doomed to lives of crime.

It did not have to be like that; she'd always said so. Look at widows' children; no one condemned them out of hand. Or did they? Anyway, they had had fathers, men they knew about, and some of whom, like murdered policemen, were heroes.

"I know, but if your friends want to do wrong things, you mustn't join in," Susan warned.

"They don't," said Mark. Steve did wrong things, but he wasn't exactly Mark's friend and it was nice not having to stick with him anymore. "I liked Mr. Morton," Mark affirmed. "He was like a granddad might be, I thought."

"Oh, Mark!" At this, Susan suddenly burst into tears, rushed over to him and hugged him.

Mark felt most uncomfortable. Why was she crying, when he had done nothing wrong except have a secret? Was that so bad?

"Don't cry," he implored, patting her anxiously.

Susan soon regained her self-control.

"Mark," she said, now speaking firmly. "You haven't got a grandfather because my parents are dead. You know that, don't you?"

"Yes," he mumbled.

"Lots of children don't have grandparents," she told him. "But lots of children don't live in nice houses or have parents who can afford to buy them mountain bikes or computer games. Lot of people haven't got jobs, you know."

"Yes," Mark repeated miserably. "I know that. It's all right, Mum. I just liked him being there," he said.

He liked Miss Darwin, too, and she had said that he could use the room where the books had been. Something told him that he had better not repeat this to his mother. As he came to this conclusion, the telephone rang.

With a mutter of annoyance, Susan released him and

went to answer it. He saw her expression of surprise, irritation, then a tiny thaw.

"Yes," she kept on saying. "Yes. Yes. Well—I don't know—no, I am free tomorrow. Thank you. Four o'clock."

She replaced the receiver and turned to Mark.

"That was your new friend, Miss Darwin," she said. "She's invited us to tea tomorrow afternoon. I couldn't very well refuse."

Tomorrow afternoon, thought Mark. That would give him time to see if Steve had done the robbery. That is, if his mother would let him go round to Ivy's.

She did. They went together. She meant to cross-examine Ivy about the license she permitted Mark while he was in her care.

Ivy still saw Susan frequently, but not as often as when Mark had had to be escorted back and forth. Susan paid her weekly, and when Mark stayed overnight there were cooperative washing arrangements regarding his clothes. Ivy rendered an account which Susan checked against her own record of the hours Mark had spent with her, and the meals she had provided. They respected one another, got on well, and had never had a serious difference of opinion.

So when Susan arrived, wearing a frown and with Mark beside her looking thoroughly abashed, she sensed trouble.

Susan did not beat about the bush, following Ivy into the kitchen where Kylie was spooning a soggy mixture into the willing mouth of her nephew. Sharon was working at the supermarket.

"Mr. Morton, Ivy," Susan said. "Who was he? Mark says you let him go visiting?"

"I did. He was a nice old man—very lonely after his wife died," said Ivy. "I cleaned for him and left him meals, but I was anxious about him at night. He'd had a stroke and could only walk with difficulty. Steve and Mark used to spend time with him. He taught them chess, and that. It was good for them to be with such a gentleman. Why?"

"Mark never told me he went there," said Susan.

"Perhaps he thought you wouldn't be interested," Ivy stated. "There was nothing wrong, Susan. He was a good old man. The boys helped him—they kept him company and did shopping for him."

"I'm not suggesting there was anything wrong," said Susan. "I just think I should have known about it."

"You don't expect me to tell you every time they've gone to the park to play football, or Mark's been to see one of his friends, do you?" asked Ivy, drawing herself up and adopting a combative expression. "I always know where he's going. Don't you trust me to look after him?"

"Of course I do, Ivy." Susan had to retreat a fraction; she could not afford to lose Ivy's goodwill; where would she find someone to replace her?

"Mr. Morton was a good influence," said Ivy firmly. "A man in their lives, two fatherless boys."

At this point, Adam began to wail because Kylie had allowed some of his pappy meal to go up his nose. Ivy, almost without seeming to move, wiped his nostrils clear, patted his back so that he ceased his cries, and spooned in another portion.

"Take Mark into the lounge, Kylie," she said. "Susan and I have to talk. We can do that and see to Adam."

Mark and Kylie left the room at speed.

"Those two get on well," Ivy said as they left. "They do jigsaws together and play cards. Steve's gone a bit past Mark now, being that bit older." She wouldn't tell Susan that she was anxious about Steve who, one night recently, had come back reeking of petrol. She'd caught a strong whiff of it from his discarded jeans. Next day she heard that a barn had been set alight some miles out of Haverscot. Challenged about his clothes, Steve said he'd helped a mate put juice in his car and they'd spilt some. Was it true? Ivy could not be certain. She knew that Steve missed his father; Joe would soon have found out the truth. When Steve was down at Tom's, she had never worried about what he was up to.

"Does Mark see much of Terry Gardner?" Susan asked,

"Quite a bit," said Ivy, who was not altogether sure.

"Have you met his mother?"

"No. Some sort of artist, isn't she?" said Ivy.

"Terry ran off one night and hid. He was reported missing," Susan said. "The police came to us and woke Mark up, wondering if he knew where Terry might be. He didn't, of course."

Ivy had not heard about this.

"Oh dear," she said. "Why did he do such a thing?"

Susan told her what she knew about the incident.

"Now Mark's visiting this Miss Darwin at The Willows," she went on. "She was burgled last night. She thought Mark might have done it because he had a key."

Ivy's glance flew to the dresser hook from which hung a batch of keys. She went to check them, though she could already see the distinctive yellow label on Tom's, duly returned by Steve after his escapade. But how had Mark got hold of one? Perhaps the old man had given it to him.

"It wasn't Mark, of course," Susan was saying. "But it wasn't nice having him suspected and then not knowing about his visits there."

"I can see that," said Ivy. "I should have told you, Susan, but I didn't realize Mark hadn't mentioned it." By the same token, perhaps Susan should have reported Terry's disappearance, which was a significant event in the children's lives, but Ivy thought it wiser not to say so.

"Well—we've cleared things up now," said Susan. She thought of seeking more assurances, but decided not to; until Mark was older, she needed Ivy. Unless she let things run on with David; part of her thought how easy it would be to give up the struggle to carry on alone; part of her wanted to remain independent.

Meanwhile, Kylie had shown Mark a pretty box that Steve had given Ivy. It was exactly like the one he had admired which Miss Darwin had decorated. He had known that his mother would love a box like that. If proof were needed that Steve had been the thief, here it was.

His mother, resolved to take more interest in how he spent his time, asked what he and Kylie had done while she and Ivy had their talk.

"Kylie showed me a box Steve gave Ivy," he said. "It was all covered with pictures of flowers, stuck on. This size." He made a shape with his hands.

"How nice of him," said Susan.

Mark could not say any more. He couldn't tell on Steve.

20.

None of her guests wanted to have tea with Miss Darwin. Even Mark and Richard would have preferred a different occasion without their families, though both saw that attendance was unavoidable.

When Verity returned from the exhibition, she was animated, looking almost pretty; she had enjoyed herself and met several acquaintances who had asked how her work was going. Richard recognized the fey charm which had originally drawn him to her, her air of helplessness. He decided to tell her about the invitation before her mood changed, as, inevitably, it must.

"I won't go," she said. "Miss Darwin's your friend, not mine."

"It's an opportunity to meet Mark's mother," said Richard. "Mark's Terry's friend. I think you ought to be there."

"What was all that about this morning?" asked Verity. "She was here then, wasn't she? Mark's mother?"

"Yes. Miss Darwin was burgled during the choral society's rehearsal," said Richard. "She knew Mark had often visited Mr. Morton, who lived there before, and wondered if he knew who could have got into the house without forcing an entry."

"You mean she wondered if Mark was the thief, because he might know how to get in," said Verity bluntly.

"She thought it possible, but unlikely," said Richard.

"And she decided Terry could have been his accomplice. Thanks very much," said Verity. "I'm certainly not going to tea if she suspects my son of stealing."

"She doesn't. She never did," said Richard. "She wants to make friends with Susan Conway herself, and she thought you would like to meet her because of Terry."

"Are the boys invited too?"

"Yes." Richard thought the tea party was doomed in advance, but saw no way to prevent it from being held.

"Mark seemed a nice enough boy," Verity conceded. "What sort of person is his mother?"

If Richard replied that she was pretty, animated and smart, he would antagonize Verity, who would suspect him of a sexual interest in her; if he said she was plain, dowdy and dull, he would soon be proved a liar. How should he answer?

He shrugged.

"I hardly noticed," he said. "She was concerned about Mark and in a hurry to get him home and find out what he knew, if anything." He was not going to say that he had met Susan before today; that would be committing kamikaze.

"Well, since you seem to have accepted without consulting me, I suppose I'll have to fall in with your plans," Verity said. "But it will be a waste of the afternoon."

"You'd be doing Miss Darwin a favor," Richard said. "She's anxious to help young Mark. His mother's working hours make things difficult, as we already know, and she thinks it's good for him to come here."

"I'm sure it is." Verity briefly felt benevolent about

exposing Mark to their large garden, tree house and other amenities.

"It turns out that she was the woman in the park who saw the boys being teased that time when Terry's football was snatched," Richard told her. "She saved them from a big problem then."

"Oh," said Verity.

He waited for her to ask why she had not been told this before. Hadn't Miss Darwin recognized Terry on Christmas Day?

But Verity said nothing. She might think about it in the middle of the night and demand an explanation then; that would give him time to think of one. New spectacles required, he thought; that might pass.

He and Verity had not discussed Terry's brush with the law after it happened. There had been no obvious problems since then, and the boy had been chastened by his visit to the police station. He had friends they had not met, and so had Justin, but Mark appeared to be eminently suitable. It was clear that Miss Darwin thought well of him, and while she might not be used to children, she was shrewd and would see through cant.

Verity remained in a reasonable frame of mind for the rest of the day and Richard seized the chance to make an attempt at family unity. *Jurassic Park* was on at a local cinema; he suggested they should go, as the boys had wanted to see it since it first became a box-office success.

"Let's all go," he dared to suggest, and when Verity agreed, his only worry was that all the seats would be sold.

But he was able to reserve four on the telephone, and Justin, though he said he'd meant to meet some friends, was persuaded to change his plans. They set off together, and for a few hours Richard imagined he might be able to salvage something of his marriage.

It was better than thinking about Caroline and her pregnancy.

Richard had been pretending that her condition had no relation to himself. A few people in the office had noticed it, though she wore loose jackets now and had made no mention of it.

Of course the father was the other man, the mystery begetter in Wiltshire, but after it was born, would either of them see the child? Would they have a chance to recognize their own son or daughter, maybe see a likeness which would mean there was no need for scientific proof as to who had scored? He wondered if the other man had been cast aside, too, now that both of them had served their purpose—and served was the operative word.

Wouldn't the child want to know who its father was?

What about young Mark? Did he see his father? Was Susan a widow? He didn't seem to spend time with a divorced father. Perhaps, like Verity's first husband, he had run away from his responsibilities.

If this was his child, Richard did not want to run away from it; he'd like to be involved. Indeed, he had fantasized about marrying Caroline.

Why had she told him? Why not leave him in ignorance? But of course, it was true that when he saw that she was pregnant, he would have wondered if the child was his.

In the cinema, these thoughts, at intervals, obtruded. Afterwards, they all went to a pizza bar nearby. The boys ate hugely, while Verity nibbled at a tiny slice of the giant pizza they had ordered. When they reached home, it was time for all of them to go to bed.

Verity had drunk nothing since the gallery viewing earlier. Richard managed to make love to her that night, but it wasn't really love, more an act of pity.

*   *   *

On Sunday morning Steve stayed in bed till twelve. He often did this at weekends, coming in late at night after an evening with his friends. He always told Ivy he was with Greg, or Bruce, or Kevin, and maybe he was, but not in any of their houses, as she supposed, except when the parents had gone out and the boys stayed in drinking beer and watching videos.

He'd taken the stolen video recorder, the toaster and the radio round to Greg's. Greg's older brother had given Steve twenty-five pounds for them—peanuts, but Steve couldn't have passed the stuff on himself, not yet. He wasn't in that league, but he'd get there.

He'd try to sell the jewelry on his own, maybe in the market next weekend. Some traders might not be too curious; he could say it was his mum's and she was sick and needed the money.

It was worth staying in for Sunday lunch. Ivy always cooked a roast and today it was pork, the crackling crisp, with applesauce. All of them enjoyed it; even Adam had gravy and the mashed inside of a roast potato. Steve went out later; he left the jewelry in a drawer in his room. He might give a piece of it to Ivy, though he didn't think that it was quite her style; that locket thing, for instance, and the brooches. Were those red stones rubies? If so, they'd be worth a bomb.

He didn't know what his friends had lined up for that afternoon. The rain had stopped. They might go looking for some girls. Steve wasn't keen on wasting time with girls, but Greg and Kevin liked chatting them up, trying to impress them, and if that didn't work, then shocking them with insults. Steve wouldn't mind parading round with one, to earn respect; otherwise, he wasn't bothered. Respect mattered, though; he'd had it from being with his dad, who turned up at school meetings and at football matches when Steve was in the team. His dad looked good and didn't cheer too loudly, just enough to show he cared. Steve was never in the team now; he wasn't interested.

His mates were quite impressed by what he'd lifted from The Willows. Naturally, he didn't tell them where he'd got the stuff. He'd get some more, and soon, and make Greg's brother pay him better next time. Those big houses in Wordsworth Road were tempting; not much traffic went that way, as the road ended at the church, and they had big gardens offering concealment. There was that place where young Mark's friend lived, Merrifields: it was much bigger than The Willows and would have more loot. He'd really need some wheels to get stuff away from there. Perhaps he could use a wheelbarrow; if he pushed it briskly, it wouldn't take long to get the stuff to Ivy's and stash it in the garden. He wasn't keen on sharing anything, but young Mark might help him get into Merrifields; he might even steal a key. How could he get the kid to do it? He was an awkward little bugger; he hadn't liked Steve's scams at Tom's. Scaring him might do it; he could say he'd torch his bike or put worms in his food.

As he ran through these possibilities in his mind, Steve had an instant's vision of his father. Joe had been scrupulously honest. But he shouldn't have died. He'd left Steve on his own.

Action was the way to banish these uncomfortable thoughts. Steve thought he might take a look round Merrifields this afternoon. Families went out on Sunday and that guy at Merrifields might do the same. Steve would go over the fields; then he wouldn't be noticed, lurking. He'd climb the fence and approach the house across the garden. He'd have a look around, size the place up, make a plan. He could trap Mark into telling him about it—describing where the bathroom window was, and so on, sorting out where it would be easiest to enter if he failed to get the kid to find a key.

A few nights ago, Steve had seen Greg and Kevin set light to a barn stacked half full with hay. He'd carried cans of petrol for them, then stood back while Kevin lit the screwed-up piece of paper he'd thrown into the soaked hay. Some other, younger boys had watched before running off. It had been a sight to see. Steve hadn't been too sure about the barn; after all, cows ate hay and they might starve if their food went up. But it was exciting, you couldn't deny that; all those flames soaring into the dark sky. They'd got away in a car Kevin had lifted to take them into the countryside, and they'd dropped Steve on the outskirts of the town; once they'd driven off, worried, he'd phoned the fire brigade from a call box, then hurried home.

What would there be at Merrifields? Maybe a computer, and cash. He'd found none at The Willows. There might be a food processor. Ivy would find one very useful with all the cooking she did. He'd like to get her one.

He ambled along the road. It was raw and damp. Some of the floodwater had abated, but it could rain again at any minute. Almost automatically, he turned towards The Willows; it was on his route to the church and the field path which would lead him past the gardens of the houses above the river. He missed the quiet evenings at The Willows, the weekend afternoons spent in the warm, peaceful house, and he missed the easy pickings. Ripping Tom off had been a cinch, like stealing from a child, but he'd liked the old man and finding him dead like that had been a dreadful shock. The kid, Mark, had been so cool; funny, really.

As he walked towards the church, Steve saw, ahead of him, a blue Vauxhall which he recognized as belonging to Mark's mother. The brake lights came on as it slowed, then, indicator flashing, it turned in at The Willows. Why had she bothered to signal when there was no car in sight? Typical of a woman driver, decided Steve, who had no experience of being driven by one but who blotted up opinions expressed by others in his hearing. Several of his friends thought women slags, good for only one thing.

What was Susan Conway doing at The Willows? Was Mark with her? The old girl must have reported the burglary to the police. Steve walked on and peered up the drive. The air was dank and the lowering sky was black. He stepped between the gateposts and, hugging the sheltering shrubs, keeping to the sodden grass beside the drive, he went closer to the house. The porch light was on and he could see slivers of light between the drawn curtains and the downstairs windows. Steve slipped round to the back of the house and was there when he heard another car arrive. Doors were banged, remarks exchanged, and when all was quiet he returned to the front to see if he could identify the new car.

It was the black Montego from Merrifields. He'd seen the man who owned it getting into it at the station when he'd been there with some other boys, including Justin Gardner, who had done brilliant patterns with spray paint on a wall. The kid was quite an artist. He'd had a few things to say about his stepfather; he didn't like the guy.

Steve stared at Richard's car. Why was he at The Willows? Was he alone? No sense of guilt about his thefts bothered Steve as he edged up to the sitting-room window and tried to peer through the chink in the curtains. He saw part of a head of tufty brown hair; that was Mark. He heard the boom of a male voice, then shriller sounds. A lot of people were in the house. Were all the Gardners there?

It seemed quite possible. If so, now was his chance to do Merrifields. Steve turned away. He'd best be quick. He'd brought no bag with him, but there would be one in the house if he could find it fast enough. There'd be the same sort of stuff as he'd taken from The Willows: a video, a radio, perhaps a camera, and the mixer. He forgot about the field approach he'd planned and ran back along the road.

*   *   *

Alan, peering through the window of the shed where the gun was buried, saw the figure of a youth flitting through the garden at The Willows. What was he up to? Nothing legal, that was certain.

It might be worth finding out.

Two days earlier, he had been released from prison and was living in his rented flat. He had hired a car, a Honda Civic, and had left it in Haverscot market square while he went on foot to The Willows. He wanted to discover if the house was still empty. Houses did not move much in the winter, he knew that, and there hadn't been a lot of time for a sale to have gone through. He'd seen no board outside, however, so, to be on the safe side, he hadn't walked straight up the drive but had come in over the fence from the field above the river, very early, just as it was getting light.

If his mother had kept her shameful secret, Tom would not have disinherited him. He'd be moving in there, now, himself, not planning a robbery to finance his future.

The dawn was gray; no sweeps of brilliance swept across the sky, and the air was heavy with moisture. He'd seen lights come on in the house, and, keeping close to the shrubs along the boundary, he'd edged his way toward it. Then he'd noticed a figure at a window as the curtains were drawn back. He'd inched up to a point where he could look into the kitchen, and had seen an old woman moving to and fro. She'd made toast, bending to the cooker to extract it from below the grill, and he'd thought it odd that she had no automatic toaster.

Was this old woman the new owner? Was her husband still upstairs? Were there other people living in the house? Cautiously, he circled the building, looking in at all the windows, leaping back when an automatic outside light, sensing him, came on. Nothing happened; if anyone had noticed, perhaps they thought a wandering cat or other animal had set it off.

He saw the new furnishings in the freshly decorated sitting room, and the table covered with Marigold's artwork in the dining room. Then he returned to the kitchen. She was sitting at the table, her back towards the window which overlooked the sink. On the wall opposite was a large picture, a rural scene, sunny, a lot of blues and greens with red flowers in a meadow—a print of one of Monet's poppy paintings which Marigold had bought at Giverny. She liked looking at it during meals. He saw her pour some coffee from a cafetière; then she stretched an arm towards a jar of marmalade; there was butter on a dish. Alan's mouth watered. Before leaving the flat he had grabbed some bread, spreading it with Flora, and had drunk a mug of instant coffee, without milk as he'd forgotten to buy some when he went to the grocer's in the small shopping area around the corner. Despite his work experience, he was still uncomfortable in shops and public places, moving awkwardly and unable to utter more than curt words during transactions.

The kitchen had been altered. New wood fitments added warmth and color to what had been pale cream and green. Alan considered breaking in and knocking out the old woman, still dawdling over breakfast. Then he could take his time over retrieving the gun and ammunition, and enjoy some food in the civilized surroundings which should, by rights, be his. But he couldn't be certain that she was alone in the house. It was so large for just one person. Once he'd got the gun, numbers wouldn't matter.

She stood up, pushing back her chair, and Alan quickly ducked away. Marigold glimpsed some movement, reflected in the glass covering of her Monet print, but it was gone in an instant and she thought it was a trick of the eye. She ignored it.

She mustn't catch sight of him as he retraced his steps towards the shed. Alan made a circuit of the garden under cover of the bushes, avoiding open spaces and the lawn.

Water still lay round the bases of the willows; he'd sometimes played with toy boats in these annual temporary ponds. His father—Tom—had helped him, fishing out a wreck that had sunk, causing him to burst into the frustrated crying of a child.

Dare he make a run for the shed? No other lights had come on in the house, and though it was lighter now outside, it was still overcast. He returned, hugging the wall, to the spot from which he'd overlooked the kitchen; the light was still on there, and, snatching a quick glance, he saw that the old bag was now standing at the table. She'd got flour out, and some bowls. She must be making a cake or pastry, just as his mother used to do in that very room. She'd be busy for some time, but if she took her bowls and spoons to the sink, she could look down the garden and might see him.

He went round the downstairs windows once again, but all the rooms were empty, with no lights burning. She had to be alone.

He reached the garage, and tried the door. It was unlocked, and when he opened it, he saw no car. The place was empty except for some old tea chests, *Miss M. Darwin*, he read on a label, and the address, *The Willows, Haverscot.*

That woman was Miss Darwin. He was right. There was no husband and no family.

It was dry in the garage, and warmer than outside. He pulled the door to and stayed there, wondering what to do. He had no weapon to use against her if he burst into the house. There was nothing in the garage; it had been swept clean and the boxes had been unpacked; they were so light when he moved them that he knew he would not find anything in them with which to hit her. He had no qualms about using violence; anyone who got in Alan's way would not be tolerated.

If she saw him crossing the garden, she could call the police. On the other hand, she couldn't remain in the kitchen forever. He hadn't noticed the time; how long had she been there, stirring up her mixture?

At this point in his thoughts, the church bells began to ring, making him jump. From so near, they were very loud. He remembered that his mother had gone to church every Sunday; it was possible that this woman might do the same. He pushed the door open a crack and peered through the gap. While the bells still rang, he saw her on the doorstep, in her coat and a dark hat, setting out. He breathed deeply. Now he could resume his plans, for she would be away at least an hour.

He didn't waste time on the house; the gun was what he wanted. Once he'd got that, he could control the woman, take the house over if he chose. He hurried back to the shed. There, below the concrete, lay his passport to freedom.

What sort of job had that man who was not his father done? He wouldn't have scrimped on things, but a workman might have. How deep was the concrete? Was there ballast underneath? He looked along the rows of tools, seeking a sledgehammer, but he couldn't see one. Surely Tom would have had one? There was a pickaxe, and a heavy spade. He swung the pickaxe at the floor and succeeded only in sending up some chips of stone. Then he tried to prize it up at the side, but it was far too firmly grounded. Of course, these would be the woman's tools, not Tom's, he told himself; that was why there was no sledgehammer among them. Without one, since he couldn't risk the noise of a pneumatic drill, he'd never break it up.

He'd have to get one. He would go to Texas or B & Q, or another of the huge stores what were open at weekends. This was the phenomenon that had most struck Alan about changed conditions during his imprisonment: You could buy almost anything on Sundays.

As he left the shed, a sudden shower fell. He need not worry about the old woman seeing him when he walked out of her front gate; she'd be praying for sinners, saving her soul. She might need to do that, he thought grimly. She'd be back again, however, by the time he returned, but he was going to get the gun out. Using the hammer would make a noise. Maybe she'd put the television on and that would drown the sound.

Returning with the sledgehammer, he parked near the church, where there was plenty of space now that the service was over. Not wanting to be seen carrying his parcel by a casual walker, or by Miss M. Darwin from her window, he entered The Willows's garden by the field route once again. It was raining gently now, and he met no one. He'd taken time to have some food, stopping at a McDonald's he'd passed on his way back from the shopping mall. She'd be eating, too, by now, that old cow, he thought. He hated her for her intrusion into his mother's kitchen. He'd strike her down if she spotted him and came out, investigating.

He should have cut the phone. That would have been a wise precaution and he could have done it while she was in church. As he wasn't a burglar, he hadn't thought of it.

He aimed a blow with his new tool at the concrete, and it split at once, but, because he'd hit it gently, not right through. He sat there on the wheelbarrow, fuming, wondering if he should stack the sledgehammer against the wall with all the other tools and return tomorrow, watch to see when she went out—she'd go shopping; all women did—then take his opportunity.

He did not hear two cars drive up to the house, but, glancing out, he saw the lights come on downstairs and then curtains were drawn across the windows. He was just planning a voyage of inspection—if she had the television on loud enough, he might be able to work unheard—when he saw the youth, like a shadow, gliding past.

Alan shoved the sledgehammer back beside two spades, left the shed, and followed him.

21.

Miss Darwin's tea party began stickily.

She did not know what boys nowadays liked eating. Dim memories of dreaded childhood parties came to mind: There had been jellies, jam sandwiches, chocolate finger biscuits, sponge cake. She had a feeling that all this was out of date, but scones and a chocolate cake would be appropriate for the parents. She had taken trouble, rising early to do her baking before she left for church. Perhaps Marmite sandwiches for the boys? Or cheese? In the end, she made both, large ones, not dainty quarters like those her mother's cook had constructed. This was a chance to return the Gardners' Christmas hospitality, as well as a means of getting the two mothers together. She wanted the occasion to succeed, which meant that however difficult it was, Verity must be humored.

It was to be drawing-room tea. If the boys had not met this before, it was time they were initiated. They could hand the plates of scones and sandwiches to the adults; it would occupy them between mouthfuls. Mark would certainly behave; the other boys were less predictable.

Dusk was falling as the time for their arrival drew near.

She pulled the curtains across the darkening windows, seeing nothing in the garden, no hint of an intruder's presence.

Susan and Mark came first, which pleased Miss Darwin as she was anxious to overcome Susan's understandable hostility at having Mark suspected of theft. She was wearing a long navy skirt and a hip-hugging pink sweater; her short fair hair shone, and she had on long silver earrings. Her expression was wary as Miss Darwin ushered her in, asking Mark to hang her coat, and his, in the cloakroom.

He seemed quite at home here, Susan thought resentfully, as he obeyed.

Miss Darwin was making comments on the weather as she led her guest into the sitting room. Susan managed to respond; she was used to meeting strangers, and was used, also, to keeping a wall between herself and them, and she did so now, not wanting to get close to this rather formidable old woman who had somehow become involved with Mark.

The house, however, charmed her; it was so unlike her own, but as she had imagined she might live if she had married Mark's father. That thought flashed through her mind as she noticed the good, antique pieces which Marigold had inherited from her parents. Everything looked cherished and the place was comfortable. Her own house, she saw now, was strictly functional. No wonder Mark liked it here.

"Miss Darwin, will you show Mum your boxes before the others come?" he asked. He tugged at her elbow, not shy with her. He no longer noticed her appearance; like Tom's white hair and lameness, it was all just part of the person, and accepted.

"What boxes?" Susan asked. "Do you collect them?"

"I decorate them," Marigold replied. She led the way into the dining room.

"Mum, you remember, I told you Steve gave Ivy a box," Mark was saying as he followed them.

On the big table Susan saw a wastepaper basket, almost complete, ready for is final coat of varnish. There were several boxes in various stages of embellishment among Marigold's materials.

"I'm afraid my nicest box was stolen when the video and radio went," Marigold explained. "None of the others are quite ready yet."

As she spoke, she and Susan realized what Mark had just said. They were staring at one another, speechless, when the doorbell rang.

"There are the Gardners," Miss Darwin remarked, reprieved from commenting, and went to let them in.

Through the murky dusk, Alan stalked the youth. When the rain stopped, mist rose, but there was no one about as he followed Steve down the road. He kept the boy in sight, and then, suddenly, his quarry vanished. Hurrying, Alan saw that he had disappeared at the entrance gates of Merrifields. He must have gone in there.

Hugging the side of the drive, Alan walked towards the house, from which exterior lights shone through the gloom. He lacked the knowledge Steve possessed: That one of the two cars outside The Willows was the owner's, and that most of the family, if not all of them, were out. Alan was wondering if this sly boy lived here; he had not been close enough to him to pick out details of his appearance; he was just a youth. There was plenty of cover in the drive; trees and shrubs dotted the shaggy grass, and he moved quietly from the shelter of one to another as he advanced.

The front of the house showed bland and undisturbed, a static light burning over the porch and a halogen one on the corner. That must have come on when its sensor detected the boy. Alan was impressed by these lights, which had become popular while he was inside. When trespassing at night, one must watch out for them.

He couldn't get near the front door of the house while that beam shone down. It would probably switch itself off in a few minutes; then, if he kept out of its range, he might get close enough to a window to look through. Why would a boy who lived in a place this size be skulking around The Willows, Alan asked himself; skulkers were rarely acting innocently.

The light remained on. It must be set to its maximum. In that case, he could use it to work his way round to the far side of the building. Staying at the rim of the lit area, Alan reached the rear of the house, where another light was on, and he could see the youth, almost floodlit, trying to open a window. Then he stooped and picked up a stone from the flower-bed near him, raising his arm, ready to throw it at the window.

Alan's immediate impulse was to stop him. Forcing an entry left traces of one's presence. When he stole the shotgun, he had opened the door and walked into the Wickenses' house without any hindrance. But this lad did not know that he was being watched. Alan decided that what followed might be interesting. He saw the youth apparently change his mind about flinging the stone; he moved on towards a French window, and cracked the stone quite gently against the glass near the catch, put his hand through the hole and opened the door. Alan, in the damp garden, nodded approvingly at this more prudent tactic, and, as the youth entered the house, prepared to follow. There might be benefits for him within, if he was lucky, even, possibly, a gun ready for the taking. Plenty of people legitimately owned shotguns.

Steve had tidily closed the French window behind him. Alan gave him a minute before opening it again and entering the house.

In a corner of the large room in which Alan now stood, the youth was on his knees disconnecting the video recorder beneath the television set, and he had a huge shock when he saw Alan's shoes beside him on the carpet. He looked up, and could not focus properly on whoever had caught him in the act because the man was behind a lit standard lamp.

"You don't live here, son," Alan remarked mildly, pinning down Steve's wrist with one heavy foot.

"Who says?" was Steve's brave answer as he struggled to get free. This wasn't Mr. Gardner.

"People don't often break the windows of their own houses," Alan said. He was wondering where the true residents were; no one seemed to have noticed what was going on, but he was poised for flight in case they appeared. "They don't nick videos, either." He raised his foot slightly. "Get up," he said. "But watch it."

As Steve stood, Alan seized his arm and twisted it behind his back. He did not see what use he could make of this captive, but an idea might come to him.

"Let me go," said Steve, now whining. Held in such a grip, his arm hurt.

"Not until you tell me what you're doing here," said Alan. "And I saw you trespassing at The Willows."

"If you saw me there, you must have been trespassing too," said Steve, his spirits reviving at this revelation. "And what are you doing here?" he added.

"Following you, because you were acting suspiciously," said Alan.

But Steve had recognized him now. Incredulous, he stared at Alan.

"You'd no business at The Willows," he declared. "Your dad's dead and it's not your house." He couldn't resist adding, "It was me and Mark that found your old man when he snuffed it."

Then Alan realized that this was one of the boys who were being baby-sat by Tom on that November night.

"Who lives here?" he asked, and his voice took on a harsher tone.

Steve was remembering about him now: Tom's son, the murderer.

"They're out," he said. "They're having tea with the old bag who's bought The Willows. That's why I knew the house was empty." He'd taken a chance; he couldn't be sure they were all there. He'd welcome discovery now, held firmly as he was by this man who scared him rigid.

"So you thought you'd see what you could find," said Alan. "Well, why not? Got an outlet, have you?"

"Course," said Steve boldly, heart thudding with fear.

"Tell me who lives here," Alan repeated, and Steve described the Gardners, adding that Justin sometimes hung out with him and his friends.

"Hm. And you're stealing from his dad?"

"It's his stepdad," Steve replied. "And I won't take anything that's Justin's. Or young Terry's," he said, as an afterthought.

"Any guns here?" Alan asked.

"Not that I know of," answered Steve. "Why?"

"I just wondered," Alan said. "I'll take a look around while you help yourself." He released Steve's arm.

He'd shot his wife, the paper had said. He was going to shoot someone else. Steve was quaking.

"That old woman lives there on her own, does she? At The Willows?" Alan asked nonchalantly, moving towards the door.

"Yes," said Steve, rubbing his arm. "Why?"

"That's my business," Alan answered. "And by the way, you haven't seen me. Understood?"

Steve nodded vigorously.

"I won't say a word," he promised.

"If you do, you'll be sorry," Alan warned. "You're stealing, remember."

He sauntered out of the room and took a quick look round the rest of the ground floor. There was no gun cupboard. It would have to be the sledgehammer.

He let himself quietly out the front door, leaving the boy, who wore no gloves, to get on with his thieving. Alan, his own hands warm inside new brown leather gloves, had left no prints.

He had no strong feelings about the Gardners' right to keep their property. Perhaps they should install a burglar alarm.

Leaving the boy to it, Alan began walking back towards The Willows. With the house occupied by the Gardner family and whoever the second car belonged to—he'd seen the Vauxhall and the Montego when he was trailing the boy—there should be enough noise and distraction going on to let him reach the shed unnoticed.

That kid—Steve was his name, Alan remembered—was local. Alan would recognize him if they met again and he'd find him if he needed him. He was just a lad; he'd be at the school, the one Alan had attended, though it had been a grammar school then and was now a comprehensive. His mother had crammed him hard to get him through his eleven-plus exam. Alan wondered if the place had changed much. In the town, some of the original shops remained, such as the butcher's which had been handed on through three generations. There was an antique dealer who had been there for a long time. Alan did not want to meet anyone who had known him previously, but he had altered since those days; his hair was graying and he now wore a bushy moustache. Even so, he did not intend to spend much time in the more populated areas of the town.

After his warning, the boy wouldn't go shouting about his

presence, especially if he had the nerve to continue with his burglary. Besides, the kid wouldn't know about his record. All that must have been forgotten long ago. His parents—or rather, his mother and the man Tom—had not been besieged by the press because his trial was in the Midlands and he was not living in Haverscot. Nowadays, the media would have traced and hounded them, and might even, by some means, have unearthed the truth about his parentage.

He must get that gun. Then he'd be in control.

How long would it take? An hour? Ten minutes? He'd have to estimate at least an hour, he thought.

He'd better not risk it while the guests were there, but he would have to deal with that old woman. He returned to his car and turned it round, driving back to The Willows, parking near its gate, ready for a quick getaway. He arrived in time to see the two cars drive off, first the Montego and then the small blue Vauxhall. He stayed in his car for quite a while, sometimes running the engine to get the heater going while he tried to work how to incapacitate the old woman.

He was still there when the church bells began to ring and Miss Darwin emerged between the gates, bound for church again. Twice in one day? Alan couldn't believe his luck.

As soon as she was out of sight, he armed himself with the powerful torch he'd had the foresight to buy, and, his passage illuminated by it and by the exterior lights she'd left on, he hurried back across the garden to the shed.

After her guests had gone, Marigold had cleared away the tea things, loading the dishwasher and putting what was left of the cake and scones in tins. The remaining sandwiches would do for her supper. She covered them with foil and put them in the fridge.

What now? The house, which had come alive that afternoon, had become a silent place.

Going to church again was a sudden impulse. Normally, her solitude was no burden, and she had plenty to do, but this evening she was not in the mood for découpage or for reading. She felt restless. Stepping the short distance down the road and singing a few hymns would soothe her. Then she could cheer herself up with a couple of whiskies and finish the sandwiches. Since her set had been stolen, she couldn't settle down to television. *Mastermind* was back again, and she liked that, pitting her wits against those of the contestants. She often scored well in General Knowledge.

The afternoon had been a strain. The two mothers, edgy Mrs. Gardner and the capable Mrs. Conway—was she a widow? Mark still hadn't said a word to her about his father—had sat at either end of the sofa and had been spiky with one another.

"You work in a hotel, I believe," Verity Gardner had begun.

"I'm the assistant manager. What do you do?" Mark's mother had replied.

Marigold, pouring tea and asking Mark to hand round plates, thought her tone acerbic.

"I'm a painter," Mrs. Gardner had answered. "Or I would have been, if I'd had more time."

"Come now, Verity," Richard had intervened. "You do yourself an injustice. Verity has had pictures in several exhibitions," he told Susan.

"How clever of you," Susan said, and her tone was warmer now. Marigold thought she might have imagined the earlier hostility.

"Milk?" she asked. "Sugar?"

Richard passed the cups.

"We've had painting weekends at the hotel," Susan said.

"Tutors come and hold classes for the guests. I'd love to be able to paint, but I can barely draw two straight lines."

Verity unbent a little.

"It's possible to acquire a certain competence," she conceded. "With patience, and good tuition. But there's no substitute for talent."

"Maybe I'll try it when I retire," said Susan, who found it difficult to look further forward than the week ahead.

Mark and Terry were sitting in two tub chairs, each with a small table at his side, both eating heartily, following one sandwich with another, eyes on the chocolate cake. Marigold had iced it after church that morning. Justin had refused to come; he was going to see a friend, he said, and when asked which one, named Bruce. He might catch a bus and go to the cinema if he could think of nothing more exciting to do. He certainly wasn't going to some old lady's tea party.

Richard did not waste time expressing disapproval. Justin, as unpredictable as his mother, might have been rude if he had come with them. As it was, everyone else was, so far, being decorous in Miss Darwin's pleasant room.

Susan could not push from her mind the discovery that Steve might be the thief who had taken their hostess's video, radio, and the decorated box—Steve, her own son's companion, stepson of the trusted Ivy. All at once her arrangements for Mark had revealed major flaws; not only was he visiting people she had never heard of, but he was also spending time with Steve, who was dishonest. This must be faced and tackled before she went to work the following day. After leaving here, she would go straight round to Ivy's once again. She longed to leave at once, not waste precious minutes chatting idly to these people, but she made an effort to be friendly.

Richard tried to help. He mentioned two pictures which Verity had sold the year before, saying he was sorry to see them leave the house for the exhibition where they were bought.

"That wasn't what you said at the time," snapped Verity. "You said you were glad."

"I said I was pleased about your success," said Richard. "You would have been disappointed if they had not been sold."

She couldn't know that he had bought them, secretly, trying to boost her confidence. While she was out, he had hidden them in sacking in the loft. How else could he dispose of them without detection? He could not bring himself to burn them or give them to some charity shop.

He'd considered hanging them in his office, but he would not have been able to live with their gloomy purples and dull browns. There would have been comments from his colleagues, too, since by any standards the paintings were remarkable.

Susan was too experienced to express a wish to see Verity's work. She changed the subject.

"We have all sorts of courses at the hotel," she said. "It's a new venture, between conferences. We have a lot of them, and business visitors. Music is popular, too. We have concerts by good local amateurs."

"Quintets? That sort of thing?" asked Richard helpfully, and Susan said that yes, they'd had quintets, and trios, but solo pianists were their most successful ventures.

"Richard plays the piano," said Verity.

"Do you?" Susan asked. "How nice to be able to do that. You are a clever family," she managed, earning Marigold's approval by this positive remark.

"I'm not much good," said Richard. "But I enjoy it. Justin, Verity's other son who hasn't come today, plays well by ear."

Marigold helped them knock this ball back and forth for a short rally, then asked Verity, who was beginning to look sulky, if the family planned a holiday this summer. The Sunday papers were full of enticing advertisements for sunny climes; doubtless Richard exported his difficult relations to some foreign spot.

"No," said Verity.

"We've made no arrangements yet," said Richard. "Last year we went to Corfu."

"Yes, and me and Justin got really sunburnt," Terry said.

"Did you? That must have been painful," Marigold replied. She peered into the teapot, which needed filling. "I'll just go and fetch some more hot water," she said. "Mark, would you help me, please?"

Mark, who had been silently stuffing, got up, still chewing, and followed her.

"I'm glad to see you've got such a good appetite, Mark," she said.

"We didn't have a big lunch," Mark confided. "Mum usually cooks something good on Sunday nights when she's in," he added loyally, but cooking was not Susan's strong point. She had many of her meals at the hotel and had never bothered to acquire Ivy's expertise.

Miss Darwin boiled the kettle and topped up the teapot and the hot water jug. She showed Mark a key.

"I had the locks changed yesterday," she said. "But I want you to feel that you can come here, just as you used to, when you want to. I'm not going to give this to you but we'll keep it in a special hiding place outside, where you can find it if you come here and I'm out. We'll choose a place next time you come."

This might be a rash action on her part, but if she changed her mind, she could have extra locks fitted to the doors and windows and end the arrangement.

"Thanks," he said, beaming, and then added, "Miss Darwin, I know who took your box. I'll get it back for you."

"The box doesn't matter, Mark," said Marigold. "But the

fact that it was stolen does. I think we both know who took it, don't we?" She should have thought of Steve earlier; of course he would have had access to his mother's key.

Mark nodded.

"There were things before," he said, looking at the ground.

"You mean he stole from Mr. Morton?"

"Not big things. Money, mostly," Mark said.

"You weren't happy about that, were you?"

"No." He shook his head.

"We'll talk about this another time," said Marigold. "Now we must go back to the others."

Mark's mother had understood the situation; the miscreant boy's stepmother was her child-minder. She might intervene. In her place, Marigold would have gone straight round to see the woman. Probably she would do exactly that.

Marigold went to church resolved to postpone taking steps about it herself. Possibly the stolen property would be returned.

22.

When she left The Willows, Susan's intention, as Marigold anticipated, had been to confront Ivy once again, this time to demand that she challenge Steve about the burglary, but, driving off, she decided that an hour or so's delay would make little difference to the result. She must ask Mark more about the box. Other things had been stolen, too; he might have seen the video recorder or the radio in Steve's room.

"We won't need much supper after such a big tea," she said, adding, "I liked Miss Darwin."

Susan was good at assessing people, or so she thought, but now she was having doubts about Ivy, whom for years she had trusted. Elderly ladies often came to The Golden Accord for the cultural weekends, and Miss Darwin would have fitted in among them. She would expect good service and, having received it, would appreciate what was done for her. She would be civil to the staff, but not ingratiating, and would not respond well to any familiarity. She was, in fact, a person to respect.

"I like her, too," said Mark. He had resolved to keep the matter of the new key a secret between himself and Miss Darwin. He hoped his mother wouldn't raise the subject.

She parked the car—they had no garage but there was hard standing outside the house—and they went indoors, where, after they had shed their coats, she asked him about the stolen box.

"You said Steve gave one just like it to Ivy. When was that?"

"Yesterday. At least, that's when I saw it," Mark replied.

"Steve could have got into Miss Darwin's house, couldn't he? Ivy had a key."

"Yes." Mark nodded.

"Do you think the box came from The Willows?"

"I don't know," said Mark.

"Stealing's wrong. It's a crime," said Susan. "People who do and get caught can go to prison."

"Will that happen to Steve?" asked Mark.

"So you do think he's the thief," asked Susan.

"He might say he'd bought the box."

"If so, to prove it, he'd have a receipt, or at least the shop might remember selling it to him," Susan said. "What about the video, Mark, and the radio?"

Mark shrugged.

"He could have sold them," he said.

"I must go and talk to Ivy about this," said Susan. "You understand that, don't you, Mark? It has to be sorted out, one way or the other."

"Yeah." Mark wanted Miss Darwin to get her things back, and he thought Steve deserved to be caught. "Isn't Steve too young to go to prison?" he asked.

"He's not too young to get some sort of punishment," said Susan. "I'll go there now," she added. "You stay here. You can watch TV or put a video on. I won't be long."

Mark was glad to stay behind. He did not want to witness Ivy's reaction to the news of Steve's crimes. When his mother had gone, he put on the tape of *The Secret Garden*, which Ivy had recorded for Sharon years ago. She had lent

it to him. He liked the scene where Mary gave Colin a piece
of her mind and he realized how selfish he was being.
Perhaps that was what Steve needed: a piece of Ivy's mind.

Richard knew that Verity had not liked Susan Conway. As
they drove away from The Willows, she made quite sure
that he understood her views.

"What a waste of time," she said. "Miss Darwin's a boring
old witch and that silly person, Mark's mother, made me
sick, pouring on the oil all afternoon, buttering her up."

"Miss Darwin wanted to return our hospitality, and she
thought it would be useful if you met Susan Conway," he
replied austerely.

"So she's Susan, is she?" Verity had heard Richard use
Susan's first name at The Willows.

"Well, of course she's Susan." Richard answered,
exasperated. "Everyone uses first names these days."

"Except Miss Darwin," said Verity.

Marigold had begun formally, until Susan, won round
because the old woman was clearly fond of Mark, asked to
be called by her first name. No one, however, had been so
casual with Miss Darwin, not even Richard, who had
discovered her unlikely name when she joined the choir.

"She's of that generation," he said, turning in at their gate.
"I wonder where Justin is," he added, trying to divert
Verity's grievance on to familiar ground.

"He'll come home when he's ready," was her answer.

Sensing that his mother was spoiling for a fight, Terry
disappeared as soon as they entered the house. He'd found
the tea party boring, but most things involving adults were.

"It was rude of him not to have come with us," Richard
said, despite the fact that he had welcomed Justin's absence
and proceeding to provoke inevitable conflict.

"Why should he? Miss Darwin is your friend. So's dear
Susan," Verity pursued. "That's where you go when you're

late home, I suppose. I should have guessed. Well, if she's your type, you're welcome to her—nasty, common little barmaid."

Richard took a deep breath.

"I first met Susan Conway after Terry disappeared," he said. "This is only the second time I've seen her. Her son and yours are friends. That's all. Why do you have to invent plots and mysteries and jealousies, upsetting everyone?"

"I saw how you looked at her," said Verity. "As if—" she sought about for a metaphor. "As if you could eat her up— lick cream from her navel," she added wildly.

Richard had never licked anything from anybody's navel.

"I give up," he said, turning away. He'd go out to his workshop. Chipping at some timber would relieve his feelings. He'd taken up carving not only as a hobby but as a means of letting out his anger.

"You stay here when I want to talk to you," cried Verity as he moved towards the door. "You humiliate me by your affairs with other women. That Susan's a tart—she's a whore, that's what she is, working on her back in that hotel. It's probably a brothel."

Richard, stung at last, said, "You're contemptible." Where did these foul thoughts of hers originate? He raised his fist.

"Yes—hit me—go on," Verity taunted him, thrusting out her pelvis. "That's what you'd like to do, isn't it?"

Yes, he would. Richard glowered at her but he lowered his hand. So far, he had never lost control, and he did not mean to do so now. He turned his back and as he left the room, she picked up a china figure from a side table and flung it after him. It hit him on the shoulder, not his head, at which she had aimed, then fell to the ground, shattering into several fragments.

Pity, he thought, walking on into the night. That was the second piece of Meissen she had smashed. The security light came on as he walked across the garden to his workshop. The key was on a ring in his pocket, with his car keys. Tonight, on impulse, he locked himself inside, something he rarely did, and when, some minutes later, Verity came banging the door, yelling at him and swearing, he made no response. She'd cool down eventually, perhaps get a drink if she could find some alcohol. Then she'd weep, but she never apologized for these scenes.

No wonder the boys' father had taken off, he thought, not for the first time.

He picked up a chisel and a mallet and began chipping at a block of wood held in the vise on his bench. He chipped and chipped, to no design, while outside in the garden, Verity shrieked and cursed. She'd give up in the end, and go away.

She did.

Justin had known his mother would fly into one of her rages either at The Willows or afterwards. He knew her so well because he was like that himself. Sometimes he was frightened by his own violent feelings, which he could not understand.

She got angry when Cat was calm and took no notice of her temper or her outrageous remarks. Justin knew they were outrageous, but she was driven to make them because of Cat's cool nature. At school, Justin would taunt other boys, trying to wind them up and start a row; if he failed, he longed to punch them, and sometimes he did, gratified by the reaction—either a fight, or tears. He was often in trouble because of his behavior, but even at primary school, it had brought him to the attention of some older boys— Bruce and Greg in particular—and now they sometimes used him to watch their backs when they went thieving out of cars at the station or on shoplifting jaunts further afield. Steve Burton was also on the fringe of their gang and he

had done a major job the other night, bringing in a VCR
and a radio for Greg's brother to sell.

Justin was impressed. If he could do something like that,
he'd earn respect from the older boys. Perhaps stealing a
car would impress them, and it would be easier. Setting a
fire would be easier still, and exciting.

He'd been there when they lit the barn. He'd gone to the
station, vaguely planning another assault on Cat's Montego,
and they'd turned up to steal a car. They'd taken him along
and he'd seen Steve carry the petrol, heard the whoosh as
the flames went up in a great roar, felt the thrill as the fire
caught. They'd made a job of it, unlike Mum when she tried
to burn Cat's books that time. Justin had been posted as the
lookout; they'd taken him back to the station where he'd
left his bike and dropped him there, then driven off. He
didn't know what they'd done about the car; torched it,
probably, after dropping Steve.

That afternoon, Cat had asked him where he was going.

"Out," Justin had answered.

"You're expected at Miss Darwin's," Cat had stated in that
neutral tone which Justin found so irritating.

"I'm not coming. It'll be boring," Justin said.

He'd seen Cat wondering whether to order him to go
with them. If he did, Justin would defy him; he couldn't
imagine calm Cat physically forcing him to obey. Anyway, it
wouldn't be possible; Justin was five feet six now, and he
could do some damage.

Cat had turned to Verity.

"Justin is refusing to come with us," he had said,
expecting her to say he must fall into line, but Justin knew
she wouldn't.

"I don't see why he should," she'd said, quite mildly for
her. "I don't want to, either," she'd added. "You're forcing
me to go."

"No one's forcing anyone," said Cat. Justin had heard the

note of strangled patience in his voice. One day, Mum would push him too far and he'd lose his cool. "I just want you to allow Miss Darwin to bring you and Mark's mother together, since the boys are such friends."

Were they, though? Justin thought Cat overestimated the importance of the friendship but he knew Terry wasn't popular; he hadn't yet acquired the toughness needed for survival. Mark seemed to have it in his nature, and hanging out with him had helped Terry.

"It's a waste of an afternoon," his mother had protested.

What else was she planning, Justin had wondered; did she mean to watch telly? Or get drunk? Or both? If she went out, it would keep her off the booze, at least.

"You go, Mum, for Terry's sake," he said, avuncularly. "Then you can feel good about it afterwards." And take it out on Cat, he thought, sloping off before any further effort could be made to stop him.

He'd got no plans, but as he'd mentioned meeting Bruce, he went to find him, only to discover that he and two other boys were working on the wreck of an old car which one of them had bought for a few pounds. The parts could be cannibalized for other cars; they were dismembering the corpse and taking out the working vitals.

This bored Justin. He thought stealing cars was amusing but he saw no point in spending a cold, damp afternoon getting filthy. Besides, there was a limit to how many heads could bend over one engine. He was told to clean off the various parts assembled on the ground, but this important task soon palled.

"Got to go," he said, and left them.

He could return to the empty house, which would be warm and where there was food and his computer, or he could watch a video. He'd seen some horrifying ones at Bruce's house; he hadn't liked them, they were too scary, though he'd laughed like the others at the gruesome bits.

Maybe he'd go round to Steve's place first, see if Steve would like to come back with him. Steve was all right, but he lived with all those women—his stepmother and Sharon, and that little kid, Kylie. Justin wasn't sure how they were all related. It was funny, really—none of them had the right fathers. Steve's was dead; Justin and Terry's had deserted them; Mark never mentioned his. Even Adam, Sharon's baby, had no dad at home. The women didn't need them except to give them money and so they could get kids. Women seemed to like small kids, and the men needed the women for sex and to cook. Tribes, that was what was wanted, he decided, aiming for Ivy's house where he knew there would be rich cake, jam tarts and a welcome. He'd been there several times.

There were all those things, but no Steve.

"Come in, Justin. I daresay he won't be long," said Ivy, who saw before her a boy who was cold and damp and had time to kill. "How about a cup of tea and a bite to eat?"

Ivy did not hand out fizzy drinks in costly cans. At her house you had tea, or sometimes cocoa, or water, and now and then fruit juice when she'd been out shopping.

Justin accepted milky tea with sugar, and a piece of sticky gingerbread which Kylie had helped her mother make. It was delicious. When he'd finished this snack, and had warmed up, he played Snap with Kylie, who wasn't a bad little kid at all; rather cute, really, with her fair curly hair. Justin looked quite warm and rosy when, at last, he left the house.

"I'll tell Steve you called in," said Ivy. "Come anytime, Justin. You're always welcome." She liked to send a child away looking happier than when he arrived. These boys were all at sixes and sevens with themselves, no longer children but far from adult, full of conflicting feelings, hormones rattling around, and being pressed to conform to what their peers were doing. Steve worried her; he was so silent and secretive, going out at all hours. She was sure he missed Tom Morton; the old man had been a steadying influence after Joe's death.

She sighed. She loved Steve for his father's sake and would always care for him, but she wasn't sure about him. She hadn't liked that petrol smell the other night, but then, just as she was fearing he'd been mixed up in that business of the barn, he'd given her a lovely box.

He'd be all right. It would work out. He knew right from wrong.

Not long after Justin left, Susan Conway rang the bell.

Alan draped his jacket over a peg in the shed on which already hung a spade. His torch was balanced on the bench. He could have done with more light but there was no hurricane lamp among the tins and flowerpots, nor a candle end. Raising the sledgehammer, he smote the solid center of the concrete path and, most satisfyingly, this time it cracked at once. It wouldn't take too long to break it up.

He was not in good condition, and it was heavy work; after breaking up a section, he took the pickaxe and prized up the jagged lumps he'd raised; then he resumed his blows. The noise echoed in his ears but he was making progress. Once the surface had been broken, he would still have to dig, but that could be done comparatively silently, even after the old girl came home. He must finish tonight.

Time passed. Alan had no sense of how long he had been working as the chunks of concrete mounted at the side of his excavated plot. He used a spade to dig down in the area where he was sure the gun lay buried; the change of movement was welcome. Then he felt resistance, something solid. He crouched, groping with his hands, and touched the plastic covering of the gun. He'd got there! As triumphant as any treasure hunter, Alan renewed his efforts, digging now more cautiously as he exposed the bundle.

He never heard the shed door open. All he saw was a sudden shaft of light from someone else's powerful torch; behind it stood a figure.

Alan's reaction was a reflex. Up came the spade.

She didn't stand a chance, though, unnervingly, she screamed before he hit her for the second time. Then he dropped the spade and grabbed the sledgehammer. He made quite sure that she was dead before he stopped his blows.

Now he had all the time in the world to complete his task.

23.

After Tom's son had gone, Steve had found money at Merrifields. Once, when he was at the house with Justin, he had seen the other boy go to a drawer in a desk in Richard's study and take out five pounds.

"Cat keeps a bit here for rainy days," Justin had said. "This is a rainy day," and he laughed in what Steve thought was a weird way, though he laughed, too.

Justin had never robbed Cat before and now he did it only to impress Steve. Later, he'd replaced the money with a five-pound note he'd got from his mother, pretending that he needed it for a school trip. Cat would have known who'd been to the drawer, and the consequences could have been unpleasant, since he had power over all of them.

Today, there were thirty-five pounds in the drawer and Steve took the lot. Upstairs, there was jewelry. He stole it neatly, not turning the place upside down because what was the point of that? He'd got no quarrel with the Gardners. He found some silver spoons and forks, and after searching vainly for a holdall, took a pillowcase from a bed and put them, with the slim video recorder, in that. You could always get money for a video. Then he took the mixer from the kitchen. He had to find a second pillowcase to carry what would not go into the loaded first one, and, once again stumped by the limit on what he could carry, Steve left, walking home laden with his spoils. He would hide everything in his room and see if he couldn't sell the video himself without using Greg's brother as a middleman; he'd get more that way, and it was time he made his own connections.

He stuffed the pillowcases under some bushes in the front garden, hoping it wouldn't start to rain; damp would do the electrical things no good. He'd have to come down to collect them after everyone had gone to bed. Give Ivy her due, she didn't pry, so she wouldn't find them in his room, which he was expected to keep clean himself. He didn't mind that; it was a fair exchange for privacy.

Whistling, he entered the house, and Sharon, the baby in her arms, came out of the kitchen, intercepting him on his way upstairs.

"You're wanted in there," she said, nodding towards the sitting room. "Trouble," she added. "Susan's here."

Steve had noticed the blue Vauxhall in the road outside but had thought nothing of it as he stuffed his bundles underneath a prickly berberis. Susan came round to pay Ivy and sometimes to drop Mark off; perhaps he was stopping over tonight.

Ivy had heard their voices. She emerged from the front room and asked Steve to come inside. Her face was quite without expression and she walked back into the room ahead of him, seating herself beside Susan on the sofa. Between them was the decorated box which Steve had given her.

"I was very touched by this lovely present which you gave me, Steve," she said. "Where did you get it?"

"Oh—a shop in High Wycombe," Steve replied. "I went

there with some mates." He grinned at them, but at the same time he shifted his feet awkwardly.

"A box like this was stolen from Miss Darwin at The Willows on Thursday night when she was out," said Ivy.

"Oh?" said Steve. "How weird. Maybe she bought it at the same place."

"She made hers. She does the decorating," Ivy said. "There's not another like it."

As soon as Susan had made her accusation, Ivy had telephoned Miss Darwin to ask her to come round and identify the box, but there was no reply. Now that Steve was back, they must proceed without her.

"Some jewelry was stolen, too," said Susan. "And a radio, a toaster, and the video."

"Well?" Steve shrugged, but his mind was racing round as he tried to see a route out of the trap.

"We've got a key to The Willows. You used it often enough to visit Tom," said Ivy. "There was no forced entry. You could have done it, Steve, and then there's this box, which you've only just given me."

"Miss Darwin was visited by Mark one day," said Susan. She wasn't going to reveal that he had acquired a key of his own and had entered the house uninvited. "He told her about being friends with Mr. Morton and she thought he might be the thief."

Steve made a wry face.

"Not Mark," he said. "He'd not steal."

"I hope you wouldn't either," Ivy said. "Steve, I want to go into your room now and look among your things in case there is any stolen property there."

"Course there isn't," Steve replied.

"Then you won't mind us looking, will you?" Ivy said. "Susan will be a witness." She stood up and left the room and Susan followed.

Steve thought about running off, but if he did, he would

stand no chance, whereas if he faced it out, Ivy wouldn't shop him to the police. Miss Darwin could have her rotten jewelry back. He'd got that other stuff outside and it was worth a bit, but he'd have to shift it as soon as this little scene was over.

He'd come clean about The Willows, get it over, produce the tatty bits and bobs and let them crucify him with their tongues. He didn't want Ivy going through his things; there were one or two items he'd rather she didn't see—a few pills he'd bought but hadn't tried, and some books she wouldn't like, not to mention the condoms. She'd think he was too young for those. He hadn't used one yet; he didn't really want to, but the guys all talked about their scores and he might change his mind.

He put on a bold expression and opened the bottom drawer of his chest where, stuffed inside a sock, was Miss Darwin's jewelry. He gave the sock to Ivy.

"It's all there," he said.

"What about the radio and the video recorder?" Susan asked. "And the toaster?"

Steve shrugged again.

"They're gone," he said. "A man took them off me." If he said he'd sold them to a mate, they'd want to know name, address, blood group, date of birth, everything. "She'll get it off the insurance."

"She wouldn't have got this." Ivy felt cold with shock at the proof of his guilt. She balanced the sock in her hand while she tried to think how Joe would have dealt with him. It wouldn't have happened if he hadn't died; he'd have kept tabs on Steve, prevented this. Though she'd been anxious about the boy, she hadn't seen it shaping up. "It's probably of sentimental value, like my ring your dad gave me," she said.

He might have been caught trying to flog the jewelry; perhaps that was what he needed: a real fright. As it was, if

Miss Darwin could be persuaded, this time he might be spared.

"Miss Darwin knows about the box," Ivy told him. "She wasn't able to be here tonight, otherwise she could have decided what to do about the rest of it. Whether to tell the police. I expect she'll have to. I'll go and see her tomorrow and ask what's to be done. You'll stay in your room now, Steve."

She felt like Atlas bearing the burden of the world as she went downstairs with Susan.

"What will you do?" asked Susan, who felt extremely sorry for her.

"It won't be up to me, once Miss Darwin knows the truth," said Ivy.

Susan resolved to postpone any drastic change in Mark's arrangements.

"Please don't let Mark go into town with Steve," was her sole request.

Steve wondered if Ivy would lock him in his room. If so, he'd have to get out of the window to move the stuff from the garden. He must shift it off the premises, hide it somewhere else, even the grounds of one of the big houses in Wordsworth Road, like The Willows.

Alan had to hide the body. He could bury it in the hole from which he'd taken the gun. He'd need to dig a lot deeper, and it would take up far more space, but there was no hurry now.

Shooting would have been a cleaner way of doing it, if she'd come a little later, when the gun was ready, cleaned and loaded. He'd rolled her with his foot under the bench while he went on digging. Luckily his torch, which had fallen to the ground during the skirmish—not that she had put up much resistance—hadn't broken. She'd dropped hers and it had gone off. He'd find it when he'd got her out of the way.

He needn't test the gun here, in this poor light, where it was cold and damp. He could do it in comfort in the house. No one would come in upon him now while he made himself at home. He could even sleep there, as was his right, but he'd better not stay long in case someone came asking for the old bag.

He let himself out of the shed, then turned to take his jacket off the hook. He put it on; the night was cold, and he had sweated while he dug. Between the trees he saw lights shining from the house, a welcome beacon in the gloom. She must have returned from church and noticed his torch beam through the window of the shed, then come inquisitively down. Nosy old bitch, she deserved what she had got. He picked up the gun and the box of cartridges and strode back towards the house, swaggering with confidence, claiming what should have been his own.

He had no key. There'd be one on the body, obviously— she'd have it in her pocket or her bag. She must have dropped that when she fell. Alan did not bother to go back and hunt for it. The door might be open, if she'd gone into the house before noticing his light; if not, there'd be no problem now.

The front door was locked, so he went in by the back door, remembering how he'd seen the kid enter the other house only a short time earlier. Good luck to him if he could get away with it, thought Alan. He broke the glass in the same manner as the boy had done, then reached in and found the key. She'd left every light on in the place; when he'd returned earlier, he'd had to remind himself that she lived there on her own because, though the curtains had been drawn, there were slits of light showing behind them at almost all the windows.

Now, standing in the brightly lit kitchen, he saw that there was blood on his clothes, and his strong new shoes were covered in mud, not so much from his excavations, which had been comparatively dry, as from his wanderings. He was very dirty, sweaty as well as muddy.

He didn't like it. He could have a bath here, get himself cleaned up, but with no man in the house there'd be no change of clothing. There would be only women's stuff, and even if he found some things to fit, he wasn't going to start cross-dressing.

He took off his shoes, and, in his socks, he moved about, seeking comfort. The kitchen had been rearranged but there was still a large store cupboard leading from it; once, it had been a larder, and was cool. Inside, on a shelf facing the door, he found whiskey, gin and sherry. He chose the whiskey and drank some from the bottle before pouring more into a tumbler he saw face down on the drainer by the sink. He topped it up with water from the tap. Neat whiskey fired him up but didn't quench his thirst. Then, nursing his glass, he went upstairs to take a look around.,

The first room he entered was his own, and he was shocked. Instead of his posters and the dozens of books he hadn't looked at for years, even before he moved out when he was nineteen, there were clean walls painted primrose yellow, and, on the newly painted shelves a few books. He picked one up. It was *Coot Club*, and he saw his name inside, and the date, in his mother's writing. He hurled it across the floor into a corner. Against one wall there was a small desk, with some pencils and crayons in a box. There was a plain blue carpet, and new curtains printed with various plants were drawn across the window.

This was his room. How dare someone change everything?

Alan seized several colored pencils and slashed them across the wall, breaking two of them, then threw them down to join *Coot Club* on the ground. He picked up the chair which stood before the desk and was about to fling it at the window when he remembered that the broken glass would cause a draft. He let it fall from his grasp, and it toppled over to lie on its side.

Damned old cow, he thought. She'd turned out all his stuff. His past had gone. Even so, he could live here till someone missed her. Maybe he could stave off queries, pretend to be her nephew—anything. People were so gullible. In prison he'd heard tales from men who had worked fiddles on the weakest of assumptions. But he must remember that the youth could give him away—the junior, apprentice thief, young Steve.

Alan had left the gun in the kitchen, and he went downstairs again to look at it, unwrapping its many layers of polythene, clicking the trigger. No rust was visible. He'd greased it well all those years ago and now he wiped it on a kitchen towel, then broke it open. An unloaded gun was useless. He peeled the protective coverings from the box of cartridges and took two out. They looked all right. Terrorists kept weapons concealed for years. He slid the cartridges into each barrel of the gun. Now, if a caller came, he was prepared.

After that, he began searching for food. In the refrigerator, covered in foil, there was a plate of sandwiches which tasted very fresh. He took them upstairs with him to his own room, where he had left his glass of whiskey, and he sat own on the floor to eat them, rocking gently to and fro.

By the time Justin returned home that evening, everyone else was back at Merrifields. Terry was in their playroom, music on, the volume turned up very loud.

"They've been fighting again," he said to Justin.

He looked very white. The rows between his mother and Richard frightened him, whereas they simply made Justin angry with their stepfather.

"Where are they?" Justin asked, turning the music down.

"Cat's gone to his workshop. I don't know where Mum is." Terry answered.

Much to his surprise, he'd liked it round at that old lady's. Terry had known his mother was seething, ready to explode, but Cat was calm, and Miss Darwin seemed to have everything under control. Mum wouldn't flare up while they were there. The food that was set out was excellent; Mark seemed quite at home, and nothing went really wrong while they were in that house. Even Mark's mother had got quite chatty, trying to be nice to Mum, who wouldn't respond. Yet she could be lovely; why did she have to be so changeable? Was it because he, Terry, was sometimes naughty, like the night he ran away? But he didn't often do bad things. Justin was the one who hung around with boys who, Terry knew, had been taken home in police cars; he had seen it happen. Maybe they hadn't done much, but if you went in one of their cars, you'd caught their attention, just as he'd done, and he didn't want that to happen a second time.

"It's all Cat's fault," said Justin. "He gets up her nose. And mine," he added, for good measure.

Terry knew this wasn't fair.

"He works hard. He pays for all of us," he said.

"And he lets us know it," Justin answered. "I'll go and look for Mum."

Terry thought she was best left till she'd had time to cool down, but it was no good telling Justin that. He turned the volume up again and lay back in his chair, rocking and gyrating to the beat.

Justin went all over the house looking for his mother, but she was not in her bedroom, nor her studio, nor the kitchen, nor her bathroom. He called her name in vain. She must have gone outside. He looked for her coat, the long loose black one with the hood which she often wore, and he could not see it. Was that what she'd had on today, going out to tea? He supposed so. Her bag was in the drawing room. He opened it to look for money and found some coins and a five-pound note in her purse; she never had a lot as she spent anything she could spare on drink. He took two pound coins; she wouldn't miss them. Where could she be? He'd go and see if Cat knew.

He didn't notice the broken glass by the French window, where Alan, after entering, had pulled the curtain across to close out the night. Alan and Steve had both left by the front door. Justin walked towards Richard's workshop.

"Cat—where's Mum?" he called, and had to repeat his question several times before his stepfather took any notice.

"I don't know," was all he said, when at last he bothered to respond.

Justin went off, fuming. How dare he stay in there, locked in, all smug and toffee-nosed when Mum was miserable? Anyone could see that she was sad, the way she drank and flew into her tempers. She wouldn't do it if she was happy. He blamed Cat for everything.

He went back to the house and checked again that his mother was not there. Then he fetched an empty bottle from the box by the back door; there were always plenty of them around—his mother's gin and vodka bottles. He took it to the garage. There was petrol there. Cat kept a can in the boot of his car; he'd had one on the day he rescued Mom, though a flat tire was the problem then.

He poured some petrol into the bottle and found a piece of rag which he stuffed in the top. He had to go back into the house to get some matches, but then he set off down the garden once again. With Cat gone, they'd be happy, him and Mum and Terry.

Justin's homemade bomb backfired on him, flaring as he lit it, catching petrol droplets which had fallen on his clothes, exploding into flames as he tried to throw it through the window of the workshop.

24.

Richard put the flames out, beating at Justin with his bare hands and rolling the boy on the ground. Justin's anorak was still damp despite its sojourn in Ivy's warm house, and its smoldering was soon extinguished, but his jeans, where petrol had dripped onto the denim, had scorched, and he was very badly burned. His screams had turned to whimpers when Richard, not daring to move him, covered him with his own jacket and hurried to the house to telephone for help.

"I'll be back in a few minutes, Justin," he said. "I've got to call an ambulance."

Terry, his music turned up loud, had not heard the noise of the exploding bottle. Now he was vaguely aware of a door banging and disturbance in the house but he took no notice until Richard burst into the room.

"Turn that noise off and go and fetch your mother," Richard, who had already telephoned, shouted at him, reaching out to Terry's music system, only to have Terry turn into a fiend, snatching at his hand. "There's been an accident. Justin's badly burned. Find your mother, and when the ambulance comes, send them to the workshop.

I'm going back to Justin. Come on, Terry," he ordered. "Get going. This is serious." He rushed out of the room again, leaving Terry staring after him, horrified.

Richard, back beside the injured boy, did not know how to help him. He knelt beside him, stroking his damp hair and talking to him, assuring him that the ambulance would soon arrive. Justin was crying with shock as much as pain. To both of them, it seemed hours before they heard the siren and saw light approaching over the garden.

As the paramedics bent over Justin, Richard rose.

"I don't know where his mother is. I'll go and find her," he said. Had Terry even looked for her?

Walking back towards the house, he saw the boy, illuminated by the outside lights, standing in the garden. He looked small and shrunken, but Richard had no time for sympathy.

"Haven't you found your mother?" he called out. "Where is she?"

"She's not in the house," said Terry. He was coatless, arms clutched across him, teeth chattering in the cold. "Is Justin dead?"

"No, of course not. He'll be all right," said Richard. "He must have been messing about with some petrol. It's very dangerous stuff. I'll find Verity. You get inside and keep warm."

He went indoors and ran all over the house, into every room, calling Verity by name but, as Terry had said, she was not there. After she'd battered at the workshop door, she must have gone storming off into the night. Had she crossed the fence and gone over the fields, where the river was in flood? He knew that the boys had made themselves a crossing point and that she used it too. Stumbling over the flooded fields in darkness was foolhardy, but at the moment she must take her chance; he would have to go with Justin to the hospital.

He went back to the team working with Justin in the garden. They had him on a stretcher now and were ready to take him to the ambulance.

"We can't tell how bad he is until we get him into casualty," said one of the crew. "He's very shocked. How did it happen?"

"I'm not sure what he was doing but I think he'd got some petrol in a bottle." Richard had scrunched his knee on broken glass when crouching by the boy. "There was a bang—a flash—almost an explosion. I was in my workshop and came out at once." He nodded at the shed.

"Lucky you were near," was the comment. "We'll get on, then."

"I can't find his mother," Richard said. "She's out somewhere. I'll leave her a message and come with you."

"Follow us in your car," he was advised. "There's the other boy to think of, isn't there? And you'll need to get back, later. I guess we'll be keeping Justin." They had asked the boy's name and used it, talking to him reassuringly. "Maybe you could get a neighbor in," the paramedic added.

"All right." Richard saw the sense of this. "Tell Justin I'm on my way and that his mother will be coming." If he could find her quickly, he could take her. Whatever she was up to, would she be fit to drive herself if she came later? She could take a taxi. He'd suggest it in his note.

When Justin had been taken away, he went into the house to write it. Terry was in the drawing room.

"We've been robbed," he said. "Look—the window's broken and the video's gone."

Richard almost didn't comprehend what Terry said: then he saw the broken windowpane and the gap where the video recorder had slotted in on a shelf under the television set.

"Oh God," he said. "Well, it will have to wait. I can't deal with that now."

"Perhaps the burglar set Justin on fire," said Terry.

"I don't think so," Richard said. "Where do you think your mother is? I'll have to go to the hospital."

"Don't leave me here on my own," said Terry, sniffing. "The burglar might come back and get me."

"He won't," said Richard. "He'll be busy hiding what he's taken, or selling it to someone." There was no time to look around to see what else was missing. "All right. Get a coat. I'm writing a note for your mother."

Composing it, and writing down the number of the taxi firm, he grew calmer. Delay here would make no difference to Justin, who was in good hands. He stuck the Post-It note to the fridge door, where, in the days when communications had been easier, messages were left. Sooner or later, everyone went to the fridge. Then he remembered the ambulance attendant's suggestion about a neighbor. Miss Darwin might try ringing Verity at intervals, or might even come to the house and be there when she came home.

He dialed her number but got no reply. He glanced at his watch; it was nearly eight o'clock. So late! Verity must have been roaming round for more than two hours. Miss Darwin had said nothing, that afternoon, about going out later, but then, why should she? For all he knew, she had made a lot of friends and had a busy social life. He could try ringing her again from the hospital.

Before leaving, he decided to telephone the police. They must be told about the burglary, following so soon after The Willows had been robbed. The thief had not attacked Justin, however; Richard had a shrewd idea of what had really happened and the hatred it revealed horrified him.

It took a little time to get the information through, because Haverscot police station had closed for the night, but eventually a voice told Richard that an officer would find him at the hospital. He mentioned that his wife, the

boy's mother, could not be found and agreed it was too
soon to consider her a missing person.

Then he left the house, not locking up because Verity
might not have a key and anyway, with a broken window,
why bother? Despite his comforting words to Terry, Richard
thought it possible for the thief to be lurking in the bushes,
waiting to get in a second time and take what he had left
behind earlier.

At the moment, Richard did not care. He stopped the car
in the drive, however, and went back to lock up his
workshop, with its array of tools, some of which could be
used as lethal weapons.

Terry, strapped into the front passenger seat, leaned
slightly towards his stepfather as they drove to Radbury
Hospital. Every now and then he sniffed, and Richard
managed not to tell him to blow his nose. When they
reached the hospital and had found a parking slot, he
reached into the car for a box of tissues and gave Terry a
handful.

"Stick them in your pocket," he said.

Terry did so, sniffing on.

Richard tried the telephone again, half an hour later.
There was no reply from Merrifields, but this time The
Willows's line was engaged. Richard now became seriously
concerned about Verity. Wouldn't she have rung the
hospital before driving over, if she ignored his advice about
taking a taxi? Perhaps she had crashed her car. Various
scenarios, all equally alarming, ran through his mind as he
returned to Terry and decided that both of them needed
food. After they'd tracked some down within the hospital,
there might be firm news about Justin's condition and
perhaps they would be allowed to see him. However,
before that could happen, the police came. Richard
described the sudden flash when he was in his workshop,

and how he went outside to find Justin screaming on the ground. He explained about the burglary, which he and Terry had discovered only later.

It seemed that other officers had already gone to Merrifields; arson was a serious crime and there had been several incidents in the area, notably the recent burning of a barn where youths were suspected of having set it alight. Specialists would want to discover exactly what had happened outside Richard's workshop, and what Justin had planned to do.

They would succeed, too, Richard thought, but that was of academic importance at the moment.

The police officer said he would get onto his colleagues at Haverscot to see if Verity had returned. While he was talking to them in a quiet corner of the hospital, a nurse said that Richard and Terry could see Justin. His burns were serious, especially those on his legs and his hands, but he would survive.

Richard propelled Terry ahead of him into the cubicle where Justin, not yet allocated to a ward, lay. His face was scorched, and tufts of his hair were singed. He did not look at Richard.

"You'll feel better soon," Richard said, encouragingly.

"It's all your fault." Justin, sedated, spoke in a feeble growl.

Richard knew then that his suspicions were correct: Justin's fiery bomb had been meant for him, with serious intent, if not to kill. He felt a shaft like ice pierce him.

"Did the burglar do it?" Terry asked. "Did you see him?"

Justin did not understand what he was saying. All he knew was that his body had become a mass of scorching pain and Richard, as always, was to blame.

"I want Mum," he croacked.

"She'll be here soon," said Richard.

At this point, a nurse told them they must go.

"Your dad can come and see you again soon, and he'll bring your mum," she said.

"He's not my dad," Richard heard Justin say in a sudden loud, clear voice, as he turned away. He did not look back, taking Terry with him, holding him by the sleeve of his jacket.

Outside, the police officers had no news of Verity, but there was evidence about what had caused Justin's injuries and Richard was needed back at Merrifields. There was no point in him and Terry staying any longer at the hospital; they had supplied all the necessary information, and could be telephoned if there was any change in Justin's condition. They drove home, with Terry very silent.

When they arrived, there was still no sign of Verity. Richard sent Terry off to have a bath and get ready for bed. Then he prepared to hear what the officers on the spot had to say.

They had found fragments of a bottle which had contained petrol, and a box of matches. There were wisps of burned rag. It was thought that there would be prints on some of the glass and on the matchbox.

"The lad lit it himself, I'm afraid," said the investigating Detective Inspector. At least the officers were not those who had come round after Terry's escapade, thought Richard wearily. Now that he knew Justin was out of danger, it was Verity about whom he was concerned. Where could she be?

He expressed his anxiety and mentioned the burglary.

"Ah yes—well, we've got some news for you about that," said the inspector. "We've caught your thief. While we were on our way here, we met a young lad with two pillowslips full of stuff whose possession he couldn't satisfactorily explain. He'd a video and some jewelry and silver. We picked him out in the headlights." He smiled. "It was quite pleasing," he declared. "He's a juvenile, so my colleagues are contacting his parents."

"If they're ours, the postcode's on the video, in that invisible ink you recommend," said Richard. "And we've got photographs of most of the jewelry and silver."

"I'm glad to hear it," said the inspector. "That'll make identification of the property much easier."

"But what about my wife?" pressed Richard. "She was in a state. We'd had a row." He took a deep breath. "I'm thinking of the river. It's in flood. She might have fallen in and been swept away." He paused, then continued, "She came banging on my workshop door and I took no notice. I'm afraid I'd had it up to here," he added, gesturing.

"We can't do much till daylight," said the inspector. "We'll use lights and dogs along the riverside, just in case. But she's probably gone round to a friend's, just to give you a fright, if you'd had words." Poor guy, he thought; a row with the wife and a wild kid trying to torch his workshop.

"I'll come with you," Richard said. Then he remembered Terry. "Oh—I suppose I can't leave my other stepson on his own." What could he do? Would Miss Darwin come round?

"We'll get a woman officer over to keep an eye on him," said the inspector. "You probably know the fields beside the river quite well—your local knowledge will be helpful to us."

It looked like being quite a night.

25.

Alan was sitting in his old room at The Willows. Before him was an open book: *Coot Club*, with his mother's inscription on the flyleaf.

It was his property. So was everything that had been in this room. Even if his father—Tom—had left him nothing in his will, surely all that had been in here, the books and furniture and his posters, rightfully belonged to him? They should have been restored, now that he was free.

Unseeingly, he turned the pages of the book. He had enjoyed the series when he was a boy, and his parents, anxious to occupy an only child, had sent him on a sailing course at a center geared to youngsters, but he hadn't liked the cold and wet when his boat capsized. He'd never liked discomfort and he'd had more than enough of it in recent years. This house, compared with his rented flat, was luxurious; now that the old girl was dead, why shouldn't he move in until Mick got out?

He couldn't, without other clothes. He couldn't stay in these dirty bloodstained things. When he'd buried her, he'd have to get back to the flat and change. Sitting there on the floor, he was still consumed with rage; the woman who had bought this place had bundled up his stuff, got rid of everything, expunged his past, and he resented it. If he hadn't already killed her, he'd have certainly set up a plan to do it now.

From somewhere in the house, he heard the telephone start ringing. On and on it went, the sound shrilling in his ears. When at last it stopped, he crossed the landing to the main bedroom where there was an extension and, snatching at the handset, took it off the hook and let it dangle. Now, anyone ringing up the old woman would just think that she was chattering away. He didn't want people to come looking for her, but when he and Mick had robbed their bank and left the country, anyone could call.

He looked around the bedroom which had been his mother's; Tom's too, of course, but that didn't count. Though it contained different furniture and the curtains were now blue, printed with yellow flowers, instead of his mother's mushroom pink, patterned with daisies, there was a similarity to it, and he was unable to make himself do what he really wanted: tear the place apart, smash the mirrors, foul the bedlinen.

Mick might enjoy a few nights here; it would impress him if Alan laid it on; there'd be respect. He could sort things out in the morning—bury the body in daylight when he could see what he was doing, then go back to the flat and get some clothes.

But he ought to make the trip to Reading in darkness, so that no one could see the state that he was in.

Undecided, he went downstairs for some more whiskey, filling the tumbler, splashing in only a little water. He took it back upstairs to the room where he had played music, made his models, sulked throughout his youth. He finished the sandwiches, eyes still on the book which Mark had recently enjoyed. He did not hear the front door open, quietly.

*　　*　　*

After church, Marigold had gone round to see Susan Conway. She was sure that, by this time, Mark's mother would have had a significant conversation with Ivy; if the box and other items were to be returned, Marigold could tell the police her property had been brought back anonymously and the matter could rest there.

Susan hid her annoyance at Miss Darwin's appearance on her doorstep once again, adopting a professional air of welcome.

"I'm sure you want to get on—I know you're busy—but I wanted to ask if you'd had a discussion with—Ivy, is it?" said Marigold.

Couldn't she have telephoned, thought Susan, not realizing that Marigold had, in any case, been out of the house and was passing the end of the road.

"Oh—Steve did do it," Susan said. "I think Ivy will be round to see you in the morning. The jewelry was in his room."

"I see," said Marigold.

"Come in, won't you?" Susan said, resigned. Tiresome though the interruption was, Miss Darwin had been very kind to Mark when she might have been extremely angry.

"Mark's upstairs having his bath," said Susan.

"Oh. Just as well, perhaps, that he shouldn't hear about this," said Marigold. "Though of course he'd caught on about the box."

"Yes," agreed Susan.

They sat facing one another on either side of the room.

"You're worried about leaving Mark with Ivy after this," Marigold pronounced.

"Yes."

"I can understand that. It's not her fault, however. You were satisfied with her when you made the original plan for Mark, after all."

"Steve was quite young then, and his father was alive," said Susan. "He was more controllable. And Mark has a lot of freedom now. It's inevitable. I want him to be able to take care of himself."

"He seems a most capable boy," said Miss Darwin.

"Bad company can damage anyone," said Susan.

"That's true. But Mark has other friends than Steve, hasn't he? Terry, for instance."

"Oh yes," said Susan. But Terry had been very silly, and she had met few others.

"I hope we can deal with this without the police pressing charges," said Miss Darwin. "Steve will have to be punished in some way. Perhaps he could help me in my garden—mow the lawn and cut down rubbish—unpaid for a while, and if he's a good worker I could offer him a regular job on Saturdays."

"That's a good idea," said Susan. "I'm sure Ivy would be very grateful."

"I don't want gratitude—just the return of my stolen property and a reformed junior criminal," said Miss Darwin. "He needs to be kept away from his dubious companions before it's too late. It would be a pity if he posed as either a hero or a martyr."

"Yes." Susan looked at the older woman. Her lips were set, her expression determined. Steve wouldn't be able to run rings round her. She smiled, and Miss Darwin's features relaxed too. She wished Susan smiled a genuine smile more often, not a superficial one which must be necessary in her job but was meaningless.

"I'll be happy to see Mark whenever he likes to call," Miss Darwin said. "And if you would like him to spend some time with me after school while you make up your mind about Ivy, he's most welcome. He can do his homework and be safe while you're at work, and I'll feed him, too. I like cooking," she added truthfully. She had enjoyed preparing nourishing meals for her parents; now she rarely took much trouble for herself.

"That's very kind of you," said Susan. "If he could—just for a week or so—till I'm sure about things. On a business footing, of course."

Marigold knew Susan would not accept what she would term as charity.

"Naturally," she said. She could put what sums Susan would insist on handing over into a fund for Mark. "That's settled, then," she added, suppressing her unfamiliar feeling of delight. "I'll expect him after school tomorrow." She rose to leave. "You've done a good job with him and it can't be easy for you. I've known several widows and their sons have turned out very well, but it's sad to lack a father, and a boy is the better for a good one." She moved towards the door. "However, there are schoolmasters in boys' lives and the fathers of their friends, good male influences. Richard Gardner, for instance, is a very pleasant man."

"Yes, he seems to be," said Susan. "That's not an easy situation, either. Being a stepfather, I mean."

"No, it's not," said Marigold, glad Susan had not taken her own remarks as implied criticism when they were intended as encouragement. "But a lot of things that are worth doing are quite difficult."

"I'm not a widow," Susan said. "I've never been married."

"Nor have I," said Marigold. "Who cares?"

Nearing home, Marigold looked forward to her drink. Now and then she had an evening totally without one, just to prove she could, but since she had found that a few stiff ones coaxed her into a mood of cheerfulness, she sometimes even sang along to the radio. In London, this was never her way; she was always strictly sober and very solemn.

It had been a long day, full of tests. Now it was nearly

over. Walking up the drive, she was glad to see the lights shining from her house, welcoming her home. She let herself in, still missing Sinbad's friendly greeting, and hung her coat in the cloakroom. She left her hat there, too, for it was rather damp; when it had dried off she'd take it upstairs. Then she went into the sitting room and helped herself to a large gin and tonic, from the bottles and glasses kept in the corner fitment. She did not bother about ice and lemon, but after swallowing a mouthful she lit the fire and sat down on the sofa. In a few minutes she would fetch the sandwiches left from tea. Soon the gin took effect and her spirits lifted. She was happy to be helping Mark, and was looking forward to his company, but she was not sanguine about Steve or Ivy, his unlucky stepmother. There would be a hard row to be hoed there, she thought, unless the boy could be given a fright about what the consequences of his crime might have been. Though nowadays, youngsters seemed to escape with a severe telling-off—a caution—for really serious offenses. It seemed that they went after anything they wanted; young thieves did not respect other people or their property.

She topped up her glass before going to fetch the sandwiches, which would soon blot up the alcohol. Her father had always believed in a nip to keep out the cold; it had never caused him to lose control or behave badly. It made you shed your inhibitions; she knew that. Your true nature would be revealed—mawkish or maudlin, merry or bellicose; she had seen it often enough in other people but until she began trying it herself, after her return to Haverscot, she had not understood that she was, herself, one of the cheerful ones. She had never let herself go that far before.

Did poor Richard Gardner ever let go? He'd certainly been drinking when she saw him at The Red Lion, in the bar. He was an unhappy man, but his wife was miserable. What a bitter woman she seemed to be.

Carrying her second drink, she went out to the kitchen. When she opened the door, she felt a draft, and, more slowly than if she were completely sober, she realized that the glass in the back door was broken. She was already opening the fridge door when she saw earth on the floor and a large pair of men's shoes on the mat. She had just noticed a bottle of whiskey, half full, on the worktop by the sink when a mustached man with wild gray hair, dirty, and with blood on his face, burst into the room from the hall. He carried a shotgun, and, as she stared at him, transfixed, he halted by the door and fired two shots straight at her.

Alan thought he had seen a ghost. He couldn't have killed the old cow after all, for here she was, as large as life and hideous, but she didn't fall after he had fired at her.

Marigold had been saved because the shelves in the fridge door, which had shielded her, had been stacked with bottles, tins and packs of juice whose fluid contents had stopped the shots, though some bits of metal flew about the room and one slightly grazed her hand. She had a brief advantage over her assailant because, although she was shocked and her ears rang with the sound of the explosions, she accepted what she saw, whereas he thought he beheld an apparition.

Milk, cream, mineral water, fruit juice and broken eggs cascaded onto the kitchen floor. As if it were a film unfolding before her, Marigold saw the man move, breaking the gun open as he did so, and he reached towards the box of cartridges which was standing near the bread bin. Marigold stretched out to grab the glass holding her drink which she had put down on the table. She picked it up and threw it at his head. It caught him on the ear and liquid splashed him but it barely put him off course. He was between her and the door: she might get to the back door before he reloaded the gun, but he could still hit her with it.

He was already shoving two new cartridges into the barrels when Marigold hit him over the head with the bottle of whiskey from which Alan himself had drunk earlier. He sank to the floor in a most gratifying way, loosening his grip on the gun, and she snatched it from him.

He was only stunned. Marigold pushed the cartridges home and cocked it again, ready to fire. She pointed it at him as he began to struggle to his feet, ramming it against his chest. He was blinking at her, trying to clear his head which was fuddled with the whiskey as well as the blow he had received. He was still sure that she must be a ghost come back to haunt him.

Marigold prodded him with the gun, then moved back, realizing he might be able to seize it by the barrel and wrench it from her grasp.

"I can use this," she said. "Never doubt that."

He didn't, but sick rage began to fill him now. He clung onto a cupboard top, managing to stand.

"You old bitch," he said. "You move into my house and take all my things away and think you're so great," and then he broke into a string of obscenities.

What was he talking about? He was obviously mad, and also extremely dangerous and violent. Marigold knew she must be very careful and take no chances; he was much younger than she was and a great deal stronger. She held the gun pointing firmly at him and then discovered that he was a coward. Later, she realized that of course he must have been one, to have fired at her at all; armed as he was, an elderly woman posed no great challenge.

But, to Alan, she did: She looked intimidating, glowering at him from under her grim gray hair, her thick brows forming another serious line across her face. She was not wearing her glasses, but she did not need them for this encounter.

"Get in there," she ordered, indicating the storeroom with the barrel of the gun. "Go on." She spoke firmly, like a general commanding his troops. "On the count of three or I'll fire," she warned. "Open the door. I'm waiting."

You naughty boy. Go up to your room at once or you'll be smacked, Alan heard his mother's voice. *I'm counting to three.* She had never had to carry out her threat.

Meekly, Alan went into the store-cupboard. There was no bolt on the outside of the door, but after she had banged it shut behind him—it opened outwards into the kitchen—Marigold pulled the table across in front of it and then, having dared to set the gun down, wedged that against the door with the fridge, which was very heavy, and difficult to move because of all the mess, but she did it. This barricade would not hold against a strong, determined man; she could not risk leaving it to telephone the police but must sit here, a sentry. In the morning when the milkman came, maybe she could shout for help. But that was hours away. It wasn't even midnight yet.

The floor was awash with the mess from the fridge. She sat clear of the worst of it, on a kitchen chair, holding the gun across her knees, ready to lift it if the cupboard door gave in to his battering as he rattled it, shouting and yelling. Maybe she should have shot him in the foot.

Then I'd have been charged with assault, she thought, resolving to hit his hands if they appeared.

Time passed, and after a while the man's cries diminished. Perhaps he had fallen asleep. Dare she risk leaving the room to telephone?

Just as she had decided to chance it, he resumed his cursing and swearing, and then he started throwing things around inside the cupboard. He must have found the light switch in there. She heard tins and bottles break, but the noise he made did not drown the sound of the front doorbell which, like angel music from the spheres, Marigold suddenly heard above the uproar. Surely whoever was there would hear the din and come to investigate? She'd add her yells to those of the intruder.

It was Richard at the door, and he did.

26.

At first he could not take in the spectacle before him. As he opened the unlocked back door, noting the broken pane of glass, he saw Miss Darwin rising from a kitchen chair, holding a double-barreled shotgun in a businesslike manner. The kitchen itself was in a chaotic state, with smashed eggs, broken glass, milk and other liquids all over the floor, and there was a loud background sound of shouting, which he had heard as he came round the side of the house when the front doorbell was not answered.

"He's in there," Marigold called above the noise. "A burglar."

She had just realized that he must have been in the house for some time before he appeared in the kitchen; he'd had some whiskey, and she'd seen, now, that the sandwiches she was counting on for supper had vanished. They weren't among the mess on the floor, nor left on a shelf inside the fridge as other things had been.

Richard had been so intent upon the search for Verity that he had almost forgotten about the break-in at Merrifields. Unable to get Miss Darwin on the telephone, he had come round to see if, by any freak chance, Verity had called at

The Willows. She might have done so, seeking sympathy; Miss Darwin might have persuaded her to telephone her parents, or even the Samaritans, thus accounting for the busy telephone line.

"Is Verity here?" he demanded, amazing Marigold by the irrelevance of the question.

"No." She shook her head impatiently. "Richard, please go and telephone the police. I daren't leave here in case he gets out. That door isn't secure." She had already banged the intruder's knuckles once, extremely hard, and had been able to close the door again when he retreated, screaming.

"The police aren't far away," said Richard. "They're searching for Verity. She's disappeared."

Marigold did not care if Verity had gone to the moon.

"Richard, there's a burglar in the store-cupboard. Don't you understand? He came here with a gun and he shot at me. Please go and telephone, now."

"Shot at you? Are you hurt?" Richard took a grip on himself.

"No. Richard, please," she implored.

"Give me the gun. You go and phone. It'll be quicker than going to call them from outside."

Outside? What did he mean? Marigold handed him the gun.

"Do you know how to use it?" she asked.

"Oh yes," he said. There was no need to wonder if she did. "You in there," he called out loudly. "Stop that racket. The police are on their way."

Thus instructed, Alan, who had briefly quietened down when he heard sounds from beyond his prison, broke into a fresh burst of swearing. Marigold left them to it, hastening off to telephone. When she found she could get no dialing tone, it took her a few minutes to realize that the extension might be disconnected. Of course; the burglar had been up there while she drank her gin. The thought made her shudder. She hurried upstairs and made the call. The police seemed slow to understand what she was saying: an armed man breaking in, and now captive. She feared they thought her an insane woman making a hoax call.

Before returning to Richard, she went thankfully to the bathroom. For some time she had been fearing that her bladder would not last out the siege and such a possibility was mortifying.

While she was gone, Richard had been having a crazy conversation with her prisoner.

"So she's gone, then, has she? The ghost?" Alan had asked, after running out of breath with his curses.

"What ghost?" Richard asked.

"That old bat," said Alan.

"If you mean the lady of the house," said Richard pompously, "she's no ghost. She's very real and she's fetching the police at this moment. They're not far away, in any case. They're looking for you," he added, which was not the truth, not yet, for Steve, held at the police station and waiting for Ivy to arrive before he could be questioned, had not told the tale he had concocted in the time since his arrest. He was going to say that Alan Morton, escaped murderer, had stolen the articles found in his possession and forced him to carry them away and hide them. It was a good story, and he had decided it would get him off the hook.

Marigold, physically relieved, recalled, as she returned to the kitchen, what Richard had been saying about Verity. Wretched, hysterical woman; she was playing another of her silly tricks. Surely, after all the fuss when Terry ran away, she'd have more sense than cause such anxiety?

"I'll take over now, if you want to get back outside and resume your hunt," she said, entering the kitchen.

"No," he said. "I'm not leaving you alone with our friend here." He took a look at her. She was always pale, her complexion sallow, but now, in the bright strip lighting in the kitchen, she looked gray. "You could use a drink. Have you got some brandy? Have a nip," he suggested.

"I was having a second gin and tonic when this creature appeared," said Marigold. "I'd better not start mixing things." She laughed, an odd, harsh, unamused sound. "I threw it at him," she continued. "The glass, I mean. I scored a direct hit on his head. Then I used the whiskey bottle. It was his fault it was handy—he'd left it out."

"How untidy," Richard answered calmly. What did she mean, she'd used it? Hit him with it? "Well, then, what about some tea? Or coffee. I'd quite like a cup," he added. "Though I don't suppose the police will be more than a few minutes."

"I expect they'd like some, too," said Marigold. "Isn't it what you're always supposed to give them, when they call?"

They went on chatting in this casual manner while Marigold, stepping carefully over the debris on the floor, filled the kettle and put it on.

"I'd better start clearing up the mess," she said, reaching in a cupboard for some cups and saucers. Marigold was not equipped with mugs. Most of her best tea things were still in the dishwasher.

"The police may want to look at it," said Richard. "The mess, I mean. It's evidence."

"Do you think so? Perhaps they'll want to see where the shots went," said Marigold. She could still smell the explosive. "The empty cartridge cases must be somewhere about. He'd unloaded them before I blipped him."

Had she been sitting there holding an unloaded weapon? Richard mouthed the question at her.

"Oh, it's loaded all right," she answered blithely. "He was doing that but I interrupted him. Fancy shooting at a woman my age," she went on. "What a—what a—" the appropriate epithet eluded her.

Richard could think of several.

At this point in their dialogue, the kettle boiled and the police arrived. The kitchen seemed suddenly to be full of men in uniforms, but in fact at first there were only two, soon joined by others from the search party.

They extracted Alan from the cupboard and clapped handcuffs on him while they cautioned him. The whole scene seemed, to Marigold and Richard, quite surreal.

"Have you found my wife?" he asked them, but they had no news of Verity.

Alan, being led away, was shuddering.

"Don't let that—that thing near me," he kept saying, peering sideways at Marigold. "She's a ghost."

"What can he mean?" asked Richard. "He went on like that while you were telephoning."

They didn't understand for quite some time. The search party seeking Verity were convinced, by now, that unless she had taken refuge with a friend, she must be in the river, and there was little more that could be done till daylight, but because of the summons to The Willows, where there was, allegedly, an armed man, they came into the grounds and played their powerful torches round the garden. They saw the muddy trail which Alan had made walking to and from the shed. They found Verity there, wrapped in her big coat, her tangled hair sticky with her own dried blood, her face unrecognizable.

It was a long night.

Eventually, Marigold went back for what remained of it to Merrifields with Richard. The policewoman left in the house had succeeded in getting Terry to bed and he was asleep, so he was not a problem for the moment. In the morning, Richard would have to tell him that his mother was dead— would have to say that she had been murdered, because he would hear the truth in time. Perhaps Justin could be spared the news till he was stronger.

Richard had been questioned thoroughly, but there was no blood on his clothes, and the man, soon identified as Alan Morton, was smothered in it; there would be scientific proof that it was Verity's. Separately, Richard and Marigold gave their statements. All this was done at The Willows. Alan, swiftly removed to Radbury police station, had left plenty of evidence, enough to lead, months later, to his second conviction for murder. The spade and the sledgehammer in the shed were stained with Verity's blood, to which adhered strands of her dyed hair. When the police realized who Alan was, his actions became easier to deduce. The gun used to shoot at Marigold might well prove to be the same weapon that had killed his wife so long ago.

"He kept calling me a ghost," said Marigold. "He must have thought he'd killed me, not someone he had never heard of. Poor Verity. I wonder what she was doing here."

"Just wandering about, I expect," said Richard. "Perhaps she came to see you at the house, and then heard something from the shed and walked on down there."

"We shall never really know," said Marigold.

"If I hadn't ignored her when she came banging at my workshop door, she wouldn't have run off," said Richard. He had described their row to Marigold as they sat by the revived fire in the drawing room at Merrifields.

"You weren't to know that she'd meet a murderer in my garden shed," said Marigold. "If I'd been in, she wouldn't have gone down there."

"She couldn't be happy," Richard sighed. "I couldn't make her happy, anyway."

"It's not your fault," said Marigold. "Some people just don't have it in them. They can't learn to count their blessings. I'm sure you did everything you could for all of them."

Richard had told her about Justin's part in causing his own injuries.

"He hates me so much," he said. "At least Verity never knew that he'd been burned."

What was he going to do about those boys? Would he have to face a future of caring for two disaffected stepsons, at least one of whom loathed him? Poor man, thought Marigold.

"Where's their own father?" she asked. "Will he come to the fore now?"

"I've no idea," said Richard. "Her parents might tell him about this, I suppose. They may know where is is. Perhaps they'll help in some way. The boys are fond of them. What a shock it's going to be for them."

"Well, when it's a reasonable enough hour, you can tell them, Richard," said Marigold. She was suffering, now, from a physical reaction to the night's events and had begun to tremble, only slightly but uncontrollably, her jaw shaking. She hoped he wouldn't notice.

He did, however.

"You're frozen. You must go to bed," he said.

"It's too late," she said. "Or do I mean too early? I'd like a bath, though. That would warm me up. And what about you?"

"I'd like one too," said Richard. "We can both be satisfied, for as you know, there are several bathrooms here now. What if I make up the fire, we both have baths, then come down again and tuck ourselves up with rugs, and put some music on? That will pass the time till the rest of the world wakes up."

Less than an hour later, they were both ensconced, Marigold on the sofa, Richard in the largest armchair with his legs resting on the second, rugs over them, and Elgar's violin concerto playing softly in the background. Richard fell asleep quite quickly; Marigold took much longer, and she woke first, hearing a gentle snore.

She smiled. Now she had, for the first time in her life, slept with a man.

He rang Caroline early in the morning, telling her that there had been an accident and that his wife was dead.

"Oh dear! I'm sorry." Caroline sounded genuinely distressed. She hesitated. "Are you coping? Shall I come down?"

He could not believe his ears. She was offering to help; this woman who might be carrying his child but did not mean to let him know the truth.

"No. It's all right. Someone very kind is helping me," he said. "A neighbor." He asked Caroline to let it be known that he would not be in the office today and possibly not tomorrow either.

At that moment, Marigold was giving Terry his breakfast in the kitchen. He had been told a sanitized version of the facts: His mother had gone out walking in the night; there had been a burglar, and tragically the two had met, with fatal consequences. It was close enough to the truth for now. Neither Marigold nor Richard yet knew about Steve's role in the Merrifields robbery.

Terry was chastened, almost stunned, but then he cried. Amid his tears, his brother's name was uttered several times and Richard assured him that Justin would recover. They would go and see him later.

"I don't have to go to school?"

"Not today."

"Oh." There were more tears, but then Richard said that Terry's grandparents were coming to stay for a while. This cheered him up and he began telling Marigold about their house in Devon, which was near the sea, and about their small sailing boat. Richard had told Marigold that the grandmother was a friendly, easy person, though the grandfather was less predictable.

"Verity was like him in some ways," he said.

Oh dear, thought Marigold, who was hoping the couple would take the children on; surely Richard could not be expected, now, to raise them? Perhaps there were aunts and uncles, even godparents.

"Before they get here, we must ring up the hospital and find out how Justin is this morning," Richard told Terry. "Then we must go round to Miss Darwin's house and clean it up. She was very brave last night. She captured the man—the villain. He was a very wicked man."

"The man who killed Mum?" Terry could say it, even if Richard could not bring himself to do so.

"Richard helped me," said Marigold. Let the poor man win some respect from these difficult children. "Is that a good idea?" she asked.

"Yes," said Richard firmly. "We need occupying and we can't do much here. I'll get some glass and fix the broken windows—yours and mine. And you can't clear all that mess up yourself."

Marigold's resolution to have stronger locks fitted could be carried out later. Whatever his fate, Steve had had a fright and wouldn't be coming round again; at least, not yet.

"Very well," she said. "Thank you both."

She was determined not to cancel her arrangement with Mark; he was due that afternoon and he would need something to eat. Maybe, while they cleaned the kitchen up, Terry could suggest a menu likely to appeal to him.

Two police officers arrived at Merrifields just as they were ready to set out for The Willows, and Richard asked if they had finished their work in Miss Darwin's kitchen.

"Oh yes," one of them said, and added, "You'll need a

new fridge, Miss Darwin. It's damaged beyond repair and it's a prime exhibit in the case."

Marigold knew that it had proved strong enough to save her life.

"I expect the insurance company will pay," she said, and she laughed. Two claims within so few days must be a record.

The cleaning operation was under way when Ivy Burton arrived at The Willows, pushing Adam, wrapped cocoonlike in his padded stroller. With her, on a set of reins, was the toddler she was minding for the morning She had brought back Miss Darwin's stolen jewelry.

"Oh, what a mess! What's happened?" Ivy said, seeing what was going on.

"There was some trouble here last night," said Miss Darwin. "Mr. Gardner and Terry are very kindly clearing up." She bustled Ivy into the sitting room, with the toddler, closing the door. Adam, who was asleep, they left parked in the hall.

"I'm sorry I had to bring them with me," Ivy said. She was almost in tears. "Sharon's at her job, you see—that's my daughter. Adam's my grandson—in the pushchair," she explained. "This one, William, I'm looking after for a few hours. I'd no one to leave them with."

"I understand," said Miss Darwin. It was a bit tough on Mrs. Burton to have a thieving stepson on her hands as well as her own children, and be expected to bring up her grandson, too.

"I'll keep him tethered," Ivy said. "You've such nice things. He's into everything, is William."

"Mrs. Burton, I must tell you quickly that Mr. Gardner's wife was killed last night, and the other boy, Justin, has been badly burned in an accident," said Miss Darwin swiftly, before Ivy could launch into an apology for Steve's misdeeds. With Richard and Terry so close at hand, she must be warned.

"Oh my God!" Ivy stared at her.

"You hadn't heard?" Marigold thought the news might have arrived by grapevine already.

Ivy shook her blond curls. Despite her difficult and checkered life, she was very well preserved, thought Marigold.

"What happened? Was it in the car?" she asked.

"No—nothing like that," said Miss Darwin. "There was an intruder here—that's why the kitchen's in that state. He broke in, but he'd already met poor Mrs. Gardner. He's been arrested for her murder."

"Alan Morton," Ivy said, exhaling.

"Yes. How did you know that?" asked Miss Darwin.

William, by now, was getting bored and making fretty noises. Ivy found some sweets in her pocket and unwrapped one, popping it into his mouth without turning her attention away from the conversation.

"He met Steve yesterday at the Gardners' place," said Ivy. "Steve's still at Radbury police station. The police found him carrying things he'd stolen from Merrifields—he'd got it all in pillowslips. Can you credit it? Walking along with them, he was, after I thought he was safely locked up in his room."

"But how did he meet Alan Morton?" Marigold was mystified.

"Steve broke into Merrifields and Alan Morton saw him and went in after him. When the police picked Steve up, he said Alan had done the job and had threatened Steve and made him carry off the stuff for him. Of course that part's not true," said Ivy. "Steve admitted it to me when I was let in to see him on our own last night. Seems Alan Morton saw him snooping round here again, yesterday afternoon, and then Steve realized with all the Gardners here that he could get into their place and help himself." She sighed heavily. "It's a fine thing if you can't go out and leave your house unoccupied without some young tearaway breaking in and thieving. My house is empty now. I hope none of his friends is in there while my back's turned. He's got into bad company since his dad died, I'm afraid." Ivy paused, and then said soberly, "What you're really saying is that Alan met poor Mrs. Gardner and went for her."

"Something like that," said Miss Darwin.

"I came here to apologize to you," said Ivy. "But now you've told me this—oh dear! I don't know what to say. He came in here and threatened you, I suppose? Alan, I mean."

"Yes, he did, but as you can see, I'm all right and the police soon came and took him away," said Miss Darwin.

"But the boy? You said he was burned?"

"That was a separate incident. He was playing about with petrol and set himself alight, by accident."

Ivy remembered Steve's petrol-smelling jeans. She knew he sometimes saw young Justin around town; better not to mention it just now.

"Oh dear," she said again. "Will he be all right?"

"I think so," said Miss Darwin. Richard had telephoned the hospital before they left the house, and had learned that Justin was in a stable condition. They told one so little, she had reflected.

Ivy's mind had returned to Steve.

"If Mr. Gardner gets his things back—he will—the police got everything—maybe he won't press charges," she said, hopefully. "What about you, Miss Darwin? I was going to ask you to let him off."

"I'd be willing to," said Miss Darwin. "But in view of last night's events, it may not be within my power. And the same may apply to Mr. Gardner."

"But Steve had nothing to do with—with Mrs. Gardner's death," Ivy protested.

"No, but you've just told me that he's blaming Alan Morton for the burglary at Merrifields. He'll involve himself if he sticks to that story," said Marigold.

Ivy looked at her, unable to reply.

"He'd better talk to a solicitor and take whatever advice he's given," said Marigold. "My own advice would be to tell the truth."

"He needn't say anything," said Ivy. "That's the law. He's only told me, so far."

"And it's the law that let Alan Morton out of prison after just a few years, when he had been given a life sentence for killing his wife," said Marigold. "If that sentence had been implemented literally he would not have been released and Mrs. Gardner would still be alive."

Ivy, searching Steve's drawers for further stolen property, had found, among other articles which had given her reason for concern, the newspaper cuttings he had hidden, with the report of Alan's trial.

"He came over to The Willows last November. Alan did," she said. "I don't know if he'd escaped or if he was on one of them shopping trips they let them out for. That's how Steve knew who he was, last night. Steve and Mark were here. Of course neither of them said a word to me, and nor did Mr. Morton, but that's when he went downhill. He died soon after. Steve told me last night, at the police station."

"We all have secrets," said Marigold, who had very few.

"Poor Mr. Gardner, though, with them two boys. How will he manage? It's funny, you never think of that, when you take on someone else's kids. When you get married, I mean. You don't think of them dying and leaving you with their kids. I never thought Steve would be a problem. He was a lovely little lad. My mother died when I was eight and my dad married a lovely woman. They had two more kids and we all got on a treat."

At this point, William had had enough and let out a bellow.

"I'd best take him off," said Ivy. "I'm ever so sorry, Miss Darwin. About everything."

"Yes," said Marigold. "So am I."

Two weeks later, Justin was discharged from hospital and soon afterwards was taken, with his brother, down to Devonshire. Verity's mother had spent the intervening time at Merrifields, with one excursion home to make some preparations, as she did not altogether trust her husband. The boys were going to live there for the present.

That evening, Richard took Miss Darwin out to dinner at The Red Lion.

"It's not a celebration, but I'm glad they've gone," he said to her, across the table. "They represent my failure."

When he picked her up, Marigold was just seeing off Susan Conway, who had come to collect Mark after his few hours spent at The Willows. It was too much to expect that anything could be sparked off between them, but Marigold hoped to contrive occasional meetings as the days grew longer. She had learned that Mark knew nothing whosoever about his father.

"We've all failed at some things," Marigold declared. "What about your daughter? When's she coming home?"

"Oh—not yet. I'm not sure when she's due for leave," he answered.

"She knows what's happened?"

"I haven't told her yet," said Richard. "Her mother may have done so, if she saw it in the paper."

There had been a brief report, but because Alan had so swiftly been charged, the case was *sub judice* and not a subject for lurid journalism. Luckily the incident involving Justin had not attracted any attention.

After an inquest into Verity's death had been opened and

adjourned, her funeral had taken place. Richard and Miss Darwin had gone together: tentatively, she had said that she would like to be there, and he had welcomed her support at what was, for him, a bizarre ordeal. Justin, still with a scarred face, bandaged hands, and, beneath his dark school trousers, dressings on his legs, had been there with Terry and their grandparents. Richard and Marigold had sat together on the other side of the aisle in the crematorium chapel. Terry had wept throughout, but Justin had been dry-eyed and he had never once glanced at Richard. A tall, broad-shouldered man with a bushy gray beard had been among the small group of mourners—the boys' father. Later, at The Red Lion, where he was staying, he and Richard had had an illuminating talk. His present wife was tired of living overseas and wanted to return. He wondered if it would be possible to come back into the boys' lives. So far, they'd scarcely spoken; he wasn't sure they even knew who he was.

"I'm sure they do," said Richard. "They missed you. After all, you are their father." He hesitated. "They are a bit confused," he felt it fair to warn. "But they never really took to me. Especially Justin."

"What happened? Some accident, I heard."

"Yes. I shouldn't be too curious," Richard suggested. "Let him tell you himself, if he wants to."

He'd gone home feeling shriven. A huge load had been lifted from his shoulders.

Tonight, he'd picked a good claret from The Red Lion's list, and it went well with the steak they had both chosen.

"I'm thinking of leaving my job," he told Miss Darwin, as they tried the cheeses. "Of course, I'll have to be here for the resumed inquest, and, I suppose, the trial, but I've more or less decided on early retirement. I've only got myself to pay for now."

He was planning to settle some money on the two boys,

if only to salve his conscience, but their grandparents were not penniless, and their father seemed willing to take on some responsibility for them. "I might start up my own business," he went on. "Perhaps in France."

"I see." Marigold was dismayed at the prospect of losing such a friend, the best one that she had ever had. "I'm going to have the shed pulled down," she told him. "As soon as the police say it can be dismantled. I'll put up another one in a different part of the garden. I thought I'd plant some roses on the site."

"That's a nice idea," he said. "She didn't like them, though. Said they were too pretty-pretty."

"Well, I like them, and I'm the one who'll be looking at them," was the answer, and Marigold finished up her wine.

"Let me fill your glass again," said Richard.

He thought of telling her about Caroline and the baby, but decided not to burden her anymore. Through no fault of her own, she had been drawn into his personal tragedy, and she had been a stalwart source of comfort.

She'd make her life here gently, calmly, without him. She'd got the choral society now, and that nice little boy Mark who had the pleasant, rather pretty, most efficient mother.

"What about Steve Burton? Do we know if he'll be prosecuted?" Richard asked her.

"Not yet. I think it's all still being decided," said Marigold. "I can't think locking him up will achieve anything."

"Let's hope Morton gets a really long sentence this time," Richard said.

"He'll get life. It's mandatory, but he'll qualify for release again unless the judge lays down a specific length of time for him to be in prison."

"Then he'll kill someone else," Richard said. "If he's thwarted."

"Yes," agreed Marigold. "Perhaps another stranger."